# Quinn, by design

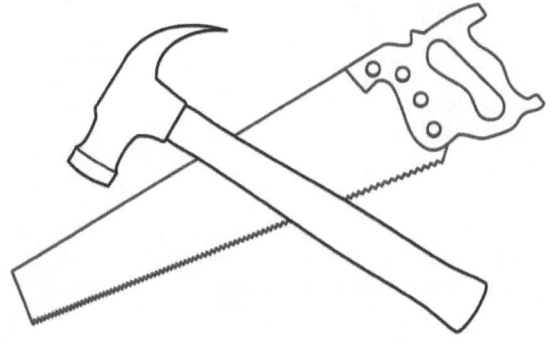

Choosing Family-Book 2

Jennifer Raines

Quimn, by design
Copyright © 2024 Jennifer Raines
All rights reserved.

ISBN: (ebook) 978-1-958136-93-5
(Print) 978-1-958136-94-2

Inkspell Publishing
207 Moonglow Circle #101
Murrells Inlet, SC 29576

Edited By Yezanira Venecia
Cover art By Emily's World By Design

# DEDICATION

**To Lesley, who's been with me since the beginning**

JENNIFER RAINES

# CHAPTER ONE

A visitor was rare enough to summon Niall Quinn to his front porch. "Don't worry about the squeak," he called to the huddled figure inspecting the hinge on his lop-sided gate. He was close enough to recognise his landlady's elegant calves and ankles. "It lets me know I've got a visitor." Noticing she had shapely legs might be excused as artistic interest, but it was a distraction he wasn't ready for.

She spun toward his voice, her coat floating on the breeze, before settling around her too-thin figure. Niall stepped out of the shadows.

"I'm Lucy McTavish." She crossed the yard and stretched out her hand.

"I know." Instead of the formal handshake she offered, Niall gripped her hand to draw her up the two wide wooden steps to his porch. Without makeup, Lucy's pallor was hauntingly evident and matched the sadness in her almond-shaped hazel eyes. She smelled of roses, with a hint of vanilla, transporting him back to carefree afternoons in his mother's cottage garden at lilac time.

"How do you know?" She withdrew her hand, pointedly reclaiming her own space.

"I saw you at your granda's funeral."

Niall had stood at the back of the church. Not a close friend, his time with Cam had been too short to claim that honour, but he'd miss the old man's advice and encouragement. Mutual respect and a passion for fine craftsmanship had forged a special bond.

Lucy's courage at the funeral had earned his respect, while her vulnerability roused protective instincts he'd tucked away for the sake of his sanity after his bust-up with his ex-fiancée, Sinead.

"I'm glad you've dropped by." Niall gentled her as he would a lost child. "Please. Come in." He gestured for her to precede him through the front door.

He'd been considering how to introduce himself since the funeral. Texting was out because he didn't have her number. Using social media seemed wrong for the words he had to say. Her arrival on a Sunday, in unrelieved black, less than ten days after the funeral, gave the encounter an ominous urgency.

"I didn't see you."

"You were too caught in your grief to see me."

She'd been too caught in her grief to see anyone. Her eyes had shimmered with tears, her fragility brittle enough to shatter with a blow. She'd held herself ramrod straight. Her self-discipline awed him, and her anguish had compounded his own, re-opening the hole left by his da's death.

Already partway down the hall, she pivoted, met his gaze, then focused on a spot over his shoulder. "I'm sorry for my rudeness."

"Whisht, lassie. There's no need for an apology. I lost my da a few years ago, didn't care who saw me cry like a baby."

The colour drained from her cheeks, leaving them chalk-white, and drawing Niall's attention to her dark auburn hair. The tight bundle at her nape punished, rather than tamed her thick tresses.

"I learned 'whisht' from Grandpa." She sounded bereft,

and he'd been raised to tend any animal in pain.

"I picked it up working in Ireland. Cam used it when he was about to impart some piece of wisdom to my eejit self." Niall smiled encouragement and waved toward the doorway at the end of the short hall. "I was in the kitchen.

"The loss is a constant, learning to live with it is the challenge," he murmured before cursing his cack-handedness.

For feck's sake. Cam had said he was Lucy's only immediate family. She probably knew more about loss than Niall hoped he ever would. He couldn't recall who'd used the expression, but the words fitted her—"*She knew her way around in the dark.*" Grief could be endlessly dark.

Neat, black, serviceable pumps continued up the narrow hall and into his neat, serviceable kitchen, their *rat-tat-tat* shutting a door on his words of condolence. She pressed a—*praise the saints*—dark-charcoal bag to her side. The woman should wear green, any shade, not this unrelenting black that made her look forbidding, when in truth she was stripped naked by mourning.

"You call him Cam." She stood stiffly beside the three-by-two-metre, bark-to-bark Huon pine table he'd finished in the early hours this morning, then muscled into the kitchen so he could live with it a few days.

"He asked me to. Said Cameron McTavish made him feel ancient." Niall stepped around her, his arm brushing against hers in the space made smaller by his table. She shivered. Not fear. Maybe cold? Grief could also make you cold from the inside out.

"I have some questions for you, Mr. Quinn." She straightened her shoulders, tilting her chin to signal her return to business.

"Please sit down, Ms. McTavish," he replied with equal formality. Then, without waiting to see what she did, he continued to the kitchen bench. "I was making tea. Share a cup?" He spoke over his shoulder. Tea was his mother's cure for every ill.

"I won't be here long." Politeness jostled with annoyance in her answer.

"Tea doesn't take long." Niall kept his back turned.

"Thank you," she said. He heard a chair being placed on the floor and learned Lucy McTavish didn't pull chairs across stone tiles. Instead, she lifted them before setting them in the correct position.

After filling the kettle, Niall opened the fridge and eyed ingredients before making his choice. A seeded sourdough loaf, a mature cheddar, tomatoes and lettuce. He added pickles. "Milk?"

"Milk, no sugar, please."

He assembled sandwiches, poured the boiling water into a large teapot, and let it sit. The overlong silence told Niall she was struggling to find the words she wanted. He slowed his movements to give her time to marshal her arguments. While he brought the kettle back to the boil, he drained the water from the pot into two waiting cups. Covering the full teapot with a cosy, he emptied the now warm cups and carried everything to the table, including two plates and the jar of pickles. "I'll let you fix your own."

"I didn't ask for that." She made a face at the oversized sandwich he'd set in front of her.

"It's lunchtime." Niall took the chair opposite her.

Her guilty glance at her smartwatch told him she'd lost track of time, while her unfashionably baggy clothes told him eating was a faint memory. Loss of appetite was another by-product of heartache.

He'd been there too. "I hate to eat alone."

"I thought you lived alone." She cut one half of her sandwich in half and added pickles. Eating his food was another nod to politeness. Referring to his living arrangements was her opening salvo in hostilities.

"What else did your granda tell you?" Niall waited for her to swallow her first mouthful, then took a bite of his own, setting himself the task of keeping her in his kitchen long enough to finish her sandwich. Food was his currency for sympathy, although Lucy McTavish's unannounced arrival declared she wasn't here for comfort.

"Months ago, Grandpa talked about meeting a furniture restorer at an antiques auction."

"I've done the odd bit of restoration." Niall was pretty positive Cam had offered those pieces as a sop to Niall's dignity. While the profit from their sale had covered the rent, over time, Niall worked out Cam had become his patron rather than his landlord.

*And wasn't that a feckin' indictment.* At thirty-four, he needed an old man's patronage because his passion for making bespoke furniture had yet to deliver a decent living.

"Three pieces." She placed her left hand on his table as if drawing strength from the age and beauty of the timber. "Three pieces of furniture were delivered to McTavish's Antiques five months ago."

"Cam said they earned a good profit." Niall wrapped both hands around his Blue Italian Spode cup, watching as she raised the Flora Danica, Royal Copenhagen to her mouth; a distraction while she framed her answer. Like most of his cups, the matching saucers were lost in the mists of time.

"They did." Her chin jut signalled a full stop on McTavish profits.

"Cam said he told you about our arrangement." Niall's doubts were growing. Furniture restorer was a half-arsed description of him.

"He told me he offered you accommodation in return for restoring furniture. Three pieces of furniture over eight months gives you a higher hourly rate than a top-class hooker." The insult rolled off her tongue, the barb sinking deeper than she could have known. Unaware, she popped the last morsel of the second quarter of sandwich into her luscious, bow-shaped mouth.

"Cam was an astute businessman." After a tussle, which had included consultation with his lawyer brother, Niall was at peace with his conscience. "He controlled how much restoration he wanted."

"From his sick bed?" She licked a pickle off her thumb, her tongue sexily practical as it brushed along her knuckle to collect the smear of sauce. The lapse in table manners gave a hint of the warm-hearted woman Cam had talked about. Today's disciplined façade was a slap at Niall.

"While I delivered the last piece five months ago, Cam spent a lot of happy hours here. Until these last two months." And when Niall had visited Cam's hospital-in-the-home, Cam had demanded updates on progress with Niall's upcoming exhibition.

Cam's favourite design was for the Huon table his granddaughter was currently stroking. Sorrow pressed on Niall's chest. A few months ago, Cam would have been in the workshop with him on a Sunday afternoon, sharing his large pot of tea and a sandwich.

"He didn't invite me to be his tenant just for my restoration."

"Why did he invite you?" She focused her irritation on sawing the second half-sandwich into two quarters. She was eating, which he counted as a win.

"Are you asking as Cam's granddaughter or as my new landlord?" Niall got that anger was better than fear or sadness for dealing with her despair. Rage gave her a purpose, a reason to get up every day. Directing it at him was disrespecting her granda's right to make his own decisions.

"You knew he was dying!" Her voice deepened into loathing, as if Niall had killed Cam.

"Not soon enough." Niall's obsession with work had fed his ignorance. Although Cam had deliberately downplayed the cancer stealing his life. "He was a kindred spirit, who talked about wood and design and what made a piece of furniture prized. More tea?" He played host, tilting the enormous teapot in her direction.

"Thank you." She was either innately polite or trained to it—another interesting discovery. He guessed politeness was the only constraint on the passion boiling below her surface.

"He told me his doctor wanted him to slow down." Niall topped off his own cup. "Cam said he'd earned the right to indulge himself."

"By letting you stay in a large inner-Sydney property rent free."

"You don't know the history to our agreement," Niall concluded, a sense of foreboding kneecapping him. Or she knew a bit, and in her distress had extrapolated from it being a mutually beneficial arrangement to something less savoury.

*Why hadn't Cam kept his promise?*

"I found a copy this morning." Her left hand returned to the table, her thumb curving around the edge, brushing the newly shellacked wood. Her unconscious fascination nourished the artist in him and vindicated his decision to make the table the centrepiece of his upcoming exhibition. "Three pieces of furniture restored in exchange for twelve months' free rent looks like fraud to me."

Niall's cup landed on the table with a thump, causing his guest to wince. She opened her mouth, and he expected her to say "Be careful of that cup." Instead, she took another bite of sandwich, probably to stop herself from taking a bite out of him. "I've made repairs. I've paid utilities and insurance for the full twelve months. With an enterprise like mine, a lease less than twelve months isn't viable."

"This is prime, commercially valuable space." She looked exhausted, as if survival was taking every ounce of energy she had. "You took advantage of him."

"My mum would tan my hide if I took advantage of anyone, much less a man old enough to be my granda." Niall tried to defuse the situation—near impossible when he was operating with minimal facts. Sharing her sense of loss handicapped him further.

"An agreement signed in the last few days of his life."

"Ms. McTavish—Lucy. I can see finding out about our

arrangement is a shock to you. I sympathise with your loss."
Niall wrapped his hands around his cup to prevent himself
reaching for her. If he offered a friendly hug in her current
mood, she'd charge him with harassment as well as fraud.
"Cam was in full possession of his faculties when we signed
our updated agreement."

"It's theft!" Having made the cruel accusation, she
deflated like a lung starved of oxygen.

"It's a legal contract," he stated. She was pissed off and
munching the last quarter of her sandwich as a gesture of
defiance. Her cheeks showed colour for the first time since
she'd arrived. Niall was pissed off Cam had left her in
ignorance, yet inexplicably grateful to see her come alive.
"There were witnesses. Cam's lawyer can answer any
questions, as can his accountant."

"But we're not talking about the eight months you've
been here and the four in your so-called updated agreement.
We're talking about another year." Her voice deepened, a
musical contralto vibrating with disbelief. "We're talking
about him changing his will in the last days of his life. He's
bequeathed you a second twelve-month occupancy of this
property, rent free."

"You're wrong." Niall's instinctive protest propelled
him to his feet and toward the window above the sink.
Cam's secure, purpose-built woodwork studio at the end of
the brick path loomed like a mirage. Niall had believed
Cam's assurances Lucy was comfortable with his tenancy.

*Or maybe he'd wanted to believe?*

"You said it yourself. Anything less than twelve months
isn't viable. So you tricked him in the last days of his life."
Her voice wobbled.

"Lucy. I'm sorry Cam didn't tell you about our
arrangement." Niall swung to face her, disquiet roiling his
gut. "I won't deny I've thought of staying here longer. On
commercial terms"—he sounded unconvincing to his own
ears—"I promise you, we never talked about his will."

She cocked her head to one side, considering him and

pronouncing him untruthful.

Her sceptical gaze dragged a clarification from Niall. "Okay, he told me he wanted to update our agreement to bring it in line with his will. Update the original twelve months to be clear I had four left. Cam said you'd be inheriting everything. Maybe a few bequests here and there."

"So you did discuss his will?"

"Making a statement is *not* a discussion." He pushed his hand through his hair, blindsided by the direction the conversation was taking. Niall feinted, she parried, and questions hung between them like rusted nails in a broken-down fence, dangerous unless handled with care. "Are you sure you haven't mixed up two things?"

*Feck! That had to be the answer.* She was muddled by grief. *I hope to hell she's muddled by grief.*

"I rang my lawyer when I found the agreement." She looked at her left hand now, fingers spread, palm flat on the golden-hued pine. She treated his table with the reverence many women reserved for precious jewels while accusing him of a scam. "Henry told me the will gave you more. So, I need to know. Who are you? And what hold did you have over Grandpa?"

"No hold." *Why the hell had Cam kept secrets?* About their relationship. About their contract. He sure as hell should have given Niall a hint of what he planned. "We were friends."

"You mean you pretended to be friends with a sick old man." The daft woman kept one hand on his table during their entire conversation, seeming blind to the tactile connection to him.

"He wasn't sick when I met him," Niall insisted. "The last time I saw him, he was alert and engaged." His last conversation with Cam had been about Cam's fear of leaving his granddaughter alone, not the will. And Cam had apologised.

*Praise the saints!* Was this what Cam was apologising for?

*A debt Niall could never repay.*

Niall's mouth dried. "You must have misunderstood."

\* \* \*

*She'd finished the sandwich.* Lucy stared at her empty plate.

He sounded sincerely baffled about the will. Baffled, with an edge of panic.

Touching the tip of her forefinger to her tongue, Lucy used it to pick up sesame seeds scattered on her plate, nibbled the seeds, then repeated the exercise. A private indulgence, not one for sharing with a stranger. Heat rose up her throat when she found Niall Quinn watching her— she a hypnotist to his willing subject.

He was charming. Conmen were supposed to be charming. The crooked grin, the laugh lines fanning out from the corners of his soulful grey eyes, the russet-coloured lock of hair hanging over his forehead, even his movements were charming.

Manly and charming, economical and practical, heroic even, with broad shoulders and the solid strength of someone who worked with his body, while his clean, sandalwood scent with its tart hint of citrus reassured. Lucy refused to be pacified. The constant parade of men through her mother's life and bedroom during Lucy's entire first decade had taught her the futility of relying on men. Still, she'd finished the sandwich. The largest meal she'd eaten in … forever.

"Whisht! You're hiding something." She'd read the first clauses of Niall Quinn's agreement and stalled at the words "rent free." Henry Dawson, her lawyer, had been at his daughter's wedding and unable to talk. He'd mentioned the changed will, Quinn as a beneficiary, and asked her to wait until they spoke. Except her rage had been liberating and propelled her straight here.

"I know nothing about a changed will," he repeated, his voice steady, his body language unthreatening.

"You're avoiding the question." *Again.* Lucy sucked in a breath. "What do you do here?"

"That would fall into the category of *my* business."

His business conducted on *her property*.

Something niggled at the back of Lucy's mind. Months ago, her grandpa had bought a supply of paintings they'd never be able to shift. When she'd queried the accounts, he said he'd bought them for a friend. Later he'd taken her to an exhibition at Leopold's Gallery. Modern, abstract art, the antithesis of Grandpa's taste. She'd followed him around completely bemused, until he'd told her to look at the frames. Cleverly made new frames from antique timbers, each one different, each crafted to showcase the artwork.

"Grandpa bought a lot of old frames earlier this year." Lucy hadn't questioned his purchases after the visit to Leopold's.

"He bought a lot of things." Quinn's expression gave nothing away.

"He never bought stock we couldn't use. Until recently." Lucy hadn't connected the furniture restorer to the friend who wanted frames either. Grandpa could easily have made the connection for her.

"And a man's not allowed to change his habits," he muttered.

"Breaking the habits of a lifetime is a reason to argue diminished responsibility." She probed more carefully. If her grandpa had deliberately kept Niall Quinn a secret, she might be making a mistake about the carpenter. She *hated* making mistakes.

"That's insulting." He looked affronted on her grandpa's behalf.

Spreading her palms on the table, Lucy leaned forward. His gaze dropped to her hands, as if mesmerised. "Did Grandpa buy those frames to provide you with timber?"

He hesitated a fraction of a second too long.

*Use that pretty Irish lilt to talk your way out of this*, she thought.

"He occasionally bought frames and antique timber on my behalf. If you can't find the repayments in your accounts, I can provide copies from mine." The charming woodworker claimed respectable accounting habits.

"I'll be checking all transactions for the last year. With our accountant." The re-energizing rage that had driven her here abandoned Lucy. Until she'd found the agreement, she'd assumed the property was hers to do with as she wished. She wished to sell it and make her current financial problems disappear. She couldn't lose the business her grandpa had spent his life building. Not after losing him.

And Niall Quinn wasn't telling her everything about his relationship with her grandpa. Guilt, or a close cousin, had flashed across his face when she'd first accused him.

"Did Henry mention anything else?" He looked more concerned for her than guilty. A charming, *disarming* hunk.

"*That* would fall into the category of *my* business." She plastered a neutral expression on her face while mimicking his earlier answer. Making sure McTavish's thrived was her first order of business.

The antiques world would be watching Lucy's moves closely. A whisper of financial difficulties and even old friends would be eyeing her stock and attempting to poach her staff.

Her grip tightened on the Flora Danica cup. A perfect example of its type. With a saucer, it would be a valuable set. Instead, someone had made a mistake—dropped it on a hard floor, thrown it in a moment of frustration, or chipped it when washing it in one of those long-gone, unforgiving porcelain sinks.

For most people, an imperfect cup and saucer were the mistake of a moment, a regrettable accident. Any breakage reminded Lucy some mistakes can never be undone.

"I don't want to know about *your* business." Impatience added a rumble to his very appealing lilt, making her toes curl in her polished court shoes. "Did Henry say anything else about *me*?"

"What should he have said?" His intense scrutiny troubled Lucy because she hadn't waited for Henry's explanation. She'd read the agreement and welcomed the righteous indignation that had flooded her numbed brain. Accusing Quinn of being a conman was better than hiding at home missing Grandpa.

"That I didn't ask for anything beyond my existing agreement with Cam." His bewilderment slowed her down.

Simple mistakes had enormous consequences. Lucy's mum and gran had died because of an instant's inattention. With Grandpa, she'd drained her personal account, then his, before taking out a personal loan to pay for twenty-four-hour-a-day professional care for the last few months of his life. She'd made sure someone was always in the room when she visited. Not within earshot, but an objective witness to her actions should one be needed. Lucy's mistake was not foreseeing the threat to McTavish's. By spending their savings, Lucy risked the business her grandpa had spent a lifetime building.

"That we were friends as well as business partners," Quinn finished quietly.

"Grandpa never said." Blaming Niall Quinn for taking advantage of her grandpa when he'd been defenceless had been a welcome distraction from her despair.

He looked poleaxed, and Lucy was terrified she was spinning out of control.

# CHAPTER TWO

The neat, single-story terrace in the inner Sydney suburb of Newtown was a good fit for Niall's brother. Better than the sterile high-rise apartment Liam had been renting when he'd met his now wife. Niall texted his identical twin en route. After ringing the bell, he paced the front path. Testing his thoughts aloud was the only way past this sense of unreality.

"Come in." Liam's grin was wide. He looked and sounded like the man he was: content, confident, married to the woman he loved, and excited about their first child. "What's up?"

"Marriage suits you." Niall sucked in a breath and released it on a grateful sigh. Eighteen months ago, he and his brother hadn't been on speaking terms because Liam had been keeping their dead father's debts a secret. Their estrangement had left Niall half whole.

"You came here to tell me that?" Liam tugged him into the hall.

"You look happy. I like that you look happy." Even if his brother's happiness highlighted his own solitary state.

"Aren't things happy in the man cave?"

"Workshop," Niall muttered, although he'd spent

enough time indoors in the last few months to develop bat-like characteristics. Like finding his way to bed in the early hours relying on echolocation rather than electric light.

"Kate's out with Anna. They're shopping for baby clothes, but won't be long." Liam pushed him into the kitchen. "Stay for dinner."

"I haven't seen Anna in ages." Old friends, Niall and Anna had indirectly introduced their respective siblings, who'd then married each other. Niall had appeared in a successful billboard campaign with Kate when Liam had needed to be invisible. The resulting snafu had forced a welcome reckoning between the brothers. "I haven't got time to stay."

"You're the one who dropped in." His brother opened the fridge door. "Sit down for five minutes. You took a raincheck on dinner last week."

"I'm too unsettled to sit." Niall paced toward the window, his gaze caught by a tree blown almost horizontal by the wind. The capacity to bend but not break was one of the characteristics that drew him so powerfully to wood. Had drawn him to Cam. "Am I wilfully blind?"

"You're focused, ambitious, and stubborn." Liam snagged a jug of orange juice and set it on the table. "That's mostly about your work. You're also kind, loyal and relentlessly honourable. Who accused you of being wilfully blind?"

"Me." Niall continued to stare through the window, as new guilt layered on old. You'd think he'd have learned from not asking Liam the right questions when their da died. "For accepting Cam McTavish's generosity without digging beneath the surface."

"For the love of Mary and Joseph, you can't still be angsting about your agreement with Cam."

"I can." Niall swung back to face his brother and held up a hand. "A recap. He offered me the use of his premises for a year in exchange for restoring three pieces of furniture." Cam had batted away Niall's objections, calling in daily to sip endless cups of tea and "give Niall the benefit of his wisdom."

"You offered to pay rent and worked punishing hours to finish intricate and bloody difficult restoration jobs in the timeframe McTavish demanded." Liam defended him. "I thought he convinced you the profit on them would cover rent for a year."

"He convinced me." Relief had been Niall's first reaction. "When I finished, Cam showed me the original purchase invoices for each piece and the final sales dockets." Even a short period of financial security was a weight lifted. Niall had pitched his exhibition to one of the most prestigious Sydney galleries on the strength of it. Then been blown away to discover he'd won the slot over a bunch of other creatives.

"I'm guessing he didn't tell his granddaughter about the agreement," Liam said.

"Worse than that," Niall growled. He'd never seen Lucy at the house with Cam. "*She's working*," Cam had said. "*She loves the work, but making sure it continues to succeed is her way of honouring her gran and me.*"

Lucy's accusation of him taking advantage of Cam had flicked Niall on the raw. A tip of the whip blow, fast and lethal, landing where all his doubts resided. Paying his way in kind, if not in cash, was one of the few choices a poor man had for keeping his self-respect.

"What's worse than keeping an agreement that materially affected her a secret?" Liam pointed to the jug of juice.

Niall nodded. "A will." Until today, he'd hoped, despite the imbalance in their bank accounts, he and Cam had met as equals. "She says he's left me a second year rent free in his will."

Liam whistled.

"She wants to hang, draw, and quarter me." Niall pictured Lucy at his kitchen table, stroking the damned wood, completely oblivious she was stroking a Quinn creation. Her delicate touch had made his artist's soul yearn and his body ache. "She used the words *fraud*, *taking advantage*, *theft*, *manipulating* and *whisht*."

"'*Whisht*.' That's quite some insult." Liam paused, the jug raised above a glass, to slant him a sideways look.

"I got the sense she was swallowing the obscenities she'd like to use. Very polite is our Ms. McTavish. On some levels." And appealingly fierce.

"Being polite and suspicious isn't enough to break a will. From what you've told me of Cam's business, the initial rental agreement was neatly calculated not to break any tax laws, not to imply any ongoing obligations, and wouldn't dent his wealth." Liam filled both glasses. "McTavish was sound in mind, and I'm guessing he was scrupulous in ensuring his last wishes were water tight."

"She suggested I took advantage of diminished responsibility at the end," Niall said the ugly words, presenting this latest sign of his insensitivity to his brother.

"For the love of …" Liam thrust the tumbler of juice into his hand. "Why didn't you fight back?"

"How do you know I didn't?" Niall took a seat and braced for the pep talk.

"Because she rattled you enough for you to break your holy rule of spending Sunday on your work for the exhibition. Tell me more about her?"

"She's an orphan. Lived with Cam and his wife since childhood, absorbed antiques and preservation through her pores." Niall met his brother's astute gaze across the table. "She's grieving. You know what that's like. People who are grieving don't always act in their own best interests. And sometimes they need a reason to get up in the morning."

"If that's a dig at me, my only regret for not telling you about Dad's debts sooner was because it led to us being estranged for a while. Then I look at the design you sent Kate for a cradle, and I can't regret your time in Ireland. Thank you. It's beautiful."

"I love you too." The words came easily. "Lucy sees

McTavish's as a sacred duty. Focusing on it is keeping her grounded while she mourns." Niall closed his eyes, but the image of Lucy sitting in his kitchen refused to budge. "Hell, she dresses like every corporate board member in Sydney wrangling balance sheets into obedient subtractions and additions. You can't distinguish one from the other, but you know they operate in some parallel world."

"So, you wouldn't be able to pick her in a police line-up?" Liam made the family joke about separating identical twins.

"She'd be the one staring back with a mixture of defiance and fear." Niall hadn't known until now he'd picked up her fear.

"You're worried about her."

"I get the sense she's lost, maybe drowning in expectations she's placed on herself. Cam wanted her to be happy." Niall frowned, trying to work out why he was unsettled about a pampered young woman who wouldn't thank him for asking if she was afraid.

"Apart from this bequest to you, is she the only beneficiary?"

"He told me she was all he had." Imagining her alone worried Niall as well. Two young women, roughly Lucy's age, had stayed close during the funeral. One had a man in tow. Lucy had seemed isolated even with their support. Most mourners were business colleagues, a few old friends—based on Lucy's eulogy. She'd made her short speech count. Had held herself erect and listed all of Cam's good qualities—like generosity.

*So why the feck is she so convinced I'm a trickster?*

"Did he tell her anything about you?"

"Not enough for her to give me the benefit of the doubt."

*A problem it would have been easy for Cam to fix.*

Niall swallowed a mouthful of the fresh juice, its acid sitting uneasily on his empty stomach. "Keeping the extent of our relationship a secret from Lucy doesn't make sense."

*Keeping me from meeting Lucy until after he died made even less.*

"What makes you so sure he did?"

"She admitted as much today. Plus, a series of coincidences, which, in hindsight, don't add up," Niall confessed. He'd almost had a nasty accident with his lathe when he'd worked out Cam had conspired to keep them apart.

"Coincidences do happen." His brother weighed the possibility with the scepticism of an experienced lawyer. "Maybe he had more important things to discuss with his granddaughter than a carpenter he was kind to." Liam's smile was sardonic. "Did you introduce yourself at the funeral?"

"It didn't seem like the right time to bring myself to her attention."

"That's what funerals are for. Perfect strangers tell you they knew your brother or your uncle or your dad, and that they're sorry for your loss." Liam folded his arms across his chest.

"And you shake their hands politely and stop yourself from screaming that *you're* sorry for your loss." Niall's father's death had hit with the finality of an axe blade levelling a sapling.

"Rituals work for some people. It helped Mum to hear words of admiration from strangers as well as friends." Liam scooped up the empty glasses and headed for the sink. "Did Lucy show you the will?" Liam wasn't making a casual inquiry.

"I'm not even sure she's seen it."

"If you weren't so focused on paying me back, you'd be free to tell her to piss off. You could stop making those frames for Leopold's and concentrate on your own work. Kate and I are more than fine. The partnership's made a huge difference to me, and Kate's books are selling. I ... we can wait for the money." His brother nudged Niall's shoulder with his fist.

"You've carried me for years. You have a wife and babe

24

on the way." Niall's sense of justice demanded he pay a share of their da's debts.

"Tell me again why you make furniture?"

"Because I can't not." Niall stared at his hands. "Because I love the feel of the wood, the excitement of seeing a shape emerge, then the smile on the face of the buyer when I finish the piece." Like Lucy's smile.

Sinead had never touched his work, or to be honest, him, with such care.

"Then why bother with an exhibition?"

"You should know the answer to that better than most."

"Because Quinns pay their way?" His brother cocked his head to one side.

Niall nodded.

"Listen up, you eejit. You were and can earn a living. The change is you're paying someone else's debts."

"Da's debts are our debts."

"I agree. But I hope you also see this exhibition as showcasing your skill, because I do." His brother smiled. "In three months everyone will want a Quinn. You won't have time to make us a cradle."

"Right," Niall muttered. "A cradle by Quinn will be the must-have item at baby showers."

Liam ignored his mini tantrum. "How does Lucy fit into this?"

"I'm not sure yet. We're from different planets. She's antiques royalty, and I'm an insistently modern designer."

"Direct her to Quinn's website. Unless she's wilfully blind, she'll see genius there and understand why Cam sponsored you."

"Thanks." His family's faith in him had always kept Niall centred and determined.

He wasn't sure why it wasn't enough now. Maybe because it irritated the hell out of him, and offended his artistic sensibility, to make more in recent months through frames for other people's artwork than his furniture. Or because Sinead's last words had fed the ever-present doubt most creatives had.

*Admit it, Quinn, some deep, barely acknowledged part of me craves the independent vindication from a successful exhibition.*

He pushed to his feet. "You'll help if I'm summoned to answer the legal equivalent of a 'please explain'?"

"You don't need to ask." Liam rested his hand on Niall's shoulder.

"Can I refuse a bequest?"

"You can," Liam admitted. "You'd have no control over where it went."

"I'm pretty sure it'll go back to her."

"Find out exactly what the will says first. And go back to the beginning of this. Cameron McTavish was of sound mind. He enjoyed your company and valued your work. It's a large estate. Unless there's some secret hidden in a closet we don't know about, the bequest to you shouldn't dent the McTavish wealth Lucy's inheriting. Lucy's ignorance of your relationship with Cam shouldn't stop you from accepting what was freely offered." Liam followed him to the door. "Did he give you a clue to why he did this?"

"He said Lucy would need a distraction." Niall gave a half-laugh. Already Lucy's well-being had started to matter. "I'd forgotten that."

"You're a hell of a distraction."

\* \* \*

Lucy glanced around the office Henry Dawson had inherited from his father. Nineteen fifties wood-framed Albert Namatjira prints hung on the walls, bookcases overflowed with musty legal tomes, and a brand-new, fresh-off-the-assembly-line laptop held pride of place on the leather-tooled desk. A nice blending of experience and currency. She'd been here for an hour, plenty of time for him to walk her through her arguments and questions once.

A knock on the door heralded the arrival of his secretary. The young man handed them each cups of tea. "Ginger helps settle an upset stomach." He placed the ginger biscuits within easy reach of Lucy. More than Lucy's stomach was upset.

"Can I fight it?" Lucy had listened closely to Henry's succinct explanation and come to her own conclusion.

"Why would you?" he asked gently, as if she needed gentle treatment.

"Grandpa was very frail at the end. Forgetful?" *Not that forgetful.*

In the weeks before his death, he'd told Lucy stories she'd never heard before of her mum as a little girl. Stories about his confusion about what made his daughter tick. How he'd loved her but not understood her; how even when he'd tried to meet her on her terms he'd never got the timing or the words right. Lucy had sensed he was apologising for leaving Lucy completely alone.

"Cameron was never easily led, if that's what you're suggesting. He knew exactly what he was doing." Henry met her gaze levelly, a straight answer from a man her grandpa trusted.

"He didn't tell me." She shook her head.

"And he told you everything?"

"Not everything." Lucy didn't know about the frequency of his visits to Niall Quinn's workshop. She looked at Namitjira's *Ghost Gum Glen Haven*, a painting she'd studied on multiple visits over the years. The tree had always reminded her of her grandpa—weathered, yet noble. Niall had a similar look. Drat the man. "But he told me about every other sizable bequest." Bequests she fretted how to honour without selling the workshop.

"You're the executor. You have certain powers regarding the management of bequests." He outlined a clause she'd examined closely.

"He intended I transfer the funds to his charities immediately." Grandpa's bequests sat on the non-negotiable side of the mental ledger Lucy had started.

"He also intended—not a whim—to use Niall Quinn's

skills to establish a lasting legacy through the creation of a foundation." He pointed to the detailed outline of the proposal in her grandpa's handwriting. "Don't you agree?"

"Yes." She was ashamed of her immediate suspicion, could admit desperation, confusion and a little jealousy had played a part. It was unlike Grandpa not to talk about his interests or his discoveries. He'd enthused about the furniture restorer, then gone strangely quiet after the three restored pieces were delivered. Yesterday, she connected the furniture restorer to the frame maker. Overnight, an internet and social media search had told her more.

"If you don't tell me the problem, I can't help you, Lucy."

She inhaled deeply and breathed out her recurring nightmare. "I emptied our savings accounts for Grandpa's medical treatment and took out a personal loan. I planned to sell the workshop to pay the bequests and boost cash flow."

Lucy had no emotional connection to the property, despite Grandpa hiding in his "shed" for hours during her high school years. Brown, unwanted furniture had repelled her, whereas she could lose herself in the timeless beauty of treasured objects in the quiet elegance of the shop. Breathing in the soothing scent of beeswax or Gran's preferred shop flowers—spicy oriental lilies—kept chaos at bay.

The workshop was a paean to chaos. Broken furniture was a reminder of numerous late-night getaways from unpaid rentals, of being hustled downstairs and hiding in garages to escape the casual violence in her mother's life.

*Why didn't I know chaos was the trigger for my unease in the workshop?*

"You're asset-rich, Lucy." He spoke reason, when she'd buried reason along with her grandpa. "The house, the shop, its contents, plus the merchandise in storage."

"My priority is the business and the staff who work there. Next are the cash bequests." *Why leave me this puzzle,*

*Grandpa?* "And Mr. Quinn is not a simple cash bequest."

"You can still sell the workshop." He leaned back in his chair, ready to listen.

"And lease it back with Quinn still in residence?" Selling a perfectly functional workshop when Grandpa's will required a workshop hinted at a panic Lucy wrestled with daily. Fitting out alternative premises was both insane and another financial black hole.

"A new owner might be prepared to do a deal and take on the property with an existing tenant?"

"I could end up paying more rent to a new owner than the cost of absorbing it myself." Lucy was thinking aloud. "Can I buy Quinn out?"

"The existing agreement runs for another four months. You can offer him money in lieu of occupancy, but your problems snowball from there. He's also invested money in the property. Some might consider you have a moral obligation to cover the costs of his alternative accommodation for the four months and reimburse his outlays."

"Grandpa would expect that." *He'd be appalled at the scenarios I'm considering.*

"You'd have a sizeable bill before you implement the conditions in your grandfather's will. That's your real issue." Henry's smile carried the patience of a man who'd been dragging her back to this point for more than an hour. Lucy could feel the noose shortening. "But you've already thought about Cameron's intentions. He wants to establish a foundation as his legacy."

"What do *you* think of Niall Quinn?" Lucy asked, envying Henry her grandpa's confidences about the carpenter, but needing his answer.

"A talented, impoverished cabinetmaker. Honest. I think Cameron saw some of his younger self in Quinn and decided to become his backer. I'd expect Quinn to be surprised and a bit embarrassed to learn of the contents of the will."

An objective observer, like Henry, might say Niall had been blindsided by what Lucy had told him. She was reserving judgment. Although, Quinn had been present at Grandpa's funeral but not forced his attentions on her. He'd given her food and drink despite her hostility, an act of service reminiscent of her gran.

And she hadn't revealed the half of Cameron McTavish's wishes to Niall Quinn.

Henry continued. "His honesty translates to a bit of stiff-necked pride. Niall Quinn doesn't want charity. I had a lot to do with him over the first agreement. He wrestled with signing it.

"This is a more complicated gift. I'd guess he'd be reluctant to translate the gift to cash, even if that was possible. He'd be more concerned if any quixotic idea he may or may not have planted in Cameron's head tipped you into financial stress."

"He doesn't need to know anything about my finances." Lucy paused.

How much did Henry know about her childhood? Grandpa had dealt with Henry Senior until the old lawyer had retired six years ago.

"I hate being in debt." Hate was an inadequate word to describe the visceral terror gripping Lucy.

"Tell me."

"I'm not ready to sell the house." She swallowed the sob caught at the back of her throat.

Ridiculous sentimentality, given her nomadic childhood. But the house held precious memories she couldn't bear to surrender: Slipping into Grandpa's library to inhale the comfort of much-loved books and the peat-scented whiskey he'd liked to sip while reading. Her gran had introduced her to perennials in her country garden, teaching Lucy the magic of living in one place long enough to bury her face in familiar blossoms year after year.

"You don't need to sell the house, Lucy. You can make your assets work harder for you." His advice made sense for someone who hadn't constantly fled insecure housing as a child.

"Can I make Niall Quinn work for me?" Lucy sat up straighter as the idea took shape. "Because you're right. Grandpa was offering patronage, and that's a reciprocal arrangement. If Quinn's as proud as you say, he'll see the fairness in providing something in return for Grandpa's generosity."

"The current agreement says he'll restore pieces on request. *Cameron* stopped requesting." He emphasised her grandpa's name.

"Do you know why?" She chose to ignore his hint.

"Cameron said he was a genius. Perhaps Cameron worked out he wanted to be more patron than employer."

"But he never said?" Lucy had been her grandpa's chief confidant after her gran's death. He'd had ample time to explain Niall Quinn. Grandpa's silence was permission of sorts for her suspicions.

"The will is making Cameron's statement for him." Henry wasn't offering her any wriggle room. But lawyers could get lost in black and white, whereas she was drowning in greys. Testing the boundaries with the erstwhile restorer made sense. "Do you like Niall Quinn?" Henry asked.

"I barely know him." But the image of him plonking a large sandwich on the table and effectively demanding Lucy eat rose in her mind's eye. He'd been kind, and kindness was rarer than most people understood.

# CHAPTER THREE

Niall debated letting the phone, linked to the loudspeaker, go through to his answering service. Debated long enough for Lucy's crisp, business-like voice to echo in the rafters, stating she was outside the workroom and expected him to open the door.

"You've changed the locks."

"Good morning, Lucy." She was wearing a gauzy, creamy blouse with some sort of ruffle at the throat. Very nineteenth century, probably perfectly suited to the hushed quiet of McTavish's antiques showroom, unlike his own dusty jeans and work shirt.

She frowned. "Shouldn't I have a set for the purposes of resumption in case of default?"

"Cam changed the locks and kept a set of keys after the insurance company asked for increased security." Niall counted to ten in his head. A generous assessment would put her motormouth down to nerves. He could afford to be generous. "If you can't find them, I'll get another set made. I won't be giving you grounds for eviction."

"Sorry. That was a genuine question." She pushed a hand through her hair, and for a heartbeat, he held his breath waiting for today's loose chignon to unravel. "I'm having trouble getting my tone right."

"With everyone, or just me?" Niall was interested she'd make the confession.

"Mostly you," she admitted. "Given I can't kick you out for not paying rent, I guess I don't have many options for eviction."

"Read the basics of commercial leases." He leaned against the doorjamb, blocking her view of his workshop. "If I damage the property, if I fail to uphold my end of the bargain, you've got grounds."

"I didn't expect to become a landlord." She rose on her toes, trying to peer over his shoulder. "What's your end of the bargain?"

"Some insurance, utilities, minor repairs, and I'm responsible for cleaning and general maintenance."

"Can I visit whenever I like?" Her heels hit the ground, and she met Niall's gaze, her eyes not as red-rimmed as yesterday. Although she was back to wearing makeup. Deftly applied, it provided camouflage.

"As my landlord, it's appropriate to make an appointment and give me a reason." Niall continued to block her view.

"Did Grandpa make appointments?" Her voice held a winsome curiosity.

"Cam called in whenever he wanted a chat. He came as a friend and mentor, not as a landlord. Occasionally, he checked if any repairs were needed."

"I called in to discuss Grandpa's will." She dangled a brown paper bag in front of his face. "And I brought sandwiches."

"I pegged you for polite." Niall registered the pink blush on her cheeks. Was she embarrassed by the compliment or yesterday's behaviour? "You didn't need to bring food."

"If I'd been properly channelling my gran, I'd have brought cake."

"Liùsaidh," he murmured, stepping back.

"Yes." Her chin jutted out, ready for a fight. "I'm named

for her."

"I didn't know." Niall decided the old-fashioned Scottish name suited her.

He'd looked up its meaning when he'd first heard it— warrior. Lucy was a warrior. He hadn't figured out what she was fighting for yet, to hoard her family's wealth or something else.

"Cam always called you Lucy. Come in."

"It surprised both of them to discover Mum named me after her." She crossed the threshold and halted. "To say Mum rebelled against everything they stood for would be an understatement."

Niall stored away the personal details she revealed. Cam had been protective of both his daughter and granddaughter. "Whereas you took to preserving old furniture with a vengeance."

"I don't see any reason to apologise for appreciating beautifully made and preserved antiques." Having made a visual assessment of the workshop, she started moving down the left side of the shed.

"You say 'preserved' as if that's a calling in itself. Art isn't something created a hundred or more years ago." Niall and Cam had debated the topic endlessly, more for the lively conversation than because they disagreed.

"That's not what I'm saying, although my personal preference is for late-nineteenth, early-twentieth-century art and furniture." She stopped in front of the stack of individual frames he'd finished this morning. "This space is different to when I was a child."

"Is that the last time you were here?"

"Chaos." She ignored his question. "That's my overriding memory. Furniture in pieces, dust everywhere. Although I realise now that's because Grandpa wasn't able to spend as much time here as he wanted." She ran a finger along a bench and held it up. "You're neat and clean, Mr. Quinn. The lighting's better, you've installed ventilation, the fire security has been updated, everything seems to have a place, and the equipment looks newer and more sophisticated." She'd identified in minutes all the key changes made since he'd moved in.

Her bravado told Niall she'd been anxious about coming here today, about him, but also about her memories. Chaos disturbed her. Being disturbed was on a continuum, from being troubled, to being unnerved, to being petrified. He guessed her instinctive discomfort with chaos had come before she'd entered her granda's workshop as a child.

Continuing her inspection, she halted in front of a large tool board mounted on the wall. It housed an old plane, a tenon saw, and ancient chisels, worn down from constant sharpening. "Antique hand tools?"

"Some of those are Cam's." Niall crossed his arms and watched her.

"*Are?*" She swivelled to face him, her expression uncertain.

"Cam let me use them. But they're yours, if you want them?" Niall's da's tools shared the same board, and he counted them among his greatest treasures.

"I'll think about it." She gripped her pearls and blew out a breath to steady herself before re-starting her inspection. "If I remember correctly, there's a small kitchenette in the passageway between here and the warehouse storage." She found it without difficulty. "I don't remember this impressive security door."

"It's new. Like the keys and other improvements. To get the insurance coverage I needed, I had to make a few changes."

"You or Grandpa?" The light of battle was back in her eyes, reminding Niall of Cam.

"This was one of the few battles I won with Cam. We split costs. Did you win many battles with him?" Niall had decided his brother was right. He'd fight back, until he gained enough facts to work out if he'd made a misstep with Cam.

She was opening a cupboard but turned to look at him

over her shoulder. "He was very strategic. He'd usually made the move before you guessed the enemy was on your left flank."

"Then you understand my dilemma." Niall let Cam's strategic rebellions sit unspoken between them. In some ways, the habit of playing his cards close to his chest explained any late changes to Cam's will.

"Royal Doulton Art Deco and Minton Pink Cockatrice." She held up his two dinner plates as if to make a point. "Do you have more than one piece of any design?"

"Not yet." Niall appreciated her knowledge of crockery—pieces he chose for their beauty as well as their job-lot prices. "Don't I get any points for recognising quality?"

"A few. Preservation is far superior to destruction."

"Are we talking about my frames again?" Niall was starting to enjoy the way her mind worked.

She unwrapped the sandwiches. Solid slabs of a country loaf. "I went for cheese and tomato again. Pickles for me, none for you."

"That works. What's in the will, Lucy?"

"It seems I misspoke on Sunday."

"I knew it." The knot of guilt he'd carried in his gut since their last meeting started to unravel and snagged on a word. "'*Misspoke*'?"

"He's left funds to establish the Liùsaidh and Cameron McTavish Foundation." She glanced around, then carried the plates across to a battered table beneath the window. Sun streaked through, magnifying each chip, scar and paint scrap on the table, a contrast to the smooth lines of his inland rosewood Boornaree fruit bowl.

"What foundation?" He took the chair she left free.

"A two-year scholarship for promising young woodworkers. In year one, the successful recipient is employed by McTavish's to learn the antiques trade. Year two is a full-time mentorship with you."

"Feck." He took a large bite of his sandwich and started

chewing.

"Do you subscribe to the thirty-two chews on average to break down food?" She stretched out a finger to stroke the edge of his crimson-toned bowl.

"Who makes that stuff up?" he muttered. When she opened her mouth to answer, he held up a hand. "That was rhetorical. Tell me the rest."

"In the first year, you get cash-in-kind to the value of twelve months rent on this property, so you can establish yourself or prepare yourself, or whatever else you have to do to take on the mentorship in year two." Her nervousness hid a deeper emotion.

"I'm presuming the foundation is an absolute. My involvement is voluntary?" What the hell had Cam hooked him into?

She pursed her lips. Pretty lips, but they twisted in disbelief. "I *assumed* Grandpa discussed the project with you."

"No." Niall listened to the silence between them. Silence could carry a thousand and one nuances. "What's the real problem? Do you resent my involvement? Or do you still think I conned him?" Niall asked because her answer mattered for whatever truce they reached.

"I was blindsided the other day. And angry because Grandpa became frail enough for people to take advantage of." She fingered her pearls again.

With sudden insight, he realised the habit was a tell. She was defensive because she didn't know what the hell Cam was playing at any more than he did.

Her voice was lower but crystal clear. "I don't think you took advantage of him. I'm sorry I accused you of theft."

"Apology accepted." Niall tasted the bewilderment lurking beneath her apology. "What's the deal after year one?" He took another bite of sandwich while he waited for her answer.

"If you agree to be the mentor, then you get rent reductions for the following four years, eighty percent off the commercial rent for year two, then sixty, then forty. By year five, you'll receive a twenty percent annual deduction on the commercial rent as payment for mentoring the scholarship holder."

"And if I don't want to be the mentor?" Niall had thought Cam's questions about his time in Ireland had been idle conversation to distract Cam from his illness. Niall had rabbited on about the sheer joy of being challenged daily by a master cabinetmaker to dig deeper, to be more than he was.

"Grandpa named you as one of the two-person panel selecting the scholarship winner each year. Being the selector is separate to being the mentor. If you choose not to be the mentor, Grandpa asked that you nominate someone to take your place." She sounded indifferent to his decision, but her body had stilled, straining for his answer.

"Who's the other person?" Niall didn't have the reputation to mentor anyone. The idea was preposterous. *And yet?* Cam had faith he could do it.

"Me."

"I feel outnumbered here." The middle of Niall's back started to itch.

"Because I favour antiques and you're relentlessly modern?" Her gaze skittered to the picture frames lined up against the wall.

"Something like that. I'm assuming I have some time to think this over." Think, rather than flail about like a beached whale with a concept Cam had never raised with him.

"The foundation needs to be in place when your initial agreement with Grandpa ends—four months." She lifted a shoulder in a half-shrug, having issued her ultimatum. "I'll get Grandpa's lawyer to send you the details."

"Please." *Why hadn't she asked Henry Dawson to set up a formal meeting?* "You didn't need to bring lunch to apologise. Henry could have explained the foundation," he said. She wrinkled her nose, revealing she had another motive. "Spit it out."

"Leopold's offers their artists a new service. Unique frames made from recycled antique timbers." She pointed. "Like those. Not to my taste, but there's creativity in the design and execution."

"I'm betting Leopold's was thrilled to get your assessment."

"Why did you ask Grandpa to source the timber?" She waited several beats. "Ashamed of what you do?"

"This is a short-term project for me." Shame had driven the search for a project to earn quick cash to repay Liam, but Niall hadn't learned how to make a second-class product. The profits from Leopold's frames were paid directly to his brother's bank account. Niall had set himself a repayment target before his nephew or niece was born.

Part payment for his share of their father's debts, a down payment in regaining his self-respect. Quinns always paid their way.

"So, you're calling the business Frames by Niall. That's not as creative as the actual frames—"

"Well, feck." Taking a leaf out of his romance author sister-in-law's playbook on pseudonyms, Niall didn't use the name Quinn for anything except his own creations.

"—but you're fetching premium prices."

"That's what counts then." He put his half-eaten sandwich back on the plate, her criticism of his mercenary intent stinging.

"It's interesting." She'd dabbed at the pickle at the side of her mouth with one of the serviettes she'd brought to go with today's sandwich. Pity, when he'd prefer to see her pink tongue take a swipe at them. "My grandpa invested quite a bit in you. You could also say you're my co-beneficiary. I've checked your website. Niall Quinn—Quinn's bespoke furniture. You're just starting to get a name."

"Next you'll be telling me I've won prizes." Niall bared his teeth, feeling like a caged hound. He hadn't received any awards for his work since his return from Ireland.

"I assume that's why he selected you as a mentor." She

looked down her nose at him, royalty dealing with a slow-thinking peasant. "Grandpa bought old frames on your behalf. I didn't really connect the dots until I remembered Leopold's."

"What dots is it you're connecting?" Niall studied her; under the makeup, there was genuine colour in her cheeks. If sparring with him had provided some of her colour, he'd let her play this game out.

"You need money," she stated.

"Everyone needs money from time to time."

"Do you accept Grandpa's generosity prevents me from earning money from this site?" For a wealthy woman, she was fixated on money. But she wasn't the first woman he'd met with a calculator for a heart.

"Yes." If Cam had been alive, Niall would have roared at him for putting Niall in this position. Her granda was a man who'd understood hard work didn't always deliver a living wage. *So, what the hell was Cam playing at?*

"You say you respected my grandpa, liked him, dare I say, admired what he achieved?" Now she'd shifted to wheedling, and seeing her beg for anything sickened him.

"Cameron McTavish was a fine man, who above all else wanted to see you secure." All the lovely colour drained from her cheeks, and Niall cursed himself for being the cause. "Why does that upset you?"

"Because he and Gran already gave me security—a bed, food, clothes, an education." She gripped her hands tightly.

*She'd needed a bed!* What the hell kind of childhood had she had? "From what Cam said, you don't have much of a family. No cousins, no aunts, no uncles."

"What's that got to do with anything?" She reached for his fruit platter, resting her hand against it. To some, a burl was a deformity on a tree. With the right touch, it became an object of beauty. Touching the wood seemed to steady her.

"No family," he repeated his point. "He valued the family he had. He loved you. It's normal to look after those you love."

"I promised to keep McTavish's in the family." She used the shop as a shield. Or maybe as a comfort blanket.

"You'll get no argument from me." He held up his hands.

"I've got a proposition for you." Colour crept up her cheeks, and wasn't that fascinating?

Lucy McTavish didn't like his frames, didn't approve of his mismatched crockery, but body chemistry wasn't as reliable as good sense. She'd just acknowledged an attraction. That makes two of us. Reluctant—definitely—but simmering below the surface just the same.

"A *business* proposition. I'll buy you more old frames if you give me what you currently have in stock and all future pieces you produce."

"You don't sell frames." Whereas despite not using the name Quinn, Niall had made peace with his need to make bespoke frames for a short time. "My current stock is promised to Leopold's, and I build to measure." Niall had a personal yardstick for dignity, and his integrity wasn't for sale.

"Don't you owe Grandpa anything?"

"I owe myself self-respect." He kept a leash on his temper. "If I reneged on the deal with Leopold's, I'd have no credibility in the marketplace."

"They're just frames." She drove him crazy, stroking his creations as if she had some special connection to them, while badmouthing items the punters couldn't get enough of. She also fascinated him.

"You've just trashed my work and my morals. What would you do if I asked you to repudiate a sale to a new customer because a regular customer asked for the piece."

"I'd explain the piece is already sold." Her bum polished his chair while she practised haughty disdain.

"You can see yourself out." He pushed back from the table. Blackmail was an ugly word. "There's not much point in making an apology only to insult me again."

"I've got a serious cash flow problem," she blurted out.

"You've just inherited one of the oldest, most respected antiques businesses in the city. The premises are elegant, the stock high quality …" he stumbled to a halt.

For no reason he could name, Niall recalled Cam's sick room. Filled with personal possessions—Cam's favourite paintings, items of furniture, photographs of his wife—an intimate space kitted out as a well-equipped twenty-four-seven private hospital. A doctor called twice daily and nurses were on permanent call. It would have cost a fortune. *Well, feck!*

"Happens to the best of businesses from time to time."
*Happens to me most of the time.*

"I'm sure Henry has some ideas, if not your accountant. Have you tried the bank?" He'd started to babble. Resuming his seat, he tried another bite of the sandwich. A bad idea. The bread and cheese congealed into a hard-to-swallow mass. Cam couldn't have foreseen this, but Cam's pipedream about a foundation with Niall in the major role had somehow tipped his granddaughter into debt.

* * *

"Yes to all three. The bank's happy to give me a mortgage or a loan." Lucy hadn't intended to admit her cash flow problem. Frames by Niall was his dirty little secret. She'd planned to embarrass him into letting her sell his frames and pocket a share of the profit. He'd gone all noble and pointed out his integrity mattered to him as much as hers did to her. "But I need to service it."

"And you hate being in debt as much as you hate chaos."

His insight silenced Lucy before his gaze settled on her. He was a brooding, creative genius if the photographs she'd seen of his prize-winning furniture were any guide. Not her preferred style, but they showcased the wood, and as Grandpa had taught her, the material was the true magic— wood or stone or glass. And the craftsmen and women were alchemists. Grandpa had wanted Niall Quinn to succeed. And was prepared to harness his legacy to Quinn's future success.

"What was your first plan?" His turn to cross-examine her.

"Selling the workshop," Lucy admitted. It was only fair to tell him he had no long-term future here. In three to four years, she might be able to nudge him out of the property by upping the rent.

He whistled, long and low. "That's quite some cash flow problem you've got."

"The foundation and you were the only surprise large bequests, but Grandpa supported a few charities. He expected them to receive the money straight away."

*I don't have the time now for my childhood demons to rematerialise.*

Still, Lucy's nightmares had returned, shaking her belief in the professional businesswoman she'd become. Debt had been the big bogeyman for the first years of her life. She was being cautious, not crazy, worrying about cash flows and money in the bank. A buffer, that's what she needed. Her panicked brain told her to keep cash reserves for six months' operating costs at a minimum—a year would be better. Time to see if she had a problem, and if so, fix it before there were irreversible consequences.

"You knew about the other bequests," he said slowly, working his way through the puzzle. "So you'd decided to sell before you found the copy of my agreement yesterday. Then Henry told you about the will. That's one house of cards to come tumbling down."

"Selling would have given me a buffer."

"If you made any mistakes," he guessed. "You're worried about stuffing up McTavish's?"

Quinn's perception rivalled that of any man Lucy had ever met.

"We keep having to draw boundaries about what is *my* and what is *your* business." She had no intention of detailing the crippling costs of the hospital-in-the-home room she'd established to make sure Cameron McTavish had twenty-four-hour professional care. Grandpa had told her he didn't need that level of care, but the shadows from her mum's death lingered. Lucy doubted she'd survive another interrogation from police and medical authorities if someone else died on her watch.

"So, we're agreed. You don't tell me why you need cash, and I don't tell you why I need it." He reached out a hand and covered hers where it sat on the table, her index finger lightly pressed up against his bowl. "Is it just wood you need to touch, or do glass and stone and clay affect you the same way?"

Lucy withdrew her hand and missed the warmth of his touch. "I'm sorry. I'm not always aware I'm doing it."

"Wood's made to be touched. I spend a bit of time stroking it myself."

"Wood's my favourite," she confessed, his gentle quizzing about materials and art easing her past the embarrassment of admitting she was scared rigid about even the tiniest whisper of debt. "Put me in front of Donatello's David, and I'd have to sit on my hands."

"Donatello's naked bronze David is magnificent." He gave a slow smile. "Nice to know you're not one of the put-a-fig-leaf-on-a-man's-genitalia brigade."

"I'd got over the sight of a naked body before I was weaned." Lucy surprised both of them. Grandpa and Gran weren't prudes, but they didn't frolic naked around the house either. Niall's smile had distracted her enough to hand him a secret.

"Take it," he said, tipping the fruit onto the table.

"I couldn't." Because she'd come intending to make him feel he owed her.

"I didn't send flowers for Cam's death. The occasion should be marked." He made his gift impossible to refuse.

"It's a Quinn? I didn't realise." She blew out a breath, feeling tears threaten. "He sat here, didn't he? Chatting about your work. What did he say about this bowl?"

"He liked it."

"Grandpa was never so mealy mouthed. If he hated something, you knew it. Hate wasn't about taste. It was about whether or not the craftsman valued what he or she did. I bet he loved this." Fate should have given her grandparents a few more years, given Lucy a few more years with them. "Thank you."

"You didn't seriously think you'd make money selling my frames, did you?" He flopped back in his seat and crossed his arms. Impressive muscles rippled beneath his shirt.

*Brute strength does not turn me on.*

"I considered it." Lucy had considered a gazillion options because debt conjured memories of skipping meals, sleeping in her mum's old car and using service station restrooms for showers.

"Like me, you worked out it would cost you too much to sell them yourself. You'd need a website or another outlet. You'd have to invest in marketing. Leopold's saves me all that work and money. Plan A was selling the workshop. Plan B, which I imagine took you about thirty seconds to discard, was financing a loan by selling my frames. By the way, I've developed a sideline with a florist." He lobbed the florist idea like a chunk of raw meat thrown to a hungry lion.

"I didn't think of that." But there must be other possibilities involving frames if Lucy gave it some thought.

"Why piss me off by suggesting it?"

"It was worth a try." Lucy deserved the scepticism evident in his raised eyebrow.

"What's Plan C?" He was inexorable.

"Your current agreement includes a clause whereby Grandpa can nominate pieces for you to restore." Her heart started pounding. Lucy hadn't intended to lay her cards so openly on the table.

He winced. "How many?"

"We can negotiate as we go along." Relief he wasn't

showing her the door anymore made her giddy.

"I'd prefer a time period."

"Like three pieces a month?" She was being provocative because the time needed for restoration would depend on the piece.

"Like a day a week of my time," he corrected her, "for the remaining term of my initial agreement with Cam. I'll give you fourteen eight-hour days."

"So, the number of pieces will depend on their size and the condition they're in." Hope was a rare green shoot for Lucy in recent months, too bright a promise to question his motives.

"That's the first genuine smile I've seen you give." His voice was gruff, and he tugged her hand away when she pressed it to her mouth. "Cam wanted you to be happy."

"I know." Her grandpa had rescued her when she'd given up hope of being found. "I'll need money to buy pieces."

"You could hock your jewels?" Mischief quirked the corner of his mouth.

Lucy fingered the perfect pearls hanging in a double strand around her neck, almost sure he was joking. "These were Gran's. Grandpa bought them for her. I couldn't sell them."

"Do you have a float to get us started?"

"I'll ask the bank to fast-track a loan."

Lucy would have time to see the manager again this afternoon. Straight after the psychologist she hadn't seen in a decade. Because after meeting the bank manager the first time, she'd had a mini meltdown—gone home, curled into a ball under the blankets and closed her eyes, as if that would make her problems go away? Ridiculous behaviour for a woman who prided herself on her business acumen. Her attitude to debt was more phobia than rational assessment of her situation. Knowing that didn't make a blind bit of difference.

"Think about picking up more frames for me at the next

auction as well."

"How did that work with Grandpa?" she asked, the glint in his eye telling her this was more teasing. She missed her grandpa's teasing. "Did you look through the catalogues and suggest stuff? Visit the auction rooms in advance?"

"Both."

"There's an estate auction next week. With no money, I wasn't planning to attend."

"Cam didn't always buy." He knew her grandpa's habits.

"He liked to look almost as much as he liked to buy." Lucy loved—*had* loved—that about him. He could admire without needing to possess, the opposite of her mum, who'd craved the shiny and new. "You should come with me?" The invitation was out before she realised. She backpedalled. "See if we can work together?"

"I haven't made a decision on the foundation yet."

"The foundation is a done deal. Whether you accept Grandpa's challenge is up to you." She held her breath, hoping he'd accept her dare to attend the auction.

"Are you sure you can bear to be seen in public with such a Philistine?"

"If you know the word, you aren't one."

The workshop comforted her in a way it never had during her grandpa's day—not that Niall Quinn's presence had anything to do with that. He was a link to her grandpa. That made him an ally of sorts, and an orphan didn't readily discard an ally.

# CHAPTER FOUR

*Put yourself in her position.* Niall scowled at the timber stacked against one side of his storeroom a few days later. *You're getting a year rent free—obligation free—to make money at will.* He tossed a piece of jarrah over his shoulder and headed back to his workbench.

For an intelligent woman, Lucy McTavish was blind. You could drive a pantechnicon through the inconsistencies in her position. She'd worked out he was making frames because he was in debt. Yet she saw no problem in asking him to work for her for free.

*So why the hell did I agree?*

He set the piece of wood on his workbench.

Because Cam had rated Lucy's peace of mind above money, the business, the house he'd built to remind him of his Scottish origins, or any foundation that might preserve his name. Niall barely managed his own cash flow, so he couldn't imagine what was involved with Cam's empire. Except, Cam hadn't intended his final bequest to Niall to tip Lucy into a panic about debt.

Saying no wasn't an option.

A bit of work for her shouldn't impact his plans.

The foundation, on the other hand, was both dare and

gift to Niall. A dare to silence potential critics by delivering a successful exhibition, and an extra year rent free as a reward. Cam's trust, even more than his generosity, made Niall want to accept the dare. The lure of a year able to focus on his work stopped his head and his heart. The idea of teaching appealed to him, and the crafty old man had teased that confession out of him in one of their many conversations.

A foundation? Niall chuckled.

People should remember Cameron McTavish. He was a great and good man. Cam hadn't told Lucy about Niall's exhibition, a secret Niall would keep. The show would be over before he needed to sign anything for the mentorship.

Niall ran his hand over the timber. A half-forgotten time ago, a friend had described a mirror he'd seen in an antiques shop. The frame was shaped like a musical note. It had cost a motza. Twenty-four hours later, when his friend had decided "to hang the expense," the mirror had been sold. His friend had never seen anything like it again. Niall planned to use the smooth-grained, reddish-brown jarrah for a mirror with a frame like a misshapen treble clef tipped on its side.

His phone vibrated in his pocket. Speak of the devil, although her voice didn't conjure images of horns and a tail, but rather memories of a smart, attractive woman, who'd triggered a wish for her to stroke him with the same delight she stroked his creations. "Hello, Lucy."

"What's your decision?" Her phone manners needed work.

"You forgot to say 'Hello, Niall, how are you?' and whether your question is about the foundation or the auction."

"Is that Candy Dulfer?" She could distinguish the wail of the alto-saxophone through the phone.

"You know Candy Dulfer?"

"Hello, Niall. How are you? You sound as astonished as the Thomas-Rhett-look-a-like music teacher at my music camp when he discovered I knew the Dutch musician." She chuckled. "I studied her like a demon with the precocious hope the teacher would single me out for attention."

"When was this camp?" If Lucy had been a minor, did Niall need to find the teacher and demand an apology?

"Shortly after I moved here. A Gran brainwave, marketed as building girls' self-esteem without any psycho-babble. Gran was sneaky like that. The teacher introduced us to talented and successful female musicians as a way to teach us to believe in ourselves."

"Did it work?" Niall hadn't met Cam's wife, but tough love fitted with Cam's stories.

"I gained respect for the women, myself and the hot teacher. His eyes never strayed to places, and in ways that made me feel uncomfortable, unlike …" She stumbled to a halt.

Niall heard her shallow breathing above the music, imagined her mouth pressed close to her phone. "Finish the thought, Liùsaidh."

"I didn't like some of Mum's friends." She offered the skimpiest, most uninformative confession he'd heard since his brother had danced around the story of their father's death leaving debts large enough to threaten their mother's home.

Niall was sickened by what she'd left unsaid. She'd been a child when she'd joined Cam's household. "Do you play an instrument?"

"I used to sing in the shower." She was giving him another piece of the puzzle. He'd always liked puzzles. "That fact's not for general consumption," she added. "And you haven't answered my question."

"There's a park around the corner from the auction venue." He made an instant decision. "Meet me there at ten-thirty."

"Why am I meeting you at ten-thirty for an auction preview that starts at eleven?"

"Because you're right." Niall stared at the open rafters.

Because he'd committed to giving her fourteen days of his time. His life would be easier if he helped her select the pieces for restoration. "We need to get to know each other better."

"I said '*See if we can work together.*'"

"Same difference." Niall paused, then asked his far-too-personal question. "What song do you sing for your granda?"

"There's an Alter Bridge song. One line is on permanent rotation in my head—'*I feel you in the wind.*'" Her voice dropped lower. "I hear Grandpa in a breeze, a zephyr, a gale. Even a puff of wind reminds me of his deep-bellied laugh."

"Cam would like that." Niall's knees threatened to buckle. She'd captured the old man's spirit in a few simple words. "I've looked at the papers on the foundation. My brother's a lawyer. He's looked at them too. I'll help with the initial stages, help you select the first scholarship holder."

"I can hear a but."

"I've not done any formal teaching before. A few friends have asked for pointers or sent family members to me to get a feel for the trade." Niall confessed one of his reservations. Fair exchange for her sharing her image of her granda. "A furniture maker with an established reputation would bring more cachet to Cam's memory."

The phone gave them the pretence of being anonymous, rather than intimate. He and Lucy barely knew each other. Niall sure as hell wouldn't have asked about her singing in the shower or admitted his reservations about being a mentor if they'd been in the same room. But he'd just handed her some of his private misgivings.

"Grandpa chose you."

Her tone told Niall that Cam's vote counted, even if she thought it was a mad or bad idea. "Yeah."

"See you at ten-thirty on Wednesday."

The tickle of anticipation at spending time with her was new.

Niall found her on a bench in the small suburban park, home to old fig trees and new children's playgrounds. Her head rested against the hard, wooden slats, and her eyes were closed, making it impossible to miss the dark smudges under them. Sleep was still eluding her, which explained why she'd nodded off on a park bench.

Lowering himself to sit beside her, he listened to her shallow breathing, ready to fend off any passer-by who strayed too close and disturbed her. A perfect day for a picnic and a nap in the park; one of those halcyon late-winter days when the wind was soft and the heat in the air promised spring. A lone kookaburra nestled in a nearby paperbark tree startled him with its raucous laugh.

Opening her eyes, she turned her head in Niall's direction. The caught-in-the-headlights look she'd worn when they'd first met was fading.

"Punctual as well as polite." Niall met her dazed gaze. "I mean you, not the kookaburra. His timing's off."

"To be punctual is to be polite." Her words carried the weight of a dictum she tried to live by.

"Was there ever a time when you weren't?"

"I can remember being regularly late for primary school."

"Just school?" Niall lifted the bag he'd been carrying, passed her a plastic food container, then lifted out a thermos, two insulated mugs and a small jar containing milk.

She pushed herself upright. "Everything."

"Did you fret?" Niall poured a mug of tea and passed it to her. "Help yourself to milk. I have a theory people are born punctual or not. If you're a punctual child, but the adults in your life aren't, it can make you a bit edgy." As a family, the Quinns were very punctual.

"I felt conspicuous."

"Ah." He took the food container from her, flipped the lid and wound back the foil packaging. "You don't like to be the centre of attention." He held the container under her nose. "Sniff."

"I beg your"—she closed her eyes and sighed—"fruit and rum."

"Kate may have overdone the rum. Although Mum subscribes to the view you can't have too much rum in Christmas cakes."

"It's a bit early for Christmas." She accepted a generous slice on a paper serviette, her rare smile rivalling the sun for warmth. "Who's Kate?"

"My brother Liam's wife. She's pregnant. Thinks she might be too pregnant later in the year to make cakes, so is starting early. This is a test. She wants feedback." Placing his slice between them, he poured his cup of tea and set the carry bag on the ground. "Moaning and hmming doesn't count as feedback."

"It's delicious."

He took a bite, savouring the rich flavour. "It's pretty good, but I might encourage her to keep practising."

"More than one slice and you probably shouldn't drive." She eyed the remaining crumbs. "It's a shame to waste any."

"I won't tell a soul you used your napkin as a funnel." He enjoyed her dilemma about the crumbs, like the smear of pickle and the sesame seeds on her plate. She wasted nothing. Most people he knew who shared her attitude had gone without at some stage in their lives.

"You're encouraging bad habits." But she followed his lead.

"You're allowed to lick your fingers at picnics."

She rolled her eyes and licked sticky fingers.

Lust hit with the suddenness of whiplash. "How old were you when you moved in with your grandparents?"

"Ten."

He swallowed, taking the empty cup from her. "Both parents dead?"

"I've never met my father." Her eyes held the bravado of a child who'd been mocked in the playground.

"You were christened McTavish?"

"Mum wouldn't have entered a church if you'd paid her." She outed her mother as the heathen daughter of Scottish Presbyterians.

"How did your mum die?" Niall tucked the items back in his bag, letting the ordinariness of his actions drain the question of any insult.

She crossed her arms over her chest, defensive but not hiding. "What makes you ask?"

"Cam never talked about how she died. He was very protective of you and your mum." Niall had put it down to being an old-style gentleman. Given Cam's silence on Niall's real work, he wasn't so sure anymore. Lucy had a feminised version of Cam's wide, intelligent brow and determined chin, although her upturned nose was her own. Her skin was lovely, not flawless, but a warm cream. Niall's fingers itched to explore whether it would feel as silky smooth as it looked. At the funeral, she'd looked fragile enough to break. Having a purpose was giving her new energy. He leaned forward, more vanilla and rose teased his senses.

*Will I taste rum if I kiss her?*

His brain told him kissing his landlord would be a mistake, though it wouldn't be the first time in his life he'd made a mistake. "There was a kid at my primary school. His mum died young."

"How did his mum die?" She stared straight ahead.

"An accidental drug overdose." Niall sensed her tremble and understood Lucy's mother hadn't intended to die the night she did. "A stronger batch than she was used to."

She turned and met Niall's gaze, resignation in the set of her jaw. "Finish your story."

"Billy was watchful, like you. When he thought no one was looking, he licked the plate. Like you'd like to." He paused. "He was part of our after-school gang."

"I know the rest of this story." She left the words "like mine" unspoken, but the bitterness was as sharp as burnt coffee. "You don't know where he is now, because you just lost track of him, or he lost track of you."

"Billy's an environmental activist on the north coast. Closer to Liam than me. Always was," Niall replied matter-of-factly, wanting to make Billy Kelly's past a non-issue. Because she'd just admitted her past had been an issue for people sitting in judgment. "Happily married. No kids, but Kate's pregnancy has given Chrissy and Billy a hurry on." Her shoulders dropped a fraction, a laying down of weapons. Niall continued. "The women beside you during the funeral ... are they school friends?"

"Friends? Yes. From school? No." Subject closed. "Did you invite me here early just to feed me?"

"I invited you for a planning meeting." Niall leaned back against the bench, mimicking her position, his legs stretched in front of him, crossed at the ankles, enjoying the moment. "Combining it with morning tea is in the nature of a time and motion exercise."

"You don't need to feed me every time we meet."

Niall changed direction. "Want to know how Cam and I met?"

She leaned toward him, greedy for stories of Cam. She could ignore hunger but not the tiniest facts about her granda.

"At an auction. I can't remember who suggested a coffee, but I found myself telling him about the frames and Leopold's." Niall had found himself explaining his plan to create unique frames for the upmarket art dealer as a short-term, money-making venture while he established his bespoke furniture business. "Cam invited himself to the workshop I rented at the time. Then he offered me his workshop."

"The workshop with a warehouse and living quarters in a mid-city-ring industrial suburb."

"We've already had that fight." Niall ignored her raised eyebrow. She'd eaten, so mission accomplished, but her scepticism suggested he'd need a new trick the next time he wanted to feed her. "That was probably the last time we attended one together. We attended a few pre-auction openings together, when the online catalogue didn't give me the information about frames I wanted. I only restored furniture he owned. Furniture he'd owned for a long time." He let that sink in. "Buying with restoration in mind pits us against a different group of competitors. Prices rise and fall based on demand, including who's generating the demand. You might want to handle this discreetly."

"So we identify some stock, and I return to purchase alone."

"If possible, we identify enough suitable stock to cover fourteen days, and you ask one of your lesser-known staff to return and purchase." Niall lifted her hand and checked the time. Her skin was as silken as he'd imagined. The compulsion to turn her wrist over and rest his lips against the softer skin there was strong enough to blindside him. He was spending too long alone in his cave. "Time to move."

"What role are you playing?" Her gaze assessed his tweed jacket and tie as he unwound and stood.

"Junior assistant, friend, confidant, whatever role we find we need me to play." Niall gestured to his clothes. "I'm not here as a carpenter."

"It's an estate auction preview, not a celebrity party." She shot to her feet and headed for the property, muttering over her shoulder, "No need to dress fancy."

*I'm attending with a McTavish, and antiques royalty has standards to maintain.* "This is the fanciest I do."

Niall let her sign in, standing back, playing the role of a not-very-interested companion. They were the first to arrive, as he'd planned, and the only viewers for the first fifteen minutes. He glanced into each of the three bedrooms, but the interest lay elsewhere—in the dining room, library and music room.

Despite the sophisticated marketing, he noticed signs the elderly owners had fallen on hard times in recent years, both financially and personally. Pieces hadn't been repaired—

burns from teapots or hot dishes not treated. He ignored the beautiful grandfather clock with its walnut casing in the library. The timepiece needed an expert clockmaker. While the harp in the music room needed someone with a musician's skill. But he noted Lucy touched both as they passed. A gentle touch, a finger held a hairsbreadth from a surface. And she struggled to restrict herself to wooden furniture. Touch was her way of interpreting her world.

*What would it feel like to have her hands on me?* Niall swallowed a groan.

A few steps into the living room, she halted, her body stiffening. "Hello, Tomas."

"Lucy." Tomas stepped close enough to Lucy for Niall to visualise his over-powering cologne landing as sticky fingers on her shirt. When Tomas puckered thick lips and blew kisses in the direction of both her cheeks, Niall saw another transgression. Lucy was uncomfortable. "Sorry I couldn't make Cameron's funeral," Tomas trilled. "He's such a loss to the industry."

"Darling"—Niall stepped up behind her and wrapped his arms loosely around her waist, pulling her rigid body back against his chest—"introduce me."

"Tomas Bechet," she said. "Bechet's Fine Furniture, a colleague of my grandfather's."

"I'm Niall, a close friend of Lucy's." He exaggerated his Irish lilt, but her body remained stiff. "I asked her to show me how she spends her day." He winked at Tomas and ignored the man's proffered hand, instead reasserting possession by rocking Lucy gently from side to side, until her muscles softened. "Really to spend my day with her."

"Nice to meet you." Tomas's smile died. "We can catch up another time, Lucy."

Stepping away from the doorway, Niall drew her with him until his back was against the wall and her back against his chest. "Smile as if you're having a wonderful time."

"What do you think you're doing?" she hissed.

"Sexual harassment is the legal term. Unforgivable to my

mind. But, you're upset, and I'm taking preventative action to confuse the half-dozen people in this room who are looking our way about whether we're here for the auction or some nooky." He nibbled at the spot where her neck and shoulder joined. The scent of rose was stronger here—old-fashioned, like a full-blown damask. Her skin was silkier, her shiver of reaction telling him she wasn't immune to his touch.

"They won't be confused if I toss you over my shoulder and sit on you," she muttered, angling her elbow into his abdomen.

"I might enjoy that."

"Whisht! We're not having a personal relationship."

"Whisht means you're pretty pissed off, so I'll apologise in any language you care to name. Later." Niall planted a kiss beneath her ear, finding this stretch of skin velvet soft, the taste reminiscent of rose-flavoured Turkish delight. Hours wouldn't be long enough to savour the taste of her. The temptation to nibble his way along her jaw to her pretty lips told him he was in serious trouble. "And we've got a personal relationship. We've had three meals together, and we've shared intimate details about our families and our cash flow." He released her, and she pivoted on her heel.

"You know what I mean." She grabbed the lapels of his jacket and tugged him close. She was hard to read; although he'd guess surprised rather than offended.

"You mean sex?" Niall forced himself to keep his hands at his sides because they'd just leapt over a metaphorical hedgerow at a full gallop, and he risked losing his balance. "Having and wanting are two separate things."

Her eyes narrowed.

"Keep that foot on the ground, Liùsaidh," he crooned. "I'm fair fascinated at the people in your past if your first reaction to a friendly conversation is to knee me in the balls."

"I'm not having sex with you," she said through clenched teeth.

"Not yet, and not while I'm working all the hours in the day and then some." Niall was tempted. It had been a long drought, and he and Lucy weren't considering deep and meaningful, just a friendly frolic.

"I have some say in this." She wasn't afraid of him, whereas in Tomas's company she'd been frozen.

"You control this." Niall brushed his lips across hers, his reward for exorcising Tomas Bechet's malign influence. "I'll apologise again if you tell me why Mr. Over-cologned Bechet upset you?"

\* \* \*

*You control this.*

The fight went out of Lucy. He meant that. There was nothing possessive or over-familiar or uncomfortable in his kiss or his touch.

*Holy hell!*

Those three words made him unlike any man she'd ever met. Sparring with him punched holes in the black fog of grief surrounding her. Which had to be the reason her body had exploded like a Roman Candle shooting stars in all directions at his touch. As if her hormones had heard the starting gun fired, and she'd won the race. The prize was Niall Quinn, cocked and loaded. She closed her eyes on a groan. Then opened them to find she hadn't disgraced herself by leaping on him.

Judging from the calm patience in Niall's expression, she hadn't spoken her thoughts aloud either. Her heart hammered in her ribcage, her hands were clammy, and her wits had abandoned her.

"Lucy?" His lilt made her stomach do a double-back flip with pike.

*Stop your dreamin'*, her Mum used to say when she'd close her eyes seemingly for no reason, except to find a place where she was safe.

She recalled Niall's question about Tomas. Had simple

concern prompted his actions? She'd already discovered he was kind. For a second, she let herself rest against the warm bulwark of his body.

He paid attention to what wasn't said, which was how he'd worked out how Lucy's mum died. And lived. But he hadn't sought to benefit from the knowledge. At school, she'd battered away sly innuendos about sleeping rough. Clementine and Kelly knew she'd had to hide from some of her mum's visitors; they didn't know it was Lucy's job to wake her mum every morning. The three of them had shared a room and friendship at the care home. Lucy missed their regular catch-ups. Kelly was making lightning visits interstate for work, and Clem was busy falling in love—a surprise to them all.

"Lucy?"

"Tomas uses dubious lighting in his shop and dodgy provenance for his products. He thinks his irresistible charm allows him to charge preposterous prices."

"He's a businessman and an extortionist?" He slipped his fingers through hers and turned her back to face the room. "Let's call the garda."

"I doubt we'd find actual evidence. He's too cagey for that, but we don't like the way he does business." Lucy stilled at hearing her use of "we." There was no "we" anymore.

"We still talk about my da. Telling stories is a way to remember him, but also to deal with his passing. I'm sure that's why wakes are so important." He understood the ebb and flow of grief. That made him easy to be around, easier still to find attractive.

"Wakes began to stop people from selling the dead for body parts. Literally someone stayed awake to protect the grave from grave robbers." Lucy cast him a sideways look. "I find those sorts of facts fascinating."

"Will you be my partner the next time I play trivia?" He steered her across the room. "You still haven't explained why Tomas makes you freeze. Another piece of trivia, fight, flight or freeze in the face of danger. Maybe I should have phrased my question differently. What about him frightens you?"

"'Frightens?'" Lucy repeated, stopping.

"Maybe I'm wrong. Maybe he reminds you of someone."

"No." She recalled the man leaving her mum's bedroom on the night her mother died. Larger than Tomas, but he'd worn the same scent or the base note was the same. Her heart raced as she made the connection. "His scent. I hadn't realised. A friend of Mum's." Her free hand reached for her pearls.

"I'm sorry to remind you." He leaned closer, a shield from prying eyes. A hint of his sandalwood scent wrapped around her. This time Lucy welcomed the reassurance.

"Poor Tomas. I've maligned him for no good reason."

"I like this washstand." He seemed content to forget Tomas. "I bet you've got a wash basin and a jug to fit the space and the period. Cam had some sheets of marble from the right period to replace the benchtop."

Lucy followed his lead. "Sounds like the McTavish's are doing all the heavy lifting if I buy this piece."

"Ah, but I thought of it." He winked, drawing her into a conspiracy of two. "And you've already spotted the mismatched leg. That, plus a few cosmetic repairs you might miss, are my contribution. Keep walking." He nudged her hip.

"You could just ask me to move along," Lucy mumbled.

He grinned, and the lines that dug around his eyes revealed genuine humour but also fatigue. *Why would he be tired?* She'd assumed selling frames was fixing his cash flow problem. Making them wasn't a physically demanding job, and yet something was keeping him awake at night.

"I'm keeping up the pretence we're interested in each other more than the items for sale." But he was scanning this room with the same intensity he'd scanned the previous rooms they'd passed through. "Ten o'clock, what do you think of the sideboard?"

"Marquetry Demilune 1890s in the style of George III."
Lucy sucked in a breath. "It's gorgeous. Damaged but
lovely."

"Depends on the price, but that's possible."

"You have a good eye," Lucy admitted, giving serious
consideration to his situation for the first time. He must be
selling the frames for a motza, whereas restoring furniture
took longer and wasn't as lucrative. But the bowl he'd given
her was stunning. The photos and testimonials on his
website confirmed his skill. Maybe he'd decided it took too
long to get rich making bespoke furniture?

*Whisht, Lucy, getting rich is a long way away from clearing debts.*
Hard-headed when he needed to be? She could respect his
decision and lament the absence of new pieces on his
website.

"Stuffs up your assumption I have no finesse or class."
He nodded in the direction of the sideboard. "The wood is
beautiful. Mahogany inlaid with satinwood. Don't know the
maker, but it's special enough to have a mark."

"Is that the sort of thing you discussed with Grandpa?"
Lucy cursed another part of her mother's legacy. Assuming
every man she met acted out of self-interest was a lonely
endowment.

"Cam knew if something was worth fixing, even if he
didn't always have the skill to do it." He steered them
around a large table, giving them a different angle on the
sideboard.

"Like the three pieces you restored for him." Henry's
words popped into Lucy's head—*Cameron stopped requesting.*

"Cam loved them. They sat in his shed for years, but he
couldn't bear to let them go. He nearly talked my ear off
while I worked on them." He turned her to face him. "Time
to look at me again as if you're besotted."

"Can Monday be the day you give to me?" The
beginnings of a plan energised Lucy. She could get a glimpse
of what Niall and her grandpa had shared. Maybe even

discover why Grandpa had kept Niall Quinn and the foundation a secret from her.

"Why?" he asked, although he must have already guessed.

"The shop's closed on Mondays, and I can visit."

"And that's a good thing because …?" He ran a finger down her nose, as if they were lovers planning a tryst.

Lucy heard the patience in his question. Kind and patient, and she pushed aside her reservations at taking advantage of his decency, of demanding more work for a debt already paid. Her first loyalty had to be the continued survival of the family business. "Because you can tell me what you're doing, so I can learn to recognise opportunities without you."

"Recognising opportunities without me has some appeal." He tugged on her earlobe, a friendly touch, which shouldn't make her pulse race. Clearly, he'd be happy if he never had to visit an auction house with her again.

"You can tell me what Grandpa would say." Lucy angled her chin higher to prove she was unaffected. "You can tell me what he told you."

"He told me he loved you." He brushed the back of his hand down her cheek, and Lucy shivered. He'd raised the stakes, flipped the mood to intimate.

"Men don't sit around talking about stuff like that," she replied, while his warm fingers did their own sweet-talking. The hands that had crafted her rosewood bowl made magic.

"It's in the tone"—his smile stalled the breath in her throat—"in the selection of stories, the small smiles, and the loud laughs, and the frequency with which Cam returned to the topic."

Niall Quin was dangerous. With his insights, with his perception, with his big, gorgeous body she wanted to play with—briefly, just to see what he offered, because entanglement wasn't a safe option for her.

# CHAPTER FIVE

Niall steered her out the front door and away from interested ears.

She'd done it again, slipped past his barriers with a simple show of courage. He'd easily understood the kind of bravery holding her spine stiff at Cam's funeral. The valour of necessity and pride, both personal and to show respect to the person you've lost. Anger had turbocharged the fearlessness propelling her to his door when she'd decided he'd cheated her granda. This was different. She'd held her ground against a hazy yet real fear, making it more terrifying.

Tomas Bechet carried the scent of a man who'd known her mum. Whatever the feck that meant, it wasn't a good memory.

Niall pieced together the bits of information he'd picked up. No father. Mother an addict, dead by the time Lucy was ten. She'd needed a bed and food. She was a fighter and a survivor. And hell, a scent could shut down the urge to fight or flee and make her freeze as the only way to protect herself.

"Cam liked to talk about the loves in his life, about establishing the business, about meeting his Liùsaidh, about you." Love had been the thread linking all the old man's stories, and another part of why Niall had been so comfortable in his company.

"Grandpa always called Gran by her full name." Lucy's mouth softened, and her gaze turned wistful at an old man's reverence for his wife's name.

Niall had used the name because he liked the way it rolled around his tongue, liked the light in Lucy's eyes when he called her Liùsaidh. *What kind of man would Lucy choose as a lover?* "I reckon he told you most of those stories."

A tender smile curved her mouth, and Niall was hooked.

"We can compare," she said.

"In his version, it was the perfect love story." Niall was beginning to think he might enjoy having Lucy around a bit more. *I'm turning into a masochist!* Her demands and her presence would make a tight timetable even tighter, before he added the hours needed to choose the first scholarship holder.

"A fairy tale?" She giggled.

Niall hadn't believed she could. Joy made her radiant, carefree for the first time since he'd met her. His chest puffed out knowing he'd wrought the miracle. "You think he made it up?"

"Maybe Grandpa embellished."

Looking at her, snatches of conversations with Cam came back to him.

"*She'll need a distraction.*" Cam had offered that morsel as part of a general conversation about loss and death.

"*It might take longer than you hope before you get the recognition you deserve.*" Cam had stared at the photo of the Huon table and sighed before throwing out his "wait for glory" line. Niall had thought the old man was giving him his regular pep talk on the patience needed for his craft.

"*I'm sorry.*" He'd been purely baffled by Cam's apology offered during Niall's last visit. At the time, he couldn't see any reason for regrets between them.

Cam was a strategic thinker, three moves ahead in any chess game. Niall had always matched Cam's offers, a matter of his pride and honour to ensure each trade was fair. Cam had changed his will for a reason. He'd never asked Niall directly to keep an eye on Lucy, but increasingly, Niall was convinced those fragments of conversation were connected.

*Did Cam propose the foundation so I'm on hand to fill some of the empty void in Lucy's life?*

Niall didn't fancy the position of guard or lap dog. He tuned back in to Lucy's words.

"The first time I asked him how they met was for a family project for school. He gave me the short version, but he pumped me every day on what the other kids were saying. And he added and added, tracing all the way back to meeting her when they were both six and stuck their tongues out at each other."

"A time-honoured way to show you care." Niall nodded. "What are you looking for in a mate?"

"Interesting word—mate. One minute we're talking about my grandparents and the next you're back to sex." She rolled her eyes.

"To hear Cam tell it, it was a mighty passion. Lots of lusty sighs, passionate glances and tackling each other onto any reasonably comfortable surface."

"I got the edited version for my school project."

"I'm asking about your life, Lucy." The inconvenient desire she'd stirred in him when she'd been in his arms made him reckless. "Everyone should have at least one passionate affair in their life."

She tilted her head and narrowed her gaze. "Are you offering?"

*Well, feck!* The rush of blood from his head to his groin made him dizzy. Having already noted her courage, he was a fool to offer her a challenge, although he was sorely tempted. "At the risk of repeating myself, you control this."

* * *

Lucy was at the workshop on the dot of eight the

following Monday, because in her experience, tradespeople started early. When she drew close enough to press the buzzer, the spine-chilling beauty of k.d.lang singing the last chords of "Hallelujah" wafted out a part-opened window. He'd sound-proofed the workshop. Another improvement since her childhood. An insurance request? Given what Lucy was learning about Niall Quinn, consideration for the neighbours probably figured as well.

He was that kind of thinker. Observing details, observing reactions—a different kind of "treat thy neighbour as you'd have them treat you" to Grandpa and Gran. Gran had fed her, bought her clothes that fitted, and read her to sleep with stories Lucy could read herself. Nothing overwhelming, just small acts of service building daily into a pattern of love. There was a different element to Niall's practical she couldn't quite put her finger on.

Compared to any man she'd met, there was a different element to his sexual challenge as well. *You control this.* He couldn't have any idea how enticing those words were to a woman who'd spent the first decade of her life with no control over anything, except her dreams. An affair with him would be discreet and harmless.

*Lucy pants-on-fire McTavish.*

An affair with Niall Quinn would be incendiary. Nuzzling his way up her throat, he'd started a fire inside her, a conflagration still blazing when he'd held her hand to inspect one piece of furniture after another. Like being close to a woodstove—the radiant heat was immediate, but the promise of bone-deep warmth over time kept you close. He'd purely smouldered when she'd asked if he was offering an affair. She'd waited for the bushes flanking the path outside the deceased estate house to spontaneously combust.

This morning he pulled open the door within seconds of her pressing the buzzer. She sensed impatience in him, as if she'd interrupted some task, then his expression cleared. Leaning forward, he sniffed the air. "Well, feck! Same scent, so it must be Liùsaidh McTavish beneath those overalls, old sweater and"—his gaze dropped to her boots—"are those steel-capped?" He patted his chest. "Be still, my beating heart."

"Are you quoting the poet Dryden or the musician Sting?" Her stomach dropped to those steel-capped boots hearing her full name roll off his tongue.

"Whoever you'd like me to quote."

"The boots are because this is a work site." She inhaled wood smoke and exhaled the jittery nerves making her question her reception. Discreet, incendiary and laced with affection—a short affair might work for both of them. "I've done basic occupational health and safety courses."

"I'm impressed." He drew her inside, and his welcome scrambled her good sense. "Why?"

"About five years ago, Grandpa organised to do some renovations at the house. I needed to do walk-throughs, keep an eye on things."

"Given your dislike of chaos and dust, you must have had a pretty strong motivation." He spun on his heel and headed toward the table under the window: their lunch spot on her first visit to his workshop.

"Gran insisted on supervising," she explained. Niall's friendship with her grandpa, and the stories Niall had to trade, neutralised her usual caution talking about family.

He glanced over his shoulder, his smile understanding. "And you supervised your gran."

"Grandpa installed an elevator, modified a bathroom, and built a balcony from the main bedroom overlooking the garden." To protect her gran, Lucy had studied in forensic detail what was safe and unsafe behaviour for an invalid in a home converted to a building site.

"Cam told me his wife was ill for some years before she died." Niall Quinn's discretion equalled his kindness.

Her grandpa had never sugar-coated hard truths. "Gran was physically frail, then was diagnosed with dementia."

"Dementia's an ugly and terrifying word." His lilt almost

disappeared under the weight of his compassion. "And unspeakably cruel to lose the love of your life twice, mentally and then physically."

"She lost the capacity to comfort others. Gran would have hated that." Lucy had hated the loss of dignity on her gran's behalf. "She was good at comforting others. In a practical way. If a family was rocked off-centre by a tragedy, she'd be the first with a casserole."

An act of service had killed her grandmother. Her cat had meowed at a closed window. In her rush to open it, Gran had fallen, hit her head on a footstool, and broken her neck. In the video clip lodged in Lucy's mental library, the cat's complaint had sounded a fraction of a second before her gran's cry. Heart pounding, Lucy had sprinted down the hall, skidding to a halt in time to see her gran roll off the footstool. Too late to be useful. Soon enough for endless what-ifs.

"You know where the kitchen is. Help yourself to tea whenever you want it." His abrupt change of topic startled her out of memories carrying the force of a stun gun.

"Do you want a cup?" She remembered her manners.

He pointed to the large teapot on the table beside him. "Just drained this."

"You've started work already? Is the furniture here?" Lucy glanced around.

"Due any minute. I was filling in my time while waiting."

A laptop sat on the table with a sketchpad to one side. She sidled closer, unable to hide her curiosity. "Can I see?"

He turned the laptop around. "I'll have to swear you to secrecy if I show you these."

"Stop." She covered her eyes after he'd scrolled through a few pages of artworks. "I think they're paintings, but I wouldn't swear to it. Conceptual art is not my style."

He laughed. "We call a spade a shovel in my family as well. Comes from growing up on the land, I thought. Then I figured out my parents valued honesty above bullshite."

"You don't like these paintings either?" At the gallery

opening with Grandpa, Lucy had decided she and the anonymous frame maker lived in wildly different universes.

"Not this particular batch. But the last lot were still lifes, painted with meticulous detail, the shadows worthy of Caravaggio at his best. The painter, a woman, lacked his volatile temperament, which made negotiation easier."

"What do you negotiate?" Another detail she hadn't considered when she'd planned to skim his profits.

"The artist has to like the frames. They send me the images. Using a software program, I send some designs, and we go from there."

"How often do you do this?" Guilt at her glib dismissal of his frames created an itch between her shoulder blades.

"Leopold's opens a new exhibition about every three weeks. Sometimes the artist has already arranged for frames or thinks frames will distract the viewer from focusing on their work. It's a balancing act, the frame and the painting. The frame has to be discreet enough not to draw attention away from the work, but to subtly enhance it." He added a few lines to a doodle on the sketchpad and recreated a section of the *Mona Lisa*'s frame.

"You've studied art." The insight explained a bit more of the Niall Quinn puzzle. Like why Grandpa enjoyed his company. But it left other questions unanswered.

"Part-time at night for a year," he admitted. "Mostly art history."

"In preparation for making frames?" Lucy asked, although that made no sense.

"Because I was interested." His mouth twisted at the implied criticism in her question.

She thought back to the frames at the exhibition she'd seen. "They're all unique."

"That's the brief."

"I mean unique to every single painting at every single exhibition." The enormity of the design task struck her. And his skill. She was the antiques expert, and she hadn't twigged to the tradition he was copying. "In eighteenth-century

France, frames stood as works of art in their own right."

"Uh-huh. Partly furniture and partly sculpture. Although I don't claim to be as good as the bloke who created the gilded frame to go with Raphael's portrait of Lorenzo de' Medici."

"The scrolling vine and foliage of the frieze echoed the leaf pattern on Lorenzo's torso." She recalled an art history class. The frame was worth more than the painting.

"That's the one."

"Why don't you make money from your furniture?" *And why haven't I asked this question before?*

"The million-dollar question." His phone buzzed. "That's your delivery. I'll open the loading dock."

"I'd like to know." Lucy's interest had become personal, not just an explanation for Grandpa's actions.

"The economy. A bespoke piece takes more time. You need to consult with the buyer, submit a design, determine a wood, make the piece. The wood's a major cost." He shrugged as his steps ate up the distance. "I use only recycled or recovered Australian timbers. Add in labour costs. We're coming out of an economic downturn. Bespoke furniture is a luxury item, and there's a sizeable part of the luxury market that likes shiny and new rather than sustainable."

"The same part of the luxury market who might buy one of these paintings neither you nor I like." She scoffed.

"Ironic, isn't it?" He unlocked the door beyond the kitchenette. It opened onto an empty space running down the right side of the building and included a long driver's bay.

"I know everyone's tastes are different, but why someone would want one of those paintings when they could have Grandpa's memorial fruit bowl is a mystery to me." She caught his arm, halting him.

"Keep moving, Lucy, and thanks for the vote of confidence. I'm focusing on the colours in this latest batch of paintings. They remind me of a valley I know—sky, hills, forest, a meandering river—so I'll make that my inspiration." He stopped short of the steel roller doors, marking the end of the bay and the shed.

"What's in these rooms?" Lucy gestured to two huge double doors on the left of the building. In her adolescence, this had been one large open space, difficult to navigate because of the amount of timber, old masonry and damaged furniture.

"Storage for what was left of Cam's materials. Storage for mine." He pressed switches on the back wall. The roller doors slid up to reveal back gates swinging open to allow the delivery truck to enter the property. With a circling gesture of his hand, he directed the driver to reverse into the bay.

"Right on time," he murmured to Lucy. "Did you threaten them with hellfire if they were late?"

"I asked if we could have the first delivery of the day," Lucy replied. "Why are you looking at me like I'm from Mars? I'm prepared to wait for a day when I can be first delivery. Nobody suffers."

"If you say so." He turned to the driver and his offsider. "Hi. I'll get you to take the sideboard through to the front. Lucy, maybe you can lead the way? I'll move the washstand into a storage bay while you're sorting that piece."

Lucy had calculated the washstand would be the fastest and therefore the first job. She had two wash basins and jugs in her car on the strength of her guess. Niall's instructions seemed to overrule that. She held her tongue while she led the men through to the workshop, held it when they returned to the loading bay to find Niall had unloaded the washstand and moved it into Cam's storage.

"Thank you." Lucy signed the delivery receipt, waited for the truck to depart and the roller doors to hit the ground. "I thought we'd discuss the order in which you restore the pieces."

"Let's discuss." Not waiting for her, he went into Cam's storage, where he'd set the washstand in an open space.

Then he hoisted three sheets of marble—as if they didn't weigh a ton—from some sort of shelves on runners and placed them nearby. "We'll have to replace the marble top. Which piece do you want? Have you chosen a wash bowl and jug?"

Miffed to discover she couldn't immediately decide between the marble slabs, she scowled at him. "I've chosen two sets."

"Why two?" He tucked his hands in his pockets, seemingly more interested in walking around the washstand and considering the marble slabs than in her uncharacteristic indecision.

"Because one set has a bowl to fit the exact dimensions of the table." She wasn't prevaricating. *Well, maybe a bit.*

"Verity is important in restoration."

"*But* the second set belonged to Gran." Lucy dug for patience because his teasing was an irritating prod to her indecision. She knew verity mattered, but Gran's wash bowl and basin set had been sitting on the deep window ledge in her bathroom when Lucy had moved in. Decorative rather than useful. Gran had sat on the floor with Lucy and woven magic into that first history lesson, a story of function, design, and how easy it was to become attached to an inanimate object.

"Wild guess here, but your gran's set doesn't have its own washstand?" He moved a rippled pink marble slab closer to the table and stood back. "Breccia Oniciata from Italy. The other possibles are the Val Venosta, another Italian marble or the Rosa Patara from Turkey."

"Right," she muttered, off-balanced by his knowledge of marble. Keeping everything that belonged to her gran and grandpa meant she'd be living in a museum, not a home. "Replacing the marble means you can adjust the cut for the basin." The idea sounded like sacrilege even as she said it. "A few millimetres. That's all." She watched his head swivel toward her.

"That's a mighty decision." His gaze was considering.

"Use your gran's set and it's not restoration, plus you could lose the set when you sell. Use the alternative set and your gran's things don't have a basin. There's a third option."

"What?"

"Look for another washstand." He sank to his haunches, the strength evident in his bunched muscles making Lucy's mouth water.

"That's another purchase."

"Haven't you stitched up the business loan yet?"

"We have room to breathe." A stupid thing to say when the breath hitched in her chest saying the words aloud. A business loan to cover the bequests, as a buffer for mistakes with the business, and to provide seed funding for the foundation hadn't come cheap.

"*You* have room to breathe." He pushed to his feet, and the bleakness in his eyes confused her. "Sounds like you're not ready to make a decision on the washstand yet. Although I'm betting the Breccia Oniciata is a perfect match for your gran's jug and basin set."

"Why did you decide on the sideboard first?" she asked, because she could hardly press him for information on his situation when she'd insisted her business was her business.

"Because the washstand needs discussion, whereas I can start straight away on the sideboard. Time is money, as they say. Sale of the sideboard will cover your first loan repayments. Isn't that the deal?"

"That's the deal." It was a bit late for Lucy to start feeling uncomfortable about her request. She, not Grandpa, had enticed him into restoring more furniture. Although "enticed" had started to smell a bit like "taking advantage." His eyebrows rose when she crossed her hands over her chest. "I'll take the basin and jug sets home then."

"Where I grew up, taking your bat and ball home the first time you're asked to share—in this case your jug and basin—was called a tantrum, not a negotiation." He gestured for her to precede him out the door.

*Great.* The noise of her boots hitting the concrete floor

echoed loudly, while he moved with the silence of a big feline. Each heavy footfall sounded like a two-year-old pummelling her fists in a tantrum. Tiptoeing would make Lucy look even more of an idiot. She'd been given a lesson, several lessons, in his ability to read his customers and his expertise at his craft.

\* \* \*

Niall pulled down his goggles and rolled his shoulders. The old railway clock on the far wall said it was a bit after one. Close enough. At the table, Lucy's head was bent, her entire focus on cleaning the handles for the sideboard. Another plait, this time for safety, and still he resented her hair being confined. Bright light streamed through the window, highlighting the subtle tones lurking in her sun-kissed auburn hair. He sought and discarded words to describe its colour—burnished copper, dark cherry, or a deep red wine, the myriad colours of his favourite timbers.

She'd been skittish when she'd arrived, rocking from foot to foot in her steel-capped boots, more appealing in work clothes than her uniform of black business suits. Not as bowed down by grief. She moved differently. Looser, more confidently, showing the decisiveness Cam had boasted about, and a weight lifted from Niall's chest. To survive the dark, you needed moments of lightness as well as anger.

Restoration required an exact replica of the original marble slab. Preservation would allow him to cut the replacement slab to fit her gran's jug and bowl. She'd been irritated because he'd called her on preserving rather than restoring the wash basin. He'd bet she was scrupulous in her requirements for McTavish's. Her hesitation revealed a secret yen to combine her granda's marble with her gran's knickknacks.

With the sideboard, he'd assessed options and begun dismantling the piece. She'd danced around him, badgering him with questions. Logical questions about the construction of the sideboard, about the steps he intended to take, why he moved in a particular order, and what materials he was going to use. Her scent had competed with the familiar workshop odours of sawdust and linseed oil, her voice drowned out by the occasional electric tool. Half an hour ago, he'd set her up at the table with the handles, rags and some brass cleaner, and to his surprise, the task silenced her.

"How's it going?' He strolled to the kitchenette to wash his hands.

"Slowly." She looked across at him. "But you expected that."

"A lot of restoration work is slow, painstakingly slow, if you want to get it right."

"I like the rhythm, the process." She picked up a second brass handle, rubbing it gently with the soft cloth. Her gaze returned to her task. "I won't finish these today." She was patient with the manual task. Another surprise. Niall had assumed she was the classy chatelaine of a famous antiques business, oozing elegance with a rehearsed patter to convince any passer-by to part with their money while never getting her hands too dirty. He'd been in McTavish's when she'd been absent on a buying trip. The genteel elegance suited her pearls and black suits.

"Let's take a break. Want some lunch?"

Her head swivelled back to him, her smile tentative. "I didn't bring food today. Didn't know if you'd send me packing after a morning of my company."

"I can feed you. You're being productive." Niall grinned. "And quiet."

"I can't guarantee the quiet will last." She wrapped the handles in the cloth he'd provided and cleared them off the table. He could add neat to patient in his list of her habits, although tidiness went with her dislike of chaos. "Can I help?"

"I've got egg salads in the fridge, if that suits?" Niall

reached for the kettle, musing on his earlier conclusion: debt was another form of chaos for her—and equally scary.

She joined him in the kitchenette, and her scent, more muted now, invaded his senses. "Better than any offering in my fridge."

"Who cooked for you and Cam?" Niall continued his tea ritual, impishly selecting two small Toby mugs from the cupboard above the bench.

"Toby mugs? For *tea*? Please, no." She dried her hands and moved behind him to reach the fridge.

"What do you use them for?"

"As little as possible. I'm not a fan." She carried the salads to the table, returning for knives, forks and serviettes.

"Has anyone ever told you you're remarkably conservative in your taste?" Niall swapped a Toby mug with a traditional Japanese teacup, this one with a handle, and carried them to the table. He enjoyed teasing her. His mismatched crockery collection was a running family joke, the result of a lifelong haunting of op shops.

"Not in such a perplexed tone of voice. Mostly, they use it to imply old-fashioned or boring. I've never been called conservative for refusing to use a mug as a teacup when it was designed for ale. You have an unusual way with an insult." She took the chair she'd taken for their first shared sandwich in his workshop.

"Swap places with me."

"Why?" She put her elbow on the table and rested her chin on her hand, her clear-eyed study flipping his stomach into a double somersault. "I sat here the other day, and you didn't see a problem."

"You don't want to get set in your ways." Niall liked distracting her, seeing her smile.

"Has anyone ever told you, you're crazy?" She took the chair Niall offered and moved the Japanese teacup to her allotted place.

"Crazy, pig-headed." Niall waved a hand in the air, acknowledging the hit. Crazy for thinking he could make a living from custom-made furniture when countries around the world churned out perfectly useful items at a fraction of the cost. Pig-headed because whenever push came to shove, his craft mattered more to him than money, his next meal and any girlfriend he'd ever had. His single-mindedness was why he missed important signals, like his brother's sudden fixation with making money after their da died. "You didn't answer my question about cooking."

"By the time I arrived, Grandpa and Gran had a rhythm. They took turns, although they each had their specialties." She let Niall doctor her tea. He hoarded these tiny surrenders of her ironclad independence because they showed she was relaxing around him. "Gran made the best casseroles; Grandpa had a delicate touch with pastries. They made me a third wheel."

"What's your speciality?" Niall guessed she'd have wanted a speciality, something she could excel at.

"From an early age, I mastered the art of a fine pasta sauce. I have more than a dozen in my repertoire." She liked contributing, which provided more context for her care with the handles.

"I'm impressed."

"After Gran died, we struggled to find a new rhythm." She nursed the delicate teacup between her hands, her words coming slowly. "We did it. I'll have to find another rhythm now."

"Cam talked about her. His Liùsaidh." Niall had caught her attention and brought the haunted look back to her eyes. Distressing her hadn't been his intention.

"What did Grandpa say?"

"That for him, talking about the people you've loved and lost helps grieving," Niall replied. She folded in on herself, a physical and emotional withdrawal painful to witness. He burned his bridges anyway. "Cam said grieving is unique to every person, and loneliness is an enticement to drunkenness and despair."

She flinched.

"Did he drink?" Niall doubted it. Cam's calm discussion of "tha demon drink" as a secret seduction showed the wry understanding of a man who'd conquered temptation. *Had Lucy's mother?*

"The occasional single malt whiskey. Self-discipline was important to him," she said.

Niall figured out she'd absorbed the lesson of self-control through her pores, along with a love of antiques, while shadowing the old man.

"Cam loved you, loved sharing a home and business with you. He was grateful you'd grown up with them, and he could talk to you about your gran after she died. This wasn't Cam's first time on grief's merry-go-round. His body and brain had fashioned a rhythm." Niall pushed ahead because she was sitting in his workshop on her one free day of the week. She'd lost her entire immediate family. How she'd jammed a stopper in the Vesuvius of emotions doing battle inside her was becoming a puzzle he wanted to solve. Accusing him of fraud had been a tiny release of steam.

"I miss him." She gripped the delicate teacup tightly enough, he feared for its survival. "I'm rational, sensible. I've always been good at managing the business." Her shoulders sagged, but tension still radiated from her. "I found a hand-written note tucked in the back of Grandpa's desk the other day. I couldn't stop crying—messy, loud sobs until it hurt to breathe." She turned her head, her gaze meeting Niall's, a mixture of confusion and embarrassment at her reaction. "It was a shopping list: coffee—beans not ground, chocolate biscuits—any sort, birthday present for Lucy."

"Do you remember what you got?" He bet she still had every gift Cam and his wife had ever given her.

"The note was dated. I was thirteen. They gave me Mum's music box." She swallowed a sob. "It played the same Brahms' lullaby she sang to me as a child."

"When I finally came home from Ireland, my mum gave me my da's tools. I didn't want to touch them at first.

Thought I'd wear them out if I used them, and then he'd really be dead." Niall had kept that bit of craziness to himself until now.

"It's like that, isn't it?" Half-question, half-statement, and her face relaxed. "You don't know yourself. You don't make sense to yourself." She sighed, adding almost inaudibly. "And if you don't know yourself, how can anyone else?"

"I should get back to work." Because Niall was tempted to stay, to ask where Lucy had been when her mum died. What she'd seen, where her friends were, and if she wanted more from life than running the family business. *Where the hell had that come from?*

"You loved him," she said, as if making a discovery.

"Yes." Niall collected the plates and turned to go.

"I'm sorry for your loss."

"Thanks."

*Praise the saints.* The woman surprised him every other minute. She'd just admitted they had common ground, and her acceptance felt every bit as good as holding her in his arms at the deceased estate viewing.

When she left, Niall finished sanding the pieces for the cradle, his hand testing the smoothness of the timber, while he absorbed the features of the grain and the marks of wear on the recycled ash. Spending time with Lucy McTavish had been easier than he'd expected. In overalls, her hair coming loose from her plait, and humming over brass handles, she fit into his workshop as easily as her be-suited persona fit McTavish's. She wasn't supposed to fit in his life.

# CHAPTER SIX

Seven o'clock on a Thursday night and Lucy was sitting in her car. She studied the solar lights lining the path to Niall's workshop, a silent guide to his man cave. This was a surprise visit. At least he'd be surprised, because when she'd left on Monday afternoon, she'd said she'd see him in a week.

She had her story prepared. A last-minute decision to attend another auction, and she needed his advice. Although her churning stomach told her a landlord should have made an appointment. The auction was only a partial truth. She wanted to sit at the table in Niall's workshop and share a meal and listen to him talk. He had a beautiful mouth, from a simply objective viewpoint—generous, sensuous, with a hint of humour. But his lovely lilt soothed, even as his words raised hard truths.

Lucy had known her grandpa was lonely, that no one and nothing could replace the time shared with his wife. She and he had joked that because of Gran's religion, he and Gran would be together again. She hadn't known he'd shared so much of himself with Niall Quinn.

*I've brought dinner*, Lucy texted, then waited.

The door opened, fast enough for her nerves to settle,

slowly enough for him to have time to hide what he was working on. *And what business is it of yours!* Inwardly, Lucy rolled her eyes.

"Hello, Lucy." He stood in the doorway, a hand braced on the opposite jamb.

The emotional connection between Niall and her grandpa bound Lucy to Niall in a more personal way than the creation of the foundation or her plea for him to restore furniture. A friend? She had few enough of those—and none of them male—to be drawn to Niall's workshop like birds drawn to nectar.

"I need some advice, and I thought you might not have eaten yet." Lucy spilled her game plan on a single breath.

"A break works." He gave a half bow to gesture her in.

The music was softer, soaring strings, and the contrast to the music he'd played on Monday revealed a complexity of character Lucy would have dismissed bare weeks ago. She strolled toward the kitchenette, aware of a largish object shrouded in drop cloths pushed to one side. Her fingers itched to flick back the coverings and see what he'd been working on.

"You were working?" Lucy glanced pointedly toward the covered item.

"Yeah," he said. He leaned toward the carry bag she'd hoisted onto the bench. "Smells good."

Lucy inhaled his blend of sandalwood, citrus, and man, and had to agree. "Tomato and caper pasta. Hope you like it."

"I'm sure I will." He set the plates in front of her. "I can offer you water, tea or a beer."

"Maybe tea later." She served the hot food, grabbed a bag full of sliced baguette rolls and headed for the table. "A cross between a picnic and fine dining."

"Thanks. I was going to nuke a frozen meal later." He followed with cutlery and some serviettes. "What's the favour?"

"Let's eat first." About to sit, Lucy stopped at the table

and reconsidered. "If you pull it out, I can sit with my back to the window."

He hooked a foot around a sturdy leg, tugged it out, set down the cutlery he was carrying, and moved the chairs. All without a word. Regret for her impulsive suggestion followed when he sat with his back to the room, his broad shoulders blocking any view, and his focus entirely on Lucy.

"What did you do today, Lucy?"

"Stock-taking," she admitted.

"What does that involve?" He spooned up another mouthful of pasta. "I can see why pasta's your speciality."

His casual compliment and his recollection of their earlier conversation were why she was here. He listened to her. "Hiding in a storeroom and checking items off a list. No brain power required at all."

"How many times did you have to start over?"

Lucy choked, then laughed, then savoured the individuality of his welcome. "At least six."

"Name three wooden pieces and describe them." He asked questions, she answered and dinner disappeared. "I'll make the tea." He stood and carried the empty plates back to the bench.

"I brought tiramisu for dessert."

"And you kept that a secret until now?" He made a smacking sound with his lips. "The tea can wait. Tell me the favour first. I'm open to bribes, but I have my principles."

She collected her laptop and opened the screen. "There's another auction coming up. I've got the catalogue and wanted to ask what you thought about a few pieces. This takes less of your time than attending the preview."

"That's thoughtful of you," he said. Did Niall think she was selfish? With his hips against the kitchen bench, his arms folded and his ankles crossed, he looked relaxed rather than wary. "Tiramisu is a big deal for a half-hour of my time."

"Can we talk about the foundation?" Lucy had buried that plan so deep in her subconscious she'd surprised herself.

"So, the tiramisu is booby-trapped."

"I didn't come here to ask you about the foundation." Lucy resented the defensiveness in her voice. "Although, Henry *did* call this morning. And we *do* need to talk. Surely this is easier for you than getting you to visit Henry with me?"

"More thoughtfulness?" He was teasing her.

"I can be thoughtful." She felt the heat rising up her throat when he grinned. "Stop being such a pain in the … whisht."

He laughed aloud. "I'll have to remember that insult next time I'm pissed off. Serve the dessert, and I'll answer your questions."

"What makes you think I have questions?"

"Do you?" He collected clean bowls and spoons.

"Yes." Lucy lifted the cooler bag onto the table.

"You have questions because cabinetmaking isn't your area of expertise, and you want to understand it." He was letting her off the hook. "I'll let you serve. Let's sort the auction out first."

Twenty minutes later, Lucy had chosen a dining set with eight chairs for the shop. They'd agreed she'd bid on a pair of late-nineteenth-century mahogany library bookcases, one of which needed restoration work. "Only if the price is right," she insisted.

"Any more tiramisu?" He eyed her cooler bag.

"Unfortunately, no." She upended it to prove in this, at least, she was telling the truth. "Next time, I'll buy the eight-person serving size instead of the four."

"Four people on starvation diets." He licked his spoon, and a little sizzle slid down her spine. "I'll make the tea." He sauntered toward the kitchenette.

He had a great butt, a delicious body but *that*, repeat *that*, was not why she'd come. He was as comfortable making tea as hefting a hunk of marble and looked good doing whatever task he turned his hand to. Lucy inhaled, absorbing the complex smell of his workspace. Linseed and wood shavings with notes she couldn't identify. Unlike McTavish's habitual scent of beeswax and oriental lilies, the workshop offered a kind of olfactory comfort for her loss.

"What about the foundation?" He set the teapot between them, returning to the kitchenette for cups and milk.

"There's an organisation that manages scholarships for families and companies. Henry thinks I should hand it over to them because of my workload." He'd said Lucy lacked the skills as well as time to take it on.

"I'm guessing you set Henry straight."

"Grandpa would have wanted me to be hands-on." Saying the words aloud solidified her decision.

"What's that involve?" He poured two cups of tea, doctored hers as Lucy liked and passed it to her. He did thoughtful on a regular basis, which was both irritating and endearing. Irritating because she wasn't as kind as she'd like to be. Endearing because kindness was baked into his character.

"The simplest way is establishing a not-for-profit organisation." Lucy organised her points in a logical order. "There are general requirements for tax purposes, like the use of funds purely for the scholarship and disbursements if we close it down."

"I'm a simple guy. It's getting late." He angled his chair away from the table, stretching out his legs and crossing his ankles. "Words of one syllable will work for me."

"We can't pay ourselves unless we have legitimate expenses related to the scholarship, and if we dissolve the foundation, any monies remaining should go to some like-minded venture."

"Makes sense. So what do you want to discuss with me?"

"Tell me what you have to do to become a cabinetmaker." Family pride demanded Lucy take an active role in the selection process, but she'd waded through pages on the internet and hadn't found answers.

"A lot, but not all, cabinetmakers in Australia do apprenticeships. A kid can be apprenticed, usually for four years, to an individual employer. Alternatively, he or she can work for an organisation, which acts as a sort of brokerage firm—farming out apprentices to different employers for shorter or longer periods of time." He perched his teacup on his chest, motionless. He didn't often stop moving.

"That's a three-way deal, isn't it? Employer, apprentice and the training organisation." Lucy had a basic understanding of the Australian apprenticeship system.

"Yeah, and if a kid's apprenticed, then they're getting a wage and have a day job."

"Wouldn't an employer want to keep them after they've finished, especially if they're exceptional?" She was looking for exceptional in the foundation's first mentee.

"Not always. Some employers only keep family members, others might take the pick of the crop, and some feel a responsibility to give a young graduate a few years' experience before they cut them loose."

"You said not all cabinetmakers do apprenticeships?" The lack of a clear answer from her research was starting to make more sense.

"Some people are self-taught. Some start in another field, like engineering or design, and gravitate to working with wood."

"Did you do an apprenticeship?" A basic fact she couldn't decipher in the general blurb on his website.

"Yeah, in Newcastle, where my parents lived. Mum still lives there. After four years with the one boss, I had a fair idea of their design style and timbers. I wanted something different."

"How different?" Her grandpa would have known every step of this journey. Another secret Grandpa had kept to encourage Lucy's ignorance of the real Niall Quinn.

"I went on the road, visited different cabinetmakers around Australia, did stints as an unpaid intern with cabinetmakers I admired, a few stints in the warehouses of auction houses, spent some time salvaging wood."

"Spent some time studying art history." Lucy recalled their conversation about the clever frame on Raphael's painting of Duke Lorenzo.

"Sydney University. Same as you. I'm betting you got your degree before training in valuation, sales and management." He flashed her a smile, reached out a long arm and topped up his cup. "Help yourself."

"Why did you go to Ireland? More wandering?" she asked. A wanderer didn't sound like a reliable person to base a foundation around. Maybe his debts were the result of years of wanderlust and low-paying, casual jobs. It wasn't her role to question his lifestyle. It was a reminder they had different dreams.

"I won an internship with a master craftsman," he said. "You said Cam left instructions."

"Grandpa provided the statement of purpose, duration of the scholarship, said recruitment was open—age and gender not relevant—and left some eligibility criteria." All neatly penned in his own hand. The will was an official document, whereas Grandpa's instructions for the foundation were personal and all the more precious.

"I'm guessing he requested, rather than specified, qualifications?" He raised a questioning eyebrow. "A portfolio of their work, how they got here, what their goals are—maybe what their dreams are?"

"He stipulated the contract was for two years on full pay."

"That's part of the legal contract I assume you and Henry are getting ready for the foundation. You should build in a cooling-off period."

"What about your cooling-off period?" Waiting until his existing agreement expired to hear his answer created a different kind of chaos for Lucy. "Have you made a decision?"

"The not-for-profit can be set up with no mention of me." He pushed himself upright, the relaxed pussy cat of the past fifteen minutes reverting to an alert king of the jungle.

"The arrangement for the workshop needs a contract. Five years at least." She studied him. He'd just detailed a history as a wanderer, and he'd spent several years in Ireland. Five years was a long time to stay in one place.

"I got the memo, Lucy." His voice was low and lethal. "But we're still in the negotiating phase."

"That's what I'm trying to do." Lucy drained her tea, unsettled by the shift from two people who loved and missed Cam chatting about cabinetmaking to two people stepping edgily around default provisions.

"Then your negotiating skills need work," he said mildly. "You can sort out the not-for-profit and start advertising for the scholarship."

"Will you make yourself available to select the scholarship holder?" She cursed herself the second she asked the pompous question.

"I said I would."

"And what!" She sent him an exasperated look. "Your word is your bond."

"As a matter of fact, it is." He was a maverick. Her grandpa would have admired his independent streak, maybe lamented a bit that his own wandering had stopped in Sydney with the birth of Lucy's mother. "Your sideboard's sitting over there because of it."

She made a strategic retreat because he was right. "The selection process will take time. What sort of short-list are we looking for?"

"No more than six, maybe less, depending on who applies. We'll want to see actual examples of their work. Ask for a demonstration of their skills." He was committing to hours more work connected to McTavish business.

"One year served at McTavish's and undertaking courses in art history and conservation, and the second with you." She was beginning to see the enormity of what Grandpa and she were asking of him. It wasn't the easy ride she'd assumed. "We need to name the mentor."

"I haven't agreed yet." His face was a mask. Did he really doubt his ability as a teacher? He had the patience for it.

"I need certainty." Another untamed legacy from her childhood.

Niall closed his eyes. Was she pushing too hard? Whatever emotion he'd wanted to hide had faded when he opened them. No smile, but his answer was clear enough. "Soon."

"I'll see you Monday."

Monday was the other side of three nights Lucy would spend rattling around at home alone. Climbing into her cold car, she worked out Niall had never once closed his door to her.

"Can you open the loading dock for me, please?" Lucy was still dithering about which of the bowls and jugs she'd use for the washstand. She couldn't delay much longer. Although calling in uninvited tonight was a yearning rather than a plan.

Gran's birthday, and she couldn't bear to be alone on the first major family anniversary since Grandpa's death.

Her real plan had been a night wrestling with the contents of the basement, until she was too tired to think, then she'd found herself driving to Niall's for the fourth time in two weeks. She'd stopped at the end of the street to call him, the muted music coming down the line tonight sounded like hard rock. She phoned again when she reached the back gates.

"That was quick. What are you bringing in?" he asked above the music. Listening to Meatloaf belting out "Two Out of Three Ain't Bad," followed by the bang of a door closing and the echo of footsteps confirmed he was walking the length of the cement-floored loading bay.

"Two wash bowls and jugs." Lucy didn't admit she'd been able to see his lights when she'd made the first call.

Now she watched the roller doors rise and spotted his figure near the control panel. The gates opened to allow her entry to the yard. She swung the van around and backed in.

"McTavish's Antiques." He opened the driver's door to let her out. Another small act of kindness, making her feel welcome when he must be itching to get to whatever he did on Friday nights. "Gran's jug deserves only the best transport?" he queried.

"I'll be collecting some new pieces in the morning." Lucy inhaled a bit deeper than necessary, filling her lungs with his increasingly familiar blend of citrus soap and sandalwood. The combination was insidiously reassuring and … addictive. "I'll go straight from home tomorrow, so thought I'd use it tonight."

"Let's get them unloaded then." He waited for her to unlock the back of the van.

"Am I interrupting anything?" Lucy blurted, her fingers tangling in her gran's pearls. "I mean, tonight? You sounded distracted when I called."

"Communing with my muse." The defeat in his voice puzzled Lucy.

*What or who did Niall Quinn use as inspiration?*

The frames for Leopold's next exhibition had been boxed up ready to go on Monday. He never talked about his own pieces, and the absence of any uploads to his website since they'd met meant she never asked. Whatever his debt was, paying it seemed all-consuming. She understood the compulsion.

"I'm your landlord, yet you never remind me I should make an appointment to visit." *Would his muse have to make an appointment?* Lucy's spurt of envy for the unknown woman he shared his creative secrets with rattled her. *Pull yourself together, Lucy.*

"You called." He shrugged, his expression unreadable. "And I'm currently working for you."

"I'm not here to check what you do in your own time." She stamped her foot, exasperated by her neediness and his rock-solid composure.

He grinned. "You're a bit too ready with foot stamping and raising your knee."

Lucy stepped closer, the urge to shock him overwhelming good sense and good manners. She'd come for his company. And to forget it was her gran's birthday, and that Lucy was the last of her family.

Sex was a kind of oblivion, and to see friendly, consensual sex as wrong was a repudiation of her mum that Lucy didn't have the hypocrisy to stomach. His gaze held steady while she lifted her knee. He stilled, maybe braced a little, but didn't step back. She slid her knee up the outside of his thigh, enjoying the slide of silk stocking over thick denim, the contrast creating a fizz in her bloodstream. He wrapped a large, calloused hand under the back of her thigh. When he tugged her closer, his blunt fingers scored gentle brands through the flimsy fabric to her skin.

"You'd best call a halt soon, Liùsaidh, or this might not end as you planned." His growl was incendiary, and he smelled like sin.

"You don't know what I've planned," Lucy purred, leaning into his chest.

"A quick tumble with the carpenter?" His second hand settled on her hip, splayed so she felt the imprint of each finger and his thumb through her skirt. His strength made her shiver in anticipation—a taste of possession. "If that's your plan, be prepared to stay all night."

"Is that an invitation?" Heat rose up her throat at his readiness to call her bluff.

"It's a warning. Just because you're twisted in knots about whether or not to use your gran's things, you shouldn't play with fire." His finger traced the figure eight at the back of her knee—her lucky number.

Lucy slid her leg out of his loosened grasp and stepped back, unsettled to find a quick tumble had lost its appeal. He wasn't a stud for hire to blot out pain and memories for a few hours. "You're a pain in the arse, Quinn."

"So I've been told. But you must be spooked to be using a word like arse."

"You and your 'fecks' are a bad example," she muttered, her stomach doing a deep dive. He was right. Cursing proved to both of them that she was flustered. She smoothed down her sweater. Toning down her expletives after her mum's death was her act of service to spare her gran's blushes.

Lucy had hooked up with men before. But if she and Niall went to bed, she wanted it to be because they liked as well as fancied each other, not a snatch-and-grab because she was afraid to be alone. *And where the hell had that thought come from!*

She never allowed herself to care too much for the men she bedded. Not because of her mum's experience, but because she wasn't built for permanence and happy families. She'd forgotten for a while with Doug, a banker who'd stumbled into McTavish's one day looking for an investment and decided she was it. Never again.

"I've packed both sets." Lucy opened the van doors and pointed at two boxes, strapped in to prevent them from rolling in the otherwise empty van. "We can sit them in the storeroom and consider our options."

Without a word, he climbed in, released the straps and pushed one toward her. "I'll bring the second."

"Have you got the keys for Grandpa's locker with you?" She stopped outside the storage door.

"You wanted to come via the loading bay." He shifted the large box labelled *fragile* to one arm and shoved his free hand in his pocket. Unlocking the door, he flicked on a light switch. "After you."

"We don't have to discuss this tonight—"

"Praise the saints," he said to the rafters.

"—but I thought if we lived with both sets for a while, we'd have made a decision by the time the sideboard is finished." She'd just left herself without an excuse to stay.

"The sideboard won't be finished for two weeks at

least." He locked the doors behind them. "Time for a cup of tea?"

Lucy glanced surreptitiously at her watch. "Maybe I could take you out for a drink? It's after seven. I thought you'd be finished for the day."

"I'm a bit behind on a commitment. I was planning to work tonight."

She made herself smile, a skill she'd developed at her mother's knee, an all-purpose squeezing of the facial muscles that covered "*It doesn't matter that you forgot my birthday*," or "*my class play*" or "*my sports carnival.*" "You don't have to be kind." She looked everywhere but at him. "Someone's probably expecting you."

"No one's expecting me, Liùsaidh. I said I planned to work. That's the truth, but I can take a break."

"Please. Not on my account." Her arms prickled with goose bumps, his practical compassion tangible enough for her to reach out and touch.

"Don't go coy on me now. It doesn't suit you," he growled. "Will a beer do? Or I might have some red wine somewhere."

"A beer'll be fine." Relief filtered through her system.

"Drive your van out and park by the house. I'll lock up here and meet you at my door."

# CHAPTER SEVEN

Something was wrong. Niall was beginning to know her, to read her moods. It had taken him a while to figure out she was lonely. Like him. Not just the loneliness of loss, but a sense of separateness he recognised because it was the backbeat of his life. She demanded very little for herself. She'd made herself useful on the Mondays she'd been in the workshop. The drop-ins outside their agreed hours had been okay as well. He was beginning to look forward to her smile, to her serious expression when he explained a technical issue to her, and the frown lines screwing up her forehead when she was concentrating.

Niall hadn't planned on her being good company. Tonight, she was disconcerted enough to need to be with another human being. Rattled enough to make a move on him, surprising both of them. Sending her home would be cold-blooded. The blood in his head had drained to his groin when she'd slid her leg up his thigh. Nothing cold about it.

A test for him or herself? She was still here, so he must have passed.

*She'll need a distraction.*

Establishing a foundation as a distraction was a bit

extreme even for Cam. Damn the old man for tying Niall in knots through his will.

"*Soon*"—a piss-poor answer to her questions the other night. She was entitled to soon. Although their definitions of soon were very different. She wanted decisions made yesterday and set in concrete. She was owed, given her childhood. He was still feeling his way.

Cam hadn't explicitly linked the exhibition to the foundation Although success would give Niall street cred and make him a viable choice as a mentor.

But each time he yielded to a diversion from Lucy McTavish, his plans slipped further behind. With two months until the exhibition, the gallery was pressing for photos of his major pieces. He had a month max before they moved into full-on publicity. Advertising on his site needed to start at the same time.

Niall pictured the almost-finished rocking chair he'd thrown a drop sheet over when Lucy arrived tonight.

He'd hidden it when she'd called in last week as well.

*Damned if I know why I haven't told her.*

Then he spotted Lucy making her way from the parked car to his porch. His gut told him she needed company. Turning her away came a close second to kicking a puppy. If he was honest, and he tried to be, he wasn't helping her because he owed Cam. Or only because he owed Cam. He liked her fierceness, her survival against the odds. They'd moved from guns drawn at fifty paces, to sharing meals and conversation, to a tentative friendship. The bells and whistles of attraction were a complication because the McTavish heiress was in a different league to a struggling woodworker.

"Are we going to the kitchen?" She stopped beside him in the dark of the porch, her delicate scent a torment. She'd come from work—a black skirt, silk stockings he'd sensed through the thick denim of his jeans and a charcoal sweater with a high neck. The severity was broken by the luminous quality of the pearls and the luxurious textures of cashmere, tweed and silk. He had to admire her love of natural fibres.

"I have a living room of sorts." Pushing open the front door, Niall flicked light switches and took the first door on the right. "See." He lifted a pile of craft magazines off the lounge and set them on a side table. Then he turned on the heater and sound system. "The room should be warm soon." As he expected, Leonard Cohen filled the room—mournful bloody sod that Niall was. "I'll be back in a minute."

"I'll help." She followed him through to the kitchen, and he fought to keep from hauling her back into his arms to finish what they'd started in the loading bay.

"Are you sure beer's okay?" He stared into his fridge, aware a beer could be downed in fifteen minutes. Not enough time for her to settle. "I've got a curry if you're hungry."

"If it's not too much trouble." She was worried about outstaying her welcome.

"A zap in the microwave, and hey, presto, we have gourmet vindaloo."

She giggled. *That was better.* He shoved the freezer containers into the microwave, set the timer and passed her a beer.

"Tell me about your friends from the funeral." A cack-handed way to go back to the beginning, but he was convinced her distress tonight was rooted in her past. "Do you want a glass?"

"What sort of glass?" She was suspicious of his glassware. He held up old Vegemite jars. Her reaction was swift. "You have got to be kidding."

"They were free." And he usually reserved them for a drop of Jameson's with his twin.

"After you consumed the Vegemite! I'll pass. To answer your question, their names are Clementine and Kelly."

"Clementine sounds like a Mississippi Delta goddess." Niall conjured an image of the two women at the funeral, both about Lucy's age. One a curly-haired compact brunette, the other taller, with a straight, neat bob. Each of them had hugged Lucy long and hard. Lucy had hugged them back; the longest physical contact Lucy had had at the ceremony. "What do they do?" He framed his questions to coax more than a yes or no. The microwave pinged, and he gave the contents a stir.

"Kelly's a teacher-librarian, works in public education. Whereabouts of mother unknown. Clem's a social worker and an orphan."

"And?" He took two mid-twentieth century Villaroy and Boch bowls from his cupboard and set them on the benchtop ready to serve. "Orphans don't automatically become social workers. Take yourself, for example. There must be something to connect those two dots?"

"Clem had a few bad foster experiences and decided she wanted to make a difference."

"Did you? Have a few bad foster experiences, I mean?" The microwave pinged again, and he took out the curry. "Cam said they had trouble finding you." She'd been ten. A mere baby. He'd bet his prized Huon table she'd had to grow up fast.

* * *

"Mum hadn't had any contact with Grandpa and Gran for years before she died," Lucy said, Niall's earlier empathy for his brother's friend giving her the courage to answer. "They didn't know I existed, and she didn't expect to die. But you worked that out."

"I did?" He swung to face her, his gaze searching.

"An accidental overdose, like your friend's mum." Saying the words always made Lucy's bones ache. "Anyway, I was fostered for a while before social security traced Grandpa and Gran. They said they wanted me." Lucy had been back in the care home a week when she got the news. She'd cried herself to sleep. Under the bedclothes, big, silent sobs she couldn't seem to stop. Hope had jostled with relief because her gran and grandpa were already on a plane to come and fetch her.

"That's half an answer. You were ten. You'd lost your mum and whatever security you'd known, and been handed over to strangers. Even if they chose Mike and Carol Brady for your foster family, you must have been terrified." His sober assessment invited the truth.

"The couple were decent, especially her," she hesitated, because she *had* been terrified. Cold and lonely, but she'd refused to be helpless. "They took in lots of foster kids."

"You don't have to tell me anything you don't want to." He deliberately didn't look at her, concentrating instead on ladling curry into the bowls. *Could he guess what was coming?* Her experience wasn't unique.

"There was an older boy there. He overheard gossip about Mum." Lucy fell silent, and Niall glanced over his shoulder. In her head the words sounded simple, unemotional, but self-loathing and anger were Sumo wrestlers circling in her belly, each trying to gain the upper hand. "That she worked as a prostitute. I woke up to find him naked in my bed one night."

"Feck!" He was at her side in seconds, his arms wrapped around her, his cheek resting on her crown.

"He didn't expect me to fight back. I screamed and screamed." Her cheek pressed against Niall's chest, the steady beat of his heart anchoring Lucy to the present. "The woman was there in seconds. They called the police."

"I'm sorry."

Lucy lifted her face. His expression held anger on her behalf. "I believe you are. He was surprised I'd fight back, given my mum. He said that." Lucy had celebrated every punch she'd thrown. It wasn't until Niall asked his question about Tomas Bechet that she worked out she froze when she was helpless.

"He was an idiot as well as a rapist." Niall kissed her forehead.

"She was and wasn't a prostitute." Lucy's hand curled in

his sweater, keeping him close because a lot of people refused to see shades of grey.

"You don't need to explain your mum." Niall Quinn respected her privacy, making it easier to confide hard truths.

"Mostly, she worked in retail. But it didn't pay enough for her habit. So she slept with men who could get her the drugs she liked." She paused. Even now, the addiction upset Lucy more than the prostitution. "Or occasionally to pay the rent."

"Addiction's an illness." His acceptance was another comfort.

"Mum was very matter-of-fact about sex. She liked it, and claimed she liked most of the men."

"You're also not responsible for your mother's actions." He worked his fingers down her spine, massaging each vertebra. "Nor for her relationship with her parents." He released her and turned back to the bench. "I need to reheat the curry."

"I'm not very hungry," Lucy apologised.

"Me neither, but we should try." He returned the bowls to the microwave and blasted them for a few seconds. "I'll bring them through. The other room should be warm by now."

"Thanks for this." Lucy sat on the edge of the lounge, taking a small mouthful of curry, the bottle of beer at her feet. "I'm sorry I disturbed you."

"I should be thanking you. Otherwise, I might have forgotten to eat tonight. And, feck, my mum would call that ungracious." He almost blushed. "It's good to have company."

"Do you mind if I put my feet on the sofa?"

"Make yourself comfortable."

Heeling off her shoes, Lucy curled her feet under her, settling more deeply into one corner of the sofa. He seemed to relax as well. "Who's singing?" she asked.

"Leonard Cohen, a poet who was famous years before

you were born. A bit depressing." He hit the remote, and silence enveloped them. The mood shifted to companionable. Lucy had eaten a few meals with him now and had the rhythm. "If you eat some more, so will I," he said.

She chewed another mouthful.

"Why haven't you seen your friends in the last few months?" he asked, before slapping a hand to his forehead. "I'm an eejit. You were at the shop all day and with Cam the rest of the time. It's also why I never bumped into you at the house."

"Life's got in the way lately. Kelly's travelling for work and Clem's swamped with work and life. Grandpa wanted me to tell him what was happening in the shop." Except she knew now that was only part of his plan.

"Cam wanted to know what I was doing as well. Did he make you show him pictures of new stock?" He set his half-empty bowl on the floor beside him.

"Grandpa wanted to distract me from the fact he was dying." It had taken every ounce of Lucy's self-control to sit with him every night without screaming at him not to leave her.

"I didn't see Cam with your clarity. I admire your fearlessness." He took her unfinished bowl and added it to his own. "But pretending he wasn't dying was never going to fly."

"He was old-fashioned in thinking the man should be the protector." Lucy sighed. She'd loved him to pieces and despaired of his traditional view of relationships. "It was one of the reasons why my mum and he parted company."

"It wasn't a problem for you?"

"You mean because I'm so determinedly independent?" She wished she was fearless. Instead, she'd built her personal force field to transmit a clear message. *I can look after myself.* A necessity for survival growing up, but being independent didn't mean she was always strong. "By the time I'd arrived they'd had time to think about what went wrong with my mum. They kept me safe"—she smiled—"so I could live with some over-protectiveness on occasion."

"Were you returning the favour?" He edged closer on the lounge. "Cam said you were insistent, said his condition didn't need that level of care. Or that cost. Is that why you installed the high-tech, twenty-four-hour nursing?"

"I didn't come here to talk about my hang-ups." She swallowed a mouthful of her beer. In care, she'd never told a soul what she'd been doing the morning her mum died.

"I put truth serum in the beer," he deadpanned. "Why did you come?"

"Gran's birthday." A partial confession.

"And last year you spent it with Cam." A rumbling lilt, and his voice, like his scent, made Lucy think of bedrock and solid foundations. She let its music settle in her bones.

"Did Grandpa tell you how she died?" Grandpa had selectively shared secrets with his protégé and Lucy—a puzzle she was determined to solve.

"A tragic accident, he said. She fell trying to let the cat in and broke her neck. Cam said having you saved his sanity. But you found her, I think." He took her empty bottle and stacked it on the bowls.

"We were worried about her." Grandpa's praise was a precious gift to receive tonight. "She was getting more forgetful, so Grandpa and I took turns working from home. I was in the kitchen getting her a cup of tea."

Linking his fingers with hers, he raised her hand to brush a kiss across her knuckles. "You must have been devastated to be so close and not be able to help." His sympathy penetrated her bones.

Lucy wanted to believe absolution was uncomplicated. But the police and the coroner and the doctor had all had questions. "The police wanted a re-enactment with timelines. *Where was I standing? How long was I in the kitchen? Did I hear the cat? Did I hear the fall? How long did it take me to reach her?*"

"When did this happen?" He rested their joined hands on his thigh.

"I called emergency. The police arrived first."

"Were you alone?"

"What do you mean? With Gran?" Confusion slowed Lucy's reactions. *Have I made another mistake? Please, no.* Doug had asked the same question.

"Did you have someone with you when you were questioned? Was Cam there?" He lifted her onto his lap. "You would have been in shock."

"Grandpa was out of town at an auction. Took a few hours to get back." Lucy sat awkwardly in his embrace. Her hand closed over the strand of pearls, an unbreakable link to her gran. "They had some base lines of my actions. The last entry on my computer, my mobile in my pocket, the call to emergency." She'd swallowed her anger during the endless interviews and pulled every emotion that dared to surface deep within her.

"Then they didn't need to make you feel guilty." His rage trickled through her, blasting away doubts she'd never been able to fully escape.

"I shouldn't have left her alone." Lucy tossed her most constant self-reproach to Niall Quinn's judgment.

"Impossible. Unless you have"—his kneading at the base of her neck stilled—"that's the real reason for the hospital-in-the-home setup."

"I couldn't trust myself to supervise him all by myself." She swallowed the lump rising in her throat. She hadn't planned to explain her motives, but he'd figured it out.

"A tragic accident, Cam said, but losing her an inch at a time was killing him." He tightened his hold and pressed her face into his shoulder, his lullaby lilt reinforcing his words. "Cam said she'd have chosen to go fast, if the choice had been hers."

"She—they—both—had living wills. Do not resuscitate." Her grandpa had told Lucy what he'd told Niall, but the similarities to her mum's death had been too raw for her to forgive herself for not anticipating a problem. Lucy had been present, but not present. *Again.* "I was seeing someone at the time," Lucy mumbled against his throat.

"Define seeing." His hand stroked her hip and thigh, a steady caress easing the tension she'd carried all day. Carried for years.

"I thought our relationship might be serious." In reality, she'd thought she was grown up and capable and no longer likely to make fatal mistakes with people she loved.

"But it wasn't."

"How very unemotional you sound, Mr. Quinn." A spurt of rebellion flashed through her. "Doug, my lover, congratulated me on being in another room at the critical time. He laughed and insinuated that I'd set it up really well, that I'd accidentally on purpose caused her accident."

"Did you knee him in the balls?" Niall's body stilled beneath Lucy's, his disgust at Doug's reaction as comforting as another caress.

"I was physically sick when I realised Doug was serious." She'd been disoriented. Like her mum after a heavy night on her favourite white powder. "His accusations were worse than the cops or anyone else. They were just doing their job."

"What did you do?" He pressed a kiss to her hair, barely a touch, but it warmed her from the outside in.

"I told him he wasn't funny. If he thought that, we'd been making a mistake." And Lucy had blessed whatever instinct had kept her from telling Doug about her mum's death.

"You built a hospital-in-the-home for Cam." He rubbed a thumb and forefinger over her pearls. "You wear your gran's pearls. You tend their business."

Her hand covered his on the pearls, and tears spilled down her cheeks. "I'm unreliable."

"You're fierce and protective where you love. You weren't responsible for your gran's death."

A pardon, one she hadn't allowed herself to accept from

her grandpa. Niall manoeuvred himself around on the lounge until he was stretched full length with Lucy cuddled against his chest. He pressed her head to his heart, and his support was echoed in the steady rise and fall of his chest.

"I don't know why I'm crying." Lucy scrubbed her cheek.

"You're crying because it's your gran's birthday, and she's not here anymore. You're crying because your granda died, and you'll never see his like again. And maybe even a bit for your mam."

"I'm sorry." She clutched his damp shirt, hiccupping to a halt.

"Nothing to be sorry for," he growled against her ear. "Look at me, Liùsaidh."

Her stomach did backflips when he used her full name. Because of the music in his Irish lilt. Because he was the only person who called her by her full name. Because using her given name made concrete the connection between her and her gran. She lifted her head. His face was close to hers. Lucy had watched him for days now, knew his patience was real, knew he took his time with a task because his self-respect demanded it. Doing something the right way was more important than speed or money to him. He wouldn't tell her something just to make her feel better.

He caressed her jaw. The pads of his fingers were rough from the honest work he did each day, yet exquisitely tender. "You control this." He brushed a kiss across her forehead and ran his nose down her cheek. Drawing his head back, his hands rested at her waist. He was offering himself without conditions.

Lucy couldn't believe she could just reach out and take. With care, she lifted the pearls from her neck and placed them on the coffee table beside them. Cupping his face in her hands, she kissed him, desire threaded through with gratitude. His kiss was lovely, slow and sumptuous, and she let herself sink into it. When his tongue traced her upper lip, she opened her mouth on a sigh.

"You kiss like you work," Lucy marvelled, her hands holding his head for the second she could bear to lift her mouth from his. "Striving for excellence."

His generosity dispelled the caution that was her constant companion. Lucy relaxed against him, knowing he'd take her weight. She nuzzled along his collarbone, searching for the source of the scent he carried with him. This unhurried dance was almost innocent: her hand sliding under his sweater, his indrawn gasp when her palm covered his nipple, her moan when he kneaded the back of her neck.

"Let me undo your hair?" His fingers slid through her plaited skein, teasing tendrils free.

"That feels wonderful." Lucy sighed. His gentle scalp massage radiated pleasure to her toes. Wanting to see him, she pushed herself upright.

"I've wanted to get my hands on your hair since the day we met," he growled, and her muscles unravelled some more. "You should wear it out more often."

"I like your hands." Lucy caught one between hers, holding it palm up while she traced the outline of each finger and thumb, then pressed a kiss to its centre. "I watch when you work. There's poetry in them and reverence and beauty. I'm babbling." She rested her forehead on his chest.

"We can babble together." He wrapped her close, his cock between them, straining against his jeans, while his caress of her spine was light.

"This doesn't mean anything," Lucy murmured, wriggling and enjoying the groan he couldn't silence. Being with him brought a kind of freedom. He allowed her to be in the moment, to take pleasure in small things, to not always be on guard.

"It might not mean anything"—he gritted his teeth—"but it sure as hell feels like something."

"We could have an affair." She walked her fingers down his chest, toward his belt buckle. An affair with him would include laughter and conversation and respect. He didn't know, but respect was his secret weapon in seduction.

"You're going to ravish me?" His hands cupped her buttocks and lifted her more comfortably onto his erection.

Lucy moved her hips.

"I think what you just did is X-rated in movies," he managed. "More please."

She stilled. "I shouldn't tease, but you've made me feel better. Thank you for tonight."

"Do you want to thank me some more?" He waggled his eyebrows, his gaze solemn.

"Mixing desire and gratitude is a recipe for disaster." Lucy kissed his chin, then unhooked her leg to sit at his hip. "Believe me, I know."

"What's the ratio?" He sounded winded. "Fifty-fifty, forty-sixty?"

"Right this minute, I'd say seventy-five percent desire to twenty-five percent gratitude." She rested her hand on his aroused cock. "You deserve one hundred percent desire."

"I can work with the current odds." He flexed against her hand.

"Never sell yourself short." Lucy pressed a kiss to his cheek.

# CHAPTER EIGHT

Niall was listening for the doorbell on Monday morning with a randy adolescent's mix of trepidation and raging hormones. The saner part of him worried that loneliness had streaked past good sense, and both of them needed to take a step back. The baser part of him was primed for a quick hello, a few of Lucy's enthusiastic kisses, and then for nature to take things from there.

The optimist in him wallowed in the vindication in her words *don't sell yourself short*. Unlike Sinead, Lucy genuinely liked his work. The realist in him was recalling the instant he'd thrown a drop cloth over the mirror he'd been finishing Friday night.

*Avoiding a conversation about my work?*

*Avoiding a conversation about what I'm doing with the pieces I'm making?*

He hadn't wanted to place her in a difficult position when they were bumbling their way from suspicion to friendship. Friendship demanded a bit more honesty than he'd given her so far. She had an analytical mind and would take about two seconds to work out Niall was committed to more work than would fit into a standard day.

And another two seconds to ask why he wasn't selling

his own work to pay down debt. If Niall told her about the exhibition, she might tell him to stop his work for her, and she needed the funds to feel safe.

He wanted her to feel safe. End of argument.

"We arrived together," Lucy explained, standing back. Her smile was tentative, while Kate barrelled through the door.

In the split-second Niall had before his sister-in-law walked into his arms, he tried to read Lucy's expression. Was she embarrassed Kate had found her in paint-spattered overalls with a plait half undone down her back, or was she embarrassed at nearly coming apart in his arms a few nights ago? She'd called a halt, and although every cell in his body had screamed a protest, he'd let her go. His promise she was in control was part of that. Her smile widened, the haunted look absent. She gave a provocative wiggle as she sidled past, and the movement went straight to his groin. He stifled a groan.

*Memo to self: this relationship is too important to stuff up with a quick tumble.*

"Your niece wants a hug." Kate slid an arm around his waist and rested her head on his shoulder. Catching his wrist with her free hand, she flattened his palm against her belly. The baby kicked. "She's frisky this morning."

"That's because she's a he." He grinned down at her and kissed her forehead. "This is a nice surprise."

"Ambush," Kate muttered, stepping back. "Necessary because you've stopped visiting."

"I'm sorry I couldn't make dinner last night." Niall should have anticipated a visit and taken evasive action.

"Or last Sunday, and"—Kate looked around, an inquisitive bird—"I'm prepared to bet real money you'll be caught up next Sunday too."

"Do you need something?" He'd find the time to help, although time was a scarce commodity, getting scarcer. He was trying to reclaim a fraction of the time spent on Lucy's work by missing Sunday nights at Liam's.

"Your brother's pining for your company."

He met his sister-in-law's gaze, signalling "some other time" for all he was worth.

"Okay." Kate rested her hand on her belly. "If Mohamed won't come to the mountain …"

"If Liam called you a mountain, I can see why you sought refuge." Niall pretended outrage. He loved Kate for herself and the besotted expression on his brother's face when Liam looked at his wife. "I'll save you."

Her mouth softened. "I've brought samples."

"Cake?" He gestured to Lucy. "Lucy loved your Christmas cake."

"You're *that* Lucy?" Kate said, as if she'd just made the connection.

He rolled his eyes. "My sister-in-law is not a good liar."

"I worked that out." Lucy smiled. "Niall already told you he shared your Christmas cake with me. I introduced myself as Lucy, and you put two and two together and came up with landlord."

"I remembered because it's rare for the caveman to share." Kate stared hard at him.

"Don't ask." Niall held a hand up to Lucy, signalling he wouldn't be explaining the "caveman" tag. "My door's always open for cake. Thank you. Is that the only reason you came, Kate?"

"I came to see the Huon table." Kate beamed at him. "Photos aren't enough. But this looks interesting." Her attention had been caught by the reassembled mahogany sideboard.

"That's Lucy's sideboard. It's coming along," Niall said, and to forestall further questions, he pointed to one of the library bookcases. "That's next."

"You've started." Lucy smiled at him, which was reward enough for the extra hours he'd spent on her work over the weekend. A substitute for fantasising about getting her between the sheets. "I've got a buyer for the sideboard and a nibble on the bookcases. They want to see the finished product." She held up a hand. "No pressure though."

"Bills have to be paid," he murmured.

Kate frowned.

"This way." He pre-empted the questions he could see forming in Kate's eyes and led them to the steel door. Once through, he unlocked his storeroom. With a flick of a switch, he flooded the space with light. More than three times the size of Cam's storeroom, one side housed a sophisticated wheeled storage system for his timber. Against the opposite wall were the pieces he was collecting for the exhibition. Lucy, who hadn't been in his space before, gasped. Kate hurried forward.

"It's beautiful." Kate waddled around the table, studying it from different angles. She let her hand rest on the surface. "It would take something special to displace this as the centrepiece."

He shook his head, a warning to Kate that this was another no-go area. Lucy was on the other side of the room, studying a large mirror with a frame resembling a treble clef. Her fingers drifted over its surface. The visceral punch rattled his composure. Niall wanted Lucy's hands drifting over him with the same mixture of curiosity and admiration. Mentally, he zapped Kate to Timbuktu. Kate opened her mouth, glanced at Lucy, then shut it again.

Four weeks since he'd started work on Lucy's furniture. The empty spaces in this room testified to his neglect. He had the designs, he had the wood, he had the dreams in his head, and time was slipping away. He should have scheduled the photoshoot for the catalogue. Kate's twin, Anna, had designed a new page for his website and social media pages. Anna pressed him daily to give the go signal, the emojis in her texts assuming ever more alarming features.

"Your niece and I thank you for the advance showing," said Kate.

"Nephew." He tried his usual distraction.

"Unless you've become an Irish mystic, I'm sticking with my prediction." Kate put her hands on her hips and turned to Lucy. The glint in her eye matched her twin's when Anna was on a mission. "Have you met my husband?" Kate had to repeat the question because Lucy had sunk to her heels to examine the carving on his rocking chair.

"Mm. Sorry?" Lucy turned her head.

"Come for dinner with Niall next Sunday?"

"I couldn't." Lucy rose to her feet slowly, her hand reaching for the pearls she wasn't wearing.

Niall's annoyance with Kate for meddling shifted to a need to understand the expressions chasing across Lucy's face. Not wanting to impose? Not wanting to back him into a polite corner?

*Eagerness?*

Feck! From what she'd let slip, she went to work, went home, visited him. Not much of a life. Stress is exhausting—he knew that—worrying about money and missing her granda was exhausting. If she got through the essentials every day, she was doing well. Lucy's friends—Clementine and, what was her name, Kelly—were missing in action—factor in an ex-boyfriend and hell!

"Niall?" Kate was asking for his interpretation, his intercession, *his what?*

Briefly, he closed his eyes. Niall missed Liam, missed having him as a sounding board, and he sure as hell needed a sounding board for the mess he'd got himself into. "Great idea." He rearranged schedules in his head. "We'll be there at six-thirty." And somehow, he'd keep to himself that he was cancelling his regular family dinners to give Lucy's work more time.

Fifteen minutes later, Lucy stood beside him as Kate waved from the corner. "I'll call Kate and cancel." She wrapped her disappointment in cheery unconcern. "I'll wait until later today, then call and say I mistook the date, and I have another commitment."

"Kate will be disappointed."

"What about you?"

"Haven't you worked out I'm a grumbling hermit?"

Rather, he was a man who'd made too many promises. There weren't enough hours in the day to keep them all. More sleep was a necessity because her rose and vanilla scent bewitched him enough to contemplate abandoning the workshop in favour of a large bed. For a week at least. "Nobody twisted Kate's arm. She invited you because she likes you. You'll like my brother."

"She's curious."

"Curiosity is often the first step in relationships. Hard to make a friend if you don't have any interest in the other person." He'd moved from curious to fascinated by all the contradictions in Lucy. Closing the door on the outside world, he turned to her. "Don't cancel. How long has it been since Cam's funeral?"

"Five weeks, five days and three hours." She could probably give him the timing to the second.

"You've worked every single day since. Come to dinner with me and meet my family." He draped his arm over her shoulder, pulling her into an encouraging hug.

She turned her face up, her lips parted. "Kiss me."

Niall took the kiss he'd been imagining since she'd walked in. His free hand cupped her cheek. Warm, silky skin, as warm and inviting as her mouth. He let himself drown in her lushness. Her tongue touched his, raising the stakes. She tasted of sin tied up with a big pink bow of goodness.

"I stayed away because I want to kiss you all the time." Her hands fisted in his shirt, her confession straining the leash he'd put on himself.

"Maybe we make some sort of pact about no kissing around power tools." Praise the saints, he'd lost the capacity to think straight. "Too dangerous."

She slid her hand over his crotch and gave it a gentle pat. "Power tools *are* dangerous." Grinning, she stepped back, whipping her hands behind her back. "Hands off in the workshop."

"I've got your pearls." A piss-poor way of saying "down

boy," but it was the only lifeline handy. She'd forgotten her gran's necklace on Friday, and he'd returned to the sofa after she'd left to stroke the damn thing. Lucy and he weren't looking long-term, so his sentimentality bewildered him. He gestured to the table under the window. "I wrapped them up for safekeeping."

A few weeks earlier, the rectangular scarf spilling over the back of an armchair in a display window had caught his eye. Ribbons of interwoven green, where he could identify shamrock, teal, mint, moss with a thread of laurel. Smooth and soft to the touch, warm where he rubbed it between his fingers, the scarf flowed with the naturalness of running water. He'd bought it with Lucy in mind. A spontaneous purchase tucked in a drawer until she'd left her pearls behind.

She unwrapped the bundle as if her fingers would discover a story in the folds of the fabric. "What a beautiful scarf."

"Keep it." He'd known green was her colour. She was like a moth emerging from its chrysalis, unaware of her beauty. When she turned her questioning gaze toward him, he shrugged. "You won't want to wear your pearls in here."

"Thank you." She let the scarf slide through her fingers, before rewrapping her pearls. "Gran had an old pouch she kept them in. This is a better home."

Tension eased from Niall's shoulders. In his experience, a debt and a gift were kissing cousins. She was wary of gifts, in the same way she baulked at words of sympathy from strangers but was comfortable with a sandwich or a fruit bowl or a protective covering for her gran's pearls.

Debt was a demon they shared. Debt and self-respect had been part of growing up in the Quinn household. In recent years, they'd become inextricably linked to the point where an unmet obligation tore at his self-respect. He wasn't sure of the exact source of Lucy's fear but would bet his da's chisel set it had something to do with her childhood.

Which brought him full circle in his thoughts. An honest

man would share his secrets before he climbed under her doona. "Maybe we should take a break until Sunday night."

"A break?" Lucy was watching him, like he guessed she'd watched every adult male until she'd moved in with Cam. Ready to run. She was beginning to trust him, but having caution as your first playmate, the habit tended to stick.

"A cooling-off period." Niall shoved his hands in his pockets and blundered ahead. "Just to check it's not loneliness juicing our …" He stumbled to a halt.

"I am lonely." She lifted her chin, fearless in the face of his incoherence. "I'm guessing you're lonely too. I'm not ashamed of considering consensual sex with you because I'm lonely." She tucked the pearls in her bag and pulled it over her shoulder. "But … I think you've forgotten. I'm the one who called a halt, Quinn."

Niall let his ute glide to a halt near his brother's home. Lucy had been waiting outside McTavish's when he'd arrived. Sunday was a busy day for the antiques shop, and he'd listened to her descriptions of customers and the sales she'd made while the quiet floral notes in her perfume soothed. He didn't have a spare slot in his timetable to miss her. He'd missed her anyway. And fretted about his half-arsed attempt to make sense of what the hell was happening to him.

"Ready?" He swivelled to face her.

"It's not an execution, is it?" She lifted one hand toward her throat, then let it drop. An expression of confidence or because her coat was buttoned so high, she couldn't reach her pearls?

"I'm probably projecting. Kate's pissed off at me for skipping a party a few weeks ago." He'd finished the Huon table that night. In hindsight, his last financially sane decision.

"I could give you a few shifts at the shop, hone your interpersonal skills." She made him sound like an unpolished schoolboy. Based on Monday morning, she'd be right.

"Pass." He banged a fist on the steering wheel, punctuating his idiocy. "I thought you might cancel tonight."

"Why?" No reason she should make this easy for him.

"Because I was an eejit on Monday talking about a cooling-off period. I hurt you." He'd hated the idea he'd joined a long list of inconsiderate boofheads who'd either abandoned or hassled her. "I like you, and I don't want to mess that up."

"I was hurt." She flayed him with his own words. "But I like that you like me. I like you too." She sighed, and the air in the cabin of the truck calmed. "I missed being in the workshop. Can I come back tomorrow?"

"I'd like that." He stepped out of the ute, aware she slid to the ground on her side. Friends. He should be happy with that, but knowing she liked him gave his ego a boost that carried to the part of his body not ruled by his brain.

"Welcome." Liam and Kate answered the door together, the brightly lit hall behind them sending its own welcome. Liam's arm rested lightly around his wife's waist.

"Hello, Kate; hello, Liam." Lucy offered a bottle of merlot. "Goodness, you brothers do look alike."

"I'm the handsome one," Niall offered.

"That makes me the smart one." Liam leaned forward to take Lucy's hand and draw her into the hall. "Come in. Let me take your coat."

Lucy shucked hers. She'd replaced the unrelenting black of her usual outfits with wide-legged, teal trousers and a grey sweater. The scarf Niall had given her replaced her gran's pearls tonight. Knotted at the base of her throat, the loose ends lovingly curled around her breasts. An image of her sitting naked on his Huon table, her legs demurely crossed to one side to preserve her modesty, flashed into his mind. Her back was straight, her smile mischievous, and the scarf was draped so that two stripes of colour covered her nipples, emphasising the lush curves of her breasts.

"I've got to make some last-minute changes, so you'll have to excuse me for a minute." Liam backed down the hall.

"Niall, why don't you show Lucy around before Anna arrives." Kate made the explanation.

"*I* didn't know Anna was coming." Niall stressed his ignorance, wanting no new misunderstandings with Lucy tonight.

"A late addition. She's got someone she 'wants us to meet.'" Kate spoke in a whisper dripping with intrigue.

"That must be a first?" Niall grinned.

"It is. And if you tease her, I'll kill you myself." Kate shooed them away. "I need to add some settings to the table."

"Come on, Lucy. I'll show you around and fill you in. The Quinn and Turner twins together is a baptism by fire." His mind raced. Kate would feign labour pains before she'd let Anna ambush him about the exhibition tonight.

"I expected it to be harder to tell identical twins apart." Lucy studied Niall's face.

"Liam could tell Kate and Anna apart from the moment he met them. Different clothes help, hairstyles, things like that," he said. Lucy looked different tonight, a woman comfortable in her own skin. "You'll see when you meet Anna."

"Show her the nursery," Kate's retreating figure instructed. "In case you've forgotten, it's the second door on the left."

"Does this room open onto the garden?" Lucy bolted into the room immediately to their right and headed toward the double French doors.

Most women Niall knew would have been in the nursery in a heartbeat. Kate's enthusiasm made talk of babies an easy topic for the dinner table. His brother changed direction mid-sentence if Niall asked about Kate's health, how Quinn Junior was travelling, or how the nursery was coming along.

Women seemed to have a second sense about these things, yet Lucy was hell-bent on getting into the winter garden.

Sensor lights lit the tiny space. Maidenhair jostled with bird's nests, stag and elk horns. Niall had helped choose the plantings, native Australian rainforest species that thrived in this dark side passage. Moss-covered sandstone paving stones interspersed with baby's breath lined the space, and the sound of trickling water came from a pond at the far end. Decorative tiles hung like outdoor paintings. Kate had tucked her arm in Niall's one day to tell him the story of each one, mementoes from her honeymoon.

"This is lovely." Lucy turned to him, a relaxed smile curving her mouth. He was starting to wait for her smiles and learn what might elicit one. "Who's the gardener?"

"Both of them. They need green around them," he replied. Green suited Lucy. She connected to the natural world through colour. "Cam said you took over as gardener when your gran died."

"I discovered gardens when I moved to Gran's." Lucy took the bench seat facing a window into the dining room, where Kate was adding settings to the table. "You seem very close to Kate as well as your brother."

"I am." He linked his fingers with hers. "The scarf suits you."

"Green's my favourite colour. I'd almost forgotten in the last few months."

"We can skip the nursery, if you like?" Niall wasn't sure what he was offering. A chance for her to absorb the serenity to be had in a tiny garden, or a chance to avoid facing the prospect of new life so soon after her loss? Life followed death, but sometimes the reminders were too raw.

She stiffened, and he'd missed his chance of having her confide in him. Maybe she was regretting how much she's told him on her gran's birthday. Maybe she'd decided liking was enough—no deep and meaningful disclosures. If they'd taken each other to bed on Monday, he'd probably still be there. His hunger for her was more complicated than lust.

Instead, he'd channelled his frustration into preparing the pieces for one of his Shanker-style sideboards.

"I'd love to see the nursery."

*Right!* That's why her face was twisted like she'd sucked an especially sour lemon.

Pushing open the nursery door, Niall flicked on lights, standing back to let her precede him. Poised in the doorway, she seemed to have some sort of mental tussle with herself, before entering the light, airy space. He sensed she was afraid, although he couldn't pinpoint a source. Had she lost a sibling or, his heart stalled, a child of her own?

"They're tirelessly boring on the subject of paint colours, mobiles, the rights of their daughter to grow up free to wield a hammer, while their son writes romance."

She moved further into the room. "Sounds like they're the kind of people who should be parents." Then she was across the room in seconds, her hand raised above the cradle. When she stroked her index finger gently over the wood, his body hummed in response.

"This is yours, isn't it?"

"Yeah." He pushed his hands in his pockets.

"It's stunning." She pivoted to face him. "Why are you making frames and restoring furniture when you can do this?" She lifted her hands and let them drop. "When you can create the magic hidden in your storage vault? It's a waste of your skills."

The passion in her accusation skittled him. She stood with a hand on his cradle, a tactile connection making it impossible to ignore her challenge. His mind shuffled through a slideshow of images. She didn't touch any of the pieces he was restoring with the same reverence. On the few times she picked up a frame to move it out of the way, she'd handled it with care, but not the veneration she reserved for his pieces.

Niall could trot out the glib answer he gave acquaintances, but prevaricating would be an insult to her intelligence, and whatever kind of relationship they might forge beyond friendship. "My da died just after I moved to Ireland to start my mentorship."

"That sounds sudden." She'd lived the disorientation of sudden death.

"A massive heart attack. I came back for about a week. Then Liam and Mum bundled me onto the plane to Ireland and my mentorship before I knew if I was on my arse or my ear." He'd been punch-drunk, unable to find his balance. "Said Da would have been devastated if I'd chucked it in."

"Were they right?" she asked, and in his guilt, Niall had never considered the question.

"Da was a carpenter, taught me how to hold my first hammer." He grimaced. Having organised the funeral, Liam was ahead of him in processing what was happening, whereas Niall hadn't known what day it was. Niall had let Liam make the decisions for him. "But he was an eco-warrior as well, which is why Liam gravitated to environmental law."

"Were they right?"

"Yeah." The admission released something in him. "And, at the time, while Liam and I knew we could never fill the gap he'd left behind, we thought he'd died with enough assets to keep Mum safe. That we'd continue with the careers we'd chosen." Niall had let himself be feted as the new kid on the block in Ireland, filling his days with work and his nights with parties to deaden the creeping emptiness in his gut.

"What happened?" She took the seat beside the cradle, her hand still resting on the wood, still daring him to confront his past.

"Within weeks Liam discovered Da was bankrupt and Mum might lose the house. But he kept it to himself."

"Why?" she persisted, as if his family's determination was something he needed to confront along with other truths.

He recoiled at the slap. "What the feck does 'why' matter?" Although he and Liam had different answers.

"Because the 'why' is the reason you haven't made peace with yourself." She nudged the cradle, and her touch reverberated in his bones.

"For complicated reasons, his job went pear-shaped. He walked away from environmental law. When I finally prised it out of the eejit, he said his dream was dead, mine was the only one left, and he and Mum needed to dream."

"Why can't you believe him?" Her beautiful green-brown eyes held sympathy.

"Because it caused a rift between us." He stopped mid-pace and glared at her. "He got a corporate law job that turned him into a soulless robot, had him working all hours of the day and night. He wouldn't talk to me in case he let something slip and I decided to leave Ireland early."

"So, your dream became a burden."

"No." She voiced a blasphemy Niall had never admitted. "In part. I knew something wasn't right. And I only made a half-arsed effort to find out what was wrong, because I didn't want to come home."

"And you can't forgive yourself for that." She rose to her feet and walked toward him. Having her close enough to hold was a blessing he didn't deserve.

"I stayed a year beyond the mentorship." He pushed his hands through his hair, surprised she wasn't telling him what a selfish bastard he was. "Wanted to hone my skills, I said. Wouldn't get another chance like that in my lifetime."

"Was that true?" She was as stubborn as he was.

"I ignored what he wasn't saying because the craft has always seduced me." He spun on his heel and walked to the window. "I can't turn my back on the wood. Not even to earn a bloody income." *Ask any girlfriend I've ever had; ask the woman I planned to marry.*

"But you have. That's what the frames are about?" Her insight rocked him, leaving no space for shame. "You need to do this. And you need to do it now? Why?" She pushed harder than his conscience.

"Because I left it too long to come home. Because

Quinns pay their way." Niall stared at her, and the truth dawned. Paying his share was core to his identity as a man and a son, and it wasn't only about money. Maybe not even primarily about money.

"You're talking about a partner in one of the most respected law firms in the country. Partner and head of their new division on environmental law. His wife, from the little I've learned, is a writer and researcher. And I don't mean to be mercenary here, Niall, but the furnishings in this house aren't cheap." Impatience gave her words an edge. "He doesn't need your money, and I bet he told you that."

"He's about to have a babe." He retraced his steps to face her, giving her the justification he'd given his brother. "He needs a nest egg, to have options."

"This is your cash flow problem. Grandpa knew this." She didn't pause when he nodded. "How much did you charge them for the cradle?"

"Don't be daft," Niall reeled.

"What's in your pockets?" She dropped her gaze to his lower body, frying his few functioning brain cells. "Empty them."

Digging into his jacket pockets, he pulled out carved alphabet figures, upper and lower case from H to P. He set them on the narrow ledge running at knee height around two sides of the room. They joined the letters A to G, large enough not to be swallowed, small enough to teach some manual dexterity by fitting them together.

"Another gift."

"I love them." And the way to show them wasn't the money, but in the practical way he knew best. "The cradle's got nothing to do with Da's debts. These"—he gestured to the carved letters—"are just baubles."

"The fruit bowl for me." She took his face between her hands. "You aren't going to get rich and famous anytime soon if you keep giving some of your finest pieces away. You need to forgive yourself, Niall. Everyone else has." She pressed her lips to his.

He pulled her into his body, releasing some of the doubts Sinead had gifted him. The warm weight of her in his arms triggered a soul-deep need. He nibbled at her bottom lip, teasing her mouth open and letting his tongue trace hers. She tasted of honey, of the sweetness of a spring day where new beginnings were everywhere. Her hands linked behind his neck. He widened his stance, letting her feel his arousal even as he slowed his kisses.

The doorbell rang. He rested his forehead on hers. "Anna will be in here in seconds." He ran Lucy's hand over the bulge in his pants. "I don't want her to know I'm quite this pleased to see you." He gave a rueful laugh and set her away from him.

"I'm pleased to see you too." She patted his cheek. "At the risk of scaring you away a second time, I just clocked desire one hundred and ten percent, gratitude non-existent."

# CHAPTER NINE

Niall watched his brother help Kate carry platters of food to the table.

"It's an Indian banquet," Liam said. "We've got a mattar paneer, that's peas and cottage cheese to anyone unfamiliar with Indian food, spicy lentils, whole baked cauliflower with panch phora, and a chicken biryani for the meat eaters. Plenty of rice and some naan. Please, help yourself."

"So, how did you two meet?" Hunter, Anna's companion, was sitting beside Lucy. He offered her lentils and a conversational gambit designed to complicate matters.

Niall considered the motives of the man opposite. He wasn't classically handsome nor body-builder ripped. A man you could pass in the street and not notice. Unless you looked into his eyes. Agate hard, they blazed with intelligence and impatience. A man in a hurry to succeed. The impatience was banked tonight, or else he'd mastered the art of speaking quietly and slowly, while he uncovered every weakness you'd ever tried to overcome.

"We met through my grandfather. Niall restored some furniture for him." Lucy's voice hitched slightly when she mentioned her grandfather.

"McTavish?" Hunter-the-architect-turned-property-developer mused. "The big antiques warehouse near Central station. Is that you?"

"It belongs to my family." Lucy had never claimed it for herself in Niall's hearing. For her, the family business still included Cam and the numerous staff members Niall had seen farewelling her when he'd picked her up tonight.

"I'm sorry for your loss." Hunter's tone betrayed familiarity with death. Niall gave him a closer look.

"Thank you," Lucy said.

"Is your father in charge now?" Hunter's persistence annoyed Niall. *Couldn't the guy talk about the weather or the baby?*

"McTavish is my mother's name. She was never interested in the business and died when I was a child." Lucy paraded the explanation with the ease of someone speaking from a script. And her casual act hid a world of hurt.

"You carry some classy stuff." Hunter swung to Niall, his gaze speculative. A stranger's curiosity was the last thing Niall needed tonight. "You must be good at the furniture restoring business. Anna told me you were a carpenter. Sounds like she sold you short."

Niall kicked Liam under the table. "I'm a carpenter. I take the work that's offered." He trusted Kate to have told Anna the exhibition was a non-starter tonight. The unknown was whether Anna got the message before, or after, she backgrounded Hunter on this evening's dramatis personae.

"Hey, I said he made stuff with wood," Anna interrupted from beside Niall. "Want to swap lentils for cauliflower?" She held up the dish nearest her. "Carpenter" was their joke, and Anna *had* briefed her inquisitive boyfriend.

"If you've been to a recent art auction at Leopold's, you'll have seen more of Niall's work. He designs and makes brilliant bespoke frames as well. They rival the artwork." Lucy offered her defence of Niall to a room he'd sworn to silence. His pride had taken a hit when he'd started Frames by Niall. Her support of his debt strategy elevated his activities to branching out rather than scrounging for cash.

"I might drop by McTavish's sometime." Hunter took the cauliflower. "Different business models interest me. I've always thought antiques are a risky business."

"Why?" Lucy played with the stem of her glass. She was shit-scared of debt, ditto chaos, and from her hospital-in-the-home plan, Niall guessed that making mistakes was another one of her demons. She'd earned the right to her fears.

"Antiques go in and out of fashion. Wasn't there a time a few years ago when priceless antiques were dismissed as so much brown furniture?" Hunter added rice to his plate, seemingly oblivious to Anna's warning look.

"A lot of businesses folded—turnover was slow for a while." Lucy shook her head when Liam held the bottle of wine aloft. "There's a lot more interest again now. Antiques prove sustainability works."

"That's why Niall uses recycled timber," Anna said, then made a face at Kate, who was sitting at the head of the table. "What? I'm talking about his frames?"

"And his cradle. Niall made the cradle for the baby," Lucy added, dragging the conversation back to Niall's work. "It'll still be around and appreciated in a hundred years."

"We love it." Kate held up another plate. "Naan anyone?"

"Don't get me wrong. I'm not risk averse." Hunter was studying Lucy with an expression that did justice to his name. When he ignored the bait of the cradle, Niall registered that Hunter, for reasons of his own, was trying to ferret out why Niall's upcoming exhibition needed to be a secret from Lucy.

Anna kicked Niall under the table to catch his attention. His family wasn't subtle. He glanced at her. Anna's eyes were signalling, "*Secret exhibition? Are you insane?*"

He shook his head. He'd promised himself a night off from juggling frames, Lucy's restoration and the exhibition pieces. Hence, his request for his family's silence. Lucy deserved to hear the truth from him. He was just waiting for the right moment. Okay, he had no feckin' idea how to find the right moment. But it sure as hell wasn't dinner with a crowd listening to every word.

"In business, calculated risks can deliver windfalls," Hunter said, seemingly unaware of the silent messages flying around him.

*Right*, Niall thought. He'd calculated he could repay Cam by helping Lucy and still manage to produce enough new pieces for his exhibition to go ahead. He wasn't looking at a windfall but a feckin' precipice.

"What's a calculated risk in your line of work?" Kate, bless her heart, leapt on the chance to redirect the conversation.

"It varies. I work with a lot of clients, from businesses about to go under to start-ups. You should only risk what you're prepared to lose." Hunter's gaze settled on Anna, a private smile curving his mouth. "Knowing what you're prepared to lose is the hardest part of the equation."

Lucy was looking at Hunter as if he was a financial genius, which he probably was. To be fair, he didn't flaunt his wealth. If you didn't count the Rolex or the chauffeured Mercedes EQS they'd arrived in. Niall rubbed his hand down his thigh, his thumb worrying on a loose thread in his jeans. His last decent pair. Frustration, he'd conquered long ago, about an unfriendly fate snapped at his heels. He hadn't factored his da's debts into establishing his business. Hadn't factored in his sense of responsibility for Lucy's debts.

"In case anyone's interested"—Anna filled the growing silence—"Hunter and I met at a work function, which would have been the end of it, except he showed up at the office with an offer I couldn't refuse. The rest, as they say, is history." Anna's smile for Hunter was sunny and carefree.

Kate played the perfect hostess. "Dessert or coffee, anyone?"

Hunter's expression was inscrutable. Then he sent Niall a glance Niall could only call pitying, as if to say "*You poor sod, you've got no idea what you're risking or what you're prepared to lose.*"

*Damn you, I know exactly what's at stake.* And I'll take Lucy's peace of mind over a Rolex any day.

Niall pulled into the driveway of Hopetoun Cottage, a name cementing the McTavish family to its Scottish origins. Although Cam had assured him Hopetoun House outside Edinburgh was a grander residence. The last time Niall had parked here, Cam had still been alive.

*She'll need a distraction.* The phrase was on permanent rotation in Niall's head.

Niall hadn't known her then. He'd imagined her as some dutiful granddaughter dedicated to the family business. Now he knew she was self-contained, uncertain about her welcome, courageous in dealing with her past, protective of her friends, and sexy as hell.

Niall didn't need a distraction.

She'd distracted him anyway. Her praise for his work was a balm to his bruised ego. Seeing her fingers on his cradle made him want to spend decades exploring the language of touch with her.

"Would you like to come in?" Her formal invitation shattered the humming quiet between them. "For coffee?"

"Finishing what we started earlier has more appeal." Niall flicked on the truck's inside light and swung to face her. He'd kept his hands to himself on the drive because making out in the back of a ute wasn't how he wanted to make love to her for the first time. Maybe she thought he'd lost interest. "But I'll understand if you've changed your mind." Understand, but be more disappointed than he was prepared to admit.

"I haven't changed my mind." Her smile stalled his heart.

Niall stood at her shoulder as she unlocked her front door, grew giddy on her rose vanilla scent while she reset a security code. "Guess you need to be careful with all the valuables in the house?"

"We had a break-in before Gran died. It rattled her, so Grandpa went overboard." Lucy might not have changed her mind, but the little tremble in her voice told him she wasn't sure how to take the next step.

He was more than happy to help her. In the wide hallway, Niall waited while she hung her coat on a hook and set her bag on some fancy, slim-line walnut sideboard. She was efficient and graceful, the Holy Grail of the best furniture. When she'd finished, he walked her backward until the door was against her back. "I wanted to leave after those clever little pre-dinner nibbles Kate served." He nuzzled the tender spot between her shoulder and neck, and was rewarded with her little shiver of pleasure.

"I nearly pleaded a headache after the main." She splayed her fingers through his hair, got a grip and tugged his head up to face her.

"Do you think they noticed anything when we both refused dessert?" Her fragrance swirled around him, making it hard to focus on the task he'd set for himself—relaxing her so she took charge.

"Yes. Do you mind?" In the half-light of the hall, shadows played across her face, but the answer was clearly important to her.

"Not about my family knowing you're special to me." Niall brushed his mouth across hers, already lost in the taste of her. "I mind how much time we've wasted. Let me free your hair." Pulling loose the few pins holding her chignon in place, he gathered her hair in his hands, exploring its weight and texture before bunching handfuls at the top of her head. She leaned into him, meeting him as an equal rather than offering a surrender.

"I like you, Liùsaidh McTavish." He started a personal inventory of her features, pressing his lips to her forehead, skimming her eyebrows, feeling her eyelids flutter at the lightest pressure. Savouring her softness was diversion enough to let his lips linger for an eternity.

"I like—" The hitch in her breathing urged him to continue his exploration.

Releasing her hair, he cupped her jaw, needing to absorb her through his fingertips, a different kind of knowing. Running his nose against hers, he let his hands drop to hips rounder than when they'd met, a delicious handle to draw her closer.

"—you." She sighed.

When he sought her mouth, she was waiting for him, sweetness in her I want-to-get-to-know-you-well kiss. He paused for a breath and to whisper, "I like the way you kiss." He ran his hands down her arms and around her backside before lifting her against him.

"You are pleased to see me." She wriggled against his arousal, and his cock saluted.

"It's an invitation, Liùsaidh," he groaned. "Not a demand."

"I can say no?"

*Only if you want to kill me.*

"You can say 'Yes, please, I'd like a bed, more, later,' or"—he stepped back, so the door wasn't supporting them both, and let her unglue herself from his length—"you can say no." He was hanging onto control by a thread, but he'd made her a promise.

While he held his breath, she gave an encouraging pat to his crotch and turned on her heel. "Then, yes, please, more, right now, and my bedroom's upstairs."

* * *

Lucy sashayed up the stairs, swinging her hips in an invitation as old as time.

"I also like the way you walk, lass." His hand landed on her backside as he followed behind, half-rubbing, half-squeezing her butt and generating a different fire.

Lucy slowed her speed to savour the weight of Niall's hand on her backside.

"Is there anything you don't like?" She smiled over her shoulder.

"Nothing that comes to mind."

Lucy had told Niall the truth. She was lonely. He was too. She fancied him. He fancied her, and a horizontal two-step was a lovely way to finish the evening. He wasn't pretending this was a stepping stone to some happily ever after. His honesty was refreshing after a life caught between her mum's memory and her grandparents' wealth. Caring for this perceptive man who served her tea out of mismatched cups, who made a cradle for his brother's child, and who bought her a beautiful, expensive scarf when he spent nothing on himself was an unlooked-for bonus.

At her bedroom door, he put his other hand on her shoulder, turning her into his arms. "Wait a minute."

"You're kidding?" She was dazzled by the affection in his gaze.

"I haven't kissed you standing on this landing." He returned to the spot between her shoulder and neck, where the warmth of his mouth on her bare skin raised goose bumps.

She bundled into him.

"We don't need to hurry." He was upending rules she'd learned before she'd wanted to know them, creating spaces for closeness rather than hunger.

"I thought we did." Lucy cupped his balls, revelling in the sheer female power of knowing her desire was reciprocated.

He groaned, turning his head to nibble his way up Lucy's throat, stopping to tend the sensitive spot behind her ear. A trail of havoc so delightful, she stopped thinking. She shivered, and he shaped her breasts through her sweater. Heaviness dragged low in her belly, and Lucy moaned, her hand loosening its hold.

"Parts we hurry, and parts we take really slowly," he drawled.

Lucy knew how to please a man. And please herself. In

cramped accommodation, sex education had been unavoidable. She'd been bombarded with the sight, sound, and smell of sex. Hard and fast was her mum's preference. Her mum had also peppered Lucy with blunt warnings. *You're responsible for your own pleasure.* Men are selfish.

Her mother had never met anyone like Niall Quinn.

*Neither have I.*

"Show me something fast." Lucy covered his hands with her own, anticipation fizzing through her bloodstream like the finest champagne.

He moved lightning fast for a big man, bunching her sweater high on her chest. His mouth closed over her left breast, drawing the nipple deep into his mouth until Lucy rocked helplessly against him. A fair man, he lavished attention on her other breast, waiting until the nipple peaked against the damp fabric, before tugging gently with his teeth. She was panting with need when he stepped back, his warm palm replacing his mouth at her breast, soothing her with his change in tempo.

"You show me slow, Liùsaidh." He scooped her into his arms, nudged her bedroom door open, and stood with her on the threshold. "Tell me about this room, starting with the bed." He slid Lucy down his side, keeping her within the circle of his arm, while he arranged pillows against the bed head. Releasing her, he toed off his boots, before settling against the pillows, making himself comfortable against her crisp white sheets and gum-tree patterned doona.

"What are you doing?" This was like no other lovemaking she'd ever known.

"Waiting for you to join me." His cock strained against his jeans. His grin was sinfully innocent.

"What if I don't?" She crossed her arms, her nipples still tingling from his touch.

"Then I fold my tent"—he patted his erection—"so to speak, and go home."

"There was a cream brass and iron bedstead in McTavish's window the day I arrived." She undid the back zipper on her green trousers and let them fall to the ground in a silky puddle. His sharp inhalation of breath told her he approved of this move. Stepping out of the trousers, Lucy bent to collect them and place them on a nearby chair, ensuring he got a clear look, both front and back, at the white cotton bikini briefs she was wearing. "Gran said I could choose one item from the shop for my bedroom. I asked for the bed."

"Join me?" He patted the spot beside him.

Moving closer to his side, Lucy gripped the bottom of her sweater and pulled it over her head. With her arms in the air, she paused, her body at full stretch—bra, panties and high-heeled boots. When she tugged the sweater free, he leaned close enough to press a work-toughened forefinger to her skin. She sucked in a breath. Tracing a line from the valley of her breasts, he dipped into her navel then slid down to rest on the elastic band of her panties. A summer heat haze sizzled through her.

"I don't want you to get cold." He caught her around the middle and tumbled her onto the mattress beside him.

"I don't think cold's going to be a problem."

"You rest there, while I get rid of your boots." He scooted far enough down to reach her feet.

"There's a design flaw here, Mr. Quinn." She studied his head bent over the zipper on her remaining boot. His hair was longer than his brother's. The thick curls crowding his shirt collar suited him. And suited her. She gave them a tug, and her second boot dropped to the floor.

"A mismatch of textures perhaps?" He straddled her ankles, his palm doing a long, slow glide down her inner thigh. "Skin feels so much better than denim." He kissed the inside of her knee, and she dissolved into a muddle of lust and tenderness.

"Take your clothes off," Lucy ordered. His patience was pure torture when she'd been primed since pre-dinner drinks for a fast lovemaking. Anticipation had sharp claws. Yet this game with him was joyful. He didn't snatch or grab or hurry.

"Whisht, lass, am I too slow for you?" His sweater dropped onto the floor. He took his time with his shirt, slipping each button in turn, then shrugging out of it. "I liked your striptease." A wicked smile, sparkling with approval, curved his mouth. Easing off the mattress, he shed his jeans and jocks in a single move. "And the pure white briefs with the little scraps of lace."

"I considered a thong." Lucy looked at him from under her lashes, testing his reaction.

"Maybe next time." He winked, causing a yearning to stir deep in her womb. "I doubt I could manage what I've planned if you'd been cavorting in a thong." His voice was gravel rough.

"Maybe I've got my own plans?" Lucy knelt on the edge of the bed, facing him, reminding him of his promise. She'd never met a man who was prepared to share, much less surrender control of lovemaking.

"I bet you do." His gaze stayed steady on hers while his hipshot stance accentuated the bold erection arrowing up his belly. "Right now, you're over-dressed."

"I want you to worship me." Through the pounding in Lucy's head, she dimly understood patience was a form of worship.

"I can do that." Niall was changing all her mother's rules. He was playful and genuinely affectionate, making her feel unbelievably precious, and she'd think about that later.

"But first"—she scampered further back on the mattress—"come back here." Nestled against the piled cushions, Lucy couldn't predict if his next move would be deliciously fast or breathtakingly slow. Not knowing was a tantalising part of his appeal. "You aren't just going to flip me on my back and have at me, are you?"

"Is that what you want?" His intent scrutiny ignited a flashfire in her blood.

"You make me question what I want," she whispered. Perhaps the first man to do so. "Roll over and lie in the middle of the bed." He followed her instructions, and she knelt beside him.

"*You're* going to have at me?"

"Is that what *you* want?" Lucy repeated his question to her.

"I want a lot of things." His eyes hid secrets. "Let's start with your bra. It's very pretty, but I suspect your breasts are even prettier."

"Don't move." Lucy straddled his thighs, unclipped her bra, and flung it over her shoulder.

"See, I was right." He leaned forward to suckle each pouting nipple, the deep pull ricocheting through her.

"I've seen you do this." Lucy closed her eyes, placing her palms on his midriff. "Seen you close your eyes and learn the piece you're working on with your other senses." She bent forward and pressed a kiss in the space between her hands.

"You've never seen me kiss a block of wood, Liùsaidh."

"No need to be embarrassed. You're mesmerising when you focus on work." Lucy didn't open her eyes, instead inhaling deeply and letting her exhalation drift across his chest. "I'm marking my starting place. Your skin carries the slightest hint of sawdust. It's a comfort and a provocation."

"Speaking of provocation." His voice was strained, but his lilt held a caress.

"You can speak all you want." Lucy began with his hair, threading her fingers through his unruly locks, tugging lightly to show him a little of her impatience, even while she was seducing herself to patience. Next, she used her forefingers to trace his eyebrows. "Nicely shaped," she murmured, brushing her fingers down the side of his face, tracing along his jaw to meet at his chin. She shaped his nose. "Some people believe a long nose is a sign of leadership."

"What about an upturned nose?" He sucked air through his teeth.

"Adventurous in bed?" Lucy let her nipples drag across

his chest, testing them both with the merest touch. She put two fingers to his lips to catch his ragged exhalations.

When he opened his mouth to nip at her fingers, she giggled.

Wriggling to settle herself more comfortably, she ran her palm down one side of his neck and followed with tiny kisses to his stretched neck muscles. "You feel a bit tense. I must be doing something right." With deliberate slowness, she learned the smooth, muscled texture of his shoulders with her fingertips, feeling her way back to his centre via his collarbone. From there she moved across his ribs, toward his flanks. "You're very well made, Mr. Quinn."

"So are you," he growled, and the sound settled low in her pelvis. His hands rested on her hips, his thumbs pressing and retreating into the softer skin at her waist, fanning her excitement.

Leaning lower, she let him take the full weight of her breasts, the friction of skin meeting skin delightful torture. She mouthed one nipple until it stood taut. His breathing was laboured, his chest rising and falling. *Because of me.* When she laid her ear against him, she was sure she could hear his heart pounding. Positive she could hear her own.

"Am I allowed to explore?" His hands cupped her buttocks.

"Soon," Lucy crooned. "I've never introduced myself to a lover this way before." *Never felt safe enough to do so.* Slithering further back, her skin cooled where his hands had been. She trailed her fingers over the concave of his belly. "You're hard here too."

"You'll find I'm harder a bit lower." His sigh was barely audible.

"I'm getting there." She chuckled at the power rushing through her, made more valuable because he was giving it to her. Uncurling her spine, she raised her hands above her head, then lowered them to brush over her breasts and her belly to where her thighs gripped him. Dipping two fingers into her heat, she lifted them to her mouth. "You've made me wet."

"You're stunning," he said hoarsely.

"Can you see me?" She smiled, before wrapping her hand around his cock, the satin smoothness making her muscles clench in wanting. The quiet light behind her closed lids, the bombardment of her other senses kept arousal bright and needy.

"I like watching you pleasure yourself."

"This is for both of us." She let her tongue drift up the length of his cock, cupping his balls gently with one hand and squeezing. *More, I want this intimacy to last forever.*

"Praise the saints!"

Lucy opened her eyes to find his hands tangled in the feather doona, as if he needed to anchor himself to remain unmoving. She loved him in that moment. His face a rictus of taut control while he trusted her with his body.

"Lucy. Let me." His fingers closed on her shoulders, and he drew her closer.

"I want your hands on me," she pleaded, craving the power and reverence of his hands for herself.

Reversing positions, he knelt between her knees, his voice a dark chocolate. "We're upping the speed for this second stanza." His cock nudged at her opening, a dance where he inched forward, barely breathed as he drew back, and finally buried himself deep inside her.

"Please," she moaned, urgent now, seeing the banked passion in his expression.

"If you insist." His hand slipped between them, encouraging her to seek release. "You do insist?"

"Niall," she cried, her body convulsing.

His back was a sheen of sweat beneath her fingers. Still, he waited for her spasms to ebb before he picked up speed and rhythm.

She was aware the instant his patience shattered. Gripping his forearms, she pulled herself up to fuse her mouth with his. Her body started to buck as another orgasm exploded through her. "Now," she demanded.

He searched her face, and his thrusts deepened, before he threw his head back with an exultant roar. Tremors rocked from him to her, the sensations powerful and humbling. When his weight settled on her, his breath was still ragged. Long seconds later, he murmured against her temple, "I should move."

"Soon," she whispered. He wasn't ready to hear she loved him. She wasn't ready to tell him, when it might be a case of the-best-sex-she'd-ever-experienced talking. Although she didn't think so.

He rolled off her. "Snuggle up."

Lucy crawled under his arm, hiding her face against his chest. "You were rather wonderful."

"You were pretty good yourself." Kissing the top of her head, he held her close, soothing her with long, slow caresses down her back.

Lucy could read the subtext, and had her mother's example in her ear. More words were dangerous when your body felt as light as air, and magic tickled all the secret spaces in your heart and mind.

When she woke, she was still nestled under his heart, the steady beat the best reminder he was real and, for the moment, hers.

"Awake?"

"Barely." She pushed herself up to see his face and remembered the dinner. "Why were you so evasive about your work?"

"I wasn't evasive. I just had nothing to talk about." His dismissal sounded off.

"You're an artist. Your work is every bit as important as Liam's or Mr. Property-developer Hunter's." She worried at his false modesty. "I mentioned the frames because he looks like the type who'd spend money on expensive, modern art."

"What did you think of him?"

"A deflection rather than an evasion." Lucy tugged his hair to let him know she knew he was prevaricating. "I know the difference, Mr. Quinn. I liked the bit of him I saw tonight. He hides behind his wealth. He's not ostentatious—"

"You don't think the Rolex or the Merc are ostentatious?" he muttered.

"Your prejudices are showing. I'm betting his relationship with wealth is complicated." Lucy recalled the caution Hunter had carried. "He wouldn't be an easy man to live with. His comment about risk was 'verra' interesting, as Grandpa would say." It occurred to Lucy she might benefit from continuing that interesting conversation about risk. Just not now. Lucy walked her fingers from Niall's sternum to his navel. "I prefer a man whose body reflects his labour."

He held up a hand and examined it. "Callouses and nicks?"

"I'm talking about your stamina and your dedication to the task at hand." Her hand drifted lower. "You *are* interested."

# CHAPTER TEN

Niall stared into space, his mind on Lucy and the bed he'd forced himself to leave. She—it—was warm and welcoming. Closing her eyes and saying she wanted to learn him by touch smashed all his barricades. She'd ambushed him with his idea to go slowly. He'd promised her self-restraint, but it was a near thing. Making love to Lucy was shockingly wonderfully intimate. She exposed needs he'd tried to lock down.

*Whisht, I'm going all dewy-eyed and daft like a girl.*

The kettle screamed. He shook his head and came back to the workshop, the pot of tea he was brewing, and the day's labour ahead of him. She'd asked to come today. But that was before they'd spent a night in each other's arms. Would she come?

*Bad idea, Quinn.*

Pouring the first cup of tea, he surveyed his workshop. A night with Lucy, and he was ready to believe he could have everything he'd dreamed of.

Leopold's would be by at ten to pick up the finished frames and deliver the new artwork. In a few weeks his twelve-month contract with the gallery would finish, his share of his da's debts paid.

His debt to Cam had become more complicated. His dealings with Lucy's granda had been based on fair exchange. Until the will.

Niall would join the foundation, but he'd pay full rent. His work for Lucy was stemming the hole in her cash flow problem. Not so different from his deal with Cam.

All up, the profits from his Mondays with Lucy would put a serious dent in a year's commercial rent. When the new contract started, he'd restore more pieces to satisfy himself he was meeting the McTavish's as equals, not sponging off their charity.

He drained his cup. Delivering on the mentorship was doable. He'd have a full year to research ideas, talk to fellow artisans, reflect on his own learning and devise a program he could be proud of.

His exhibition was the lynchpin. Recent professional success would attract the high-quality candidates Cam and Lucy envisaged.

*"Your work is every bit as important as Liam's or Mr. Property-developer Hunter's."* He grinned at the recollection. Thank heavens Lucy understood it took time to craft beauty. She'd chosen him as her lover, not a man who hired a Merc. She would always be antiques royalty, but he was finding his place. They were finding their rhythm.

He gave himself a few hours on the sideboard he'd started for the exhibition. Hoped to get a few more in this evening. Hoped even more he'd get another invitation from Lucy. She'd found her feet as Cam had prophesied and was as lovely and loving as her granda had declared.

"You can do this, Quinn." Falling for Lucy convinced him he could move mountains. Scaling back his designs for the exhibition to smaller pieces was a workable compromise. He'd tell her when he put the exhibition catalogue in her hands.

\* \* \*

Lucy was smiling when she finally woke. Niall had cast a spell over her body, so she responded to his slightest touch—the glide of his palm on her flank, a nudge from his nose under her breast and the slide of his ankle up her calf. Snuggling back under the blankets, she inhaled sandalwood, a hint of her own rose perfume and the musky fragrance of splendid and repeated sex. She'd expected pleasure and discovered the serious carpenter was a virtuoso at lovemaking.

With a single finger trailing a path from her breastbone to her navel, he'd fashioned desire. She should have guessed from all the times she'd seen his work-roughened hands handle a table, a Blue Italian Spode cup, a frame, her pearls, even a Vegemite jar as if they were precious. Seeing the elegant turn of his wrist and the spread of his fingers tracing patterns in rare, recovered timbers, she hadn't fathomed the turmoil of having his hands on her. Her world had shifted on its axis. Her glance strayed to the open bedside table drawer, and a gurgle of smug satisfaction bubbled up from deep within her. They'd made good use of the condoms she stored there, after Niall rescued the two in his wallet.

Light sneaked under the Holland blind at her window, when she pushed herself into a sitting position, pillows propped at her back. The sky had been a dark inky blue the last time Niall had loved her, the street light casting shadows on her blind. He'd pressed his goodbye kiss to her inner thigh. She touched the spot.

He hadn't just turned her understanding of sex on its head, he'd pulled her clear of the fog dulling her judgment for weeks. Her search of his website after their first meeting had been a trawl for clues to his sneakiness. She'd missed a key detail. None of the pieces she'd glimpsed in his storeroom during Kate's visit were on the website.

*Why wasn't he advertising his work?*

Lots of people didn't have spare cash, because of the recession, but her grandpa had taught her there was always a market for quality. With the right promotion, Niall's work would sell faster than he could produce it.

"*Quinns pay their way.*" The puzzle and solution to Niall Quinn.

"Whisht, Lucy. You've been wilfully blind."

Rolling out of bed, she headed for the shower. With shampoo dripping into her eyes, the gears of her mind clicked into place.

*He's waiting until his debts to his brother are paid before focusing on his work.*

Waiting until he could devote himself full time to his craft. And she and Grandpa had casually thrown more hurdles into his path. The foundation spelt more unpaid work.

*And I arrogantly demanded he restore furniture for me.*

A cash flow problem for an estate worth millions and she'd thrown a tantrum worthy of a two-year-old. Shutting off the water, she rested her forehead against the cream porcelain wall tiles. Dozens of expletives sprang to her tongue, and only her long-ago vow to her gran kept her from uttering them. But they bounced around inside her skull, forcing her to clearly see what she'd done.

She could fix this. Briskly, Lucy rubbed herself dry. A two-pronged attack—prove to him she wasn't facing financial ruin and pay Niall for all his work.

"Child's play," she muttered to the ceiling. And then the barest inkling of a possible idea started to take shape. "Yes." Maybe Sleeping Beauty had felt this optimistic, kissed awake by her prince?

Having spent weeks of Mondays there, Lucy could picture Niall in his workshop. A pot of tea finished, crumbs from hastily consumed raisin toast clinging to his discarded plate. Leopold's driver would be around sometime to collect the latest batch of frames. Niall might well be poring over the new set of artworks, and the urge to share his morning had her hurrying out the door.

Leopold's team was unloading the new set of paintings when she arrived. She parked off to one side and followed them through the warehouse.

"You came." Niall's smile banished her tiny doubt she was the only one changed by last night's lovemaking.

"Hi." She planted a chaste kiss on his cheek while her body and mind rioted.

*Whisht! It isn't the fabulous sex confusing me. I'm really falling in love with him.*

Since Doug, she hadn't let herself believe in love. Niall made her feel lovable, that lovemaking wasn't the same as sex. Being his lover made her smile at the oddest times, and made her want to tend and nurture in return.

"One more load," the delivery man said.

She inspected the fifteen paintings lining the wall while Niall followed the delivery man to the back of the warehouse. The roller door hit the concrete. Niall's steps drew closer to the accompaniment of the jazz riffs on Katie Noonan's album *The Sweetest Taboo*. It wasn't the first time she'd arrived to Niall playing remixed songs from the seventies. Noonan was currently crooning "I Wanna Dance With Somebody" as a piano ballad, while Lucy itched to jitterbug.

"They're richer in the flesh," Lucy commented when he stopped beside her. He'd shown her the images weeks earlier.

"Yeah." His approach, she'd worked out, was to look at the paintings and let their shapes and colours and features roll around in his mind before he started on the designs—designs he'd bring to life now the paintings had arrived.

Surreptitiously, she glanced around the workshop. No piece in a corner shrouded with a cloth. She knew now the cradle had been under one of those drop sheets. Her first sighting of the cradle was at Kate and Liam's home, yet his habit was to live with his designs. Like he'd lived with his Huon Pine table or the cherry wood fruit bowl. He'd stopped his own work except for incidental pieces.

*Had he also stopped advertising it because he only had the pieces in the storeroom—not enough to build a business?*

"I wasn't sure you'd come today." Wrapping an arm around her shoulders, he pulled her close. His scent a promise of passion and shared delight.

"I thought of staying away." A part truth, because the child in her feared Niall was a creation of her imagination, the hero her adolescence had conjured when she'd dreamed of a man she could love. "Then decided we could be trusted to be responsible during office hours."

"Maybe you've got more self-discipline than me." He slid a hand down to cup her backside and press her into his body.

"I doubt it." She gripped two fistfuls of his hair and tugged his face away from hers. "Maybe you could follow me home and have dinner with me?"

"Just dinner?" The circles he was rubbing on her butt made forming words of more than one syllable difficult.

"I'm open to other offers."

"You control this—" he started to say.

She covered his mouth with her fingers. "Then I'll have to be more explicit with my invitation. Please, Niall, come to dinner, make love to me until I'm dazed and boneless, then hold me while I sleep."

"That's a lovely invitation." His slow smile blossomed from a quirk at the corner of his mouth to a wide grin—an even lovelier response. "Will seven work for you?"

"Seven's fine." She eased herself out of his arms. "Pasta and beer okay?"

"Perfect."

"Okay." Time to start fleshing out her plan. "If you don't have a specific job for me today, I'd like to work on a new project from here. I promise I won't disturb you."

"You can work in this noise?" He waved a hand around the workshop.

"I can work anywhere." One of the useful skills she'd retained from a childhood of perpetual upheaval.

"What's your project?"

"I've decided to hold Grandpa's annual spring gala."

She'd intended to cancel this year, but the hairs on the back of her neck prickled with anticipation. The gala usually delivered a profit and attracted a whole host of existing and new clients. Clients who might be interested in a gifted restorer. She'd surrender her Mondays, and Niall would be paid for his work.

"What's involved?" He followed her to the kitchen, leaning against the bench while she made tea.

"I'll need to identify inventory from storage to shift to the shop. Choose a theme, price a few pieces competitively to attract regular customers. Grandpa did this every year. A fancy opening to clear out stock we've held for a year or longer. We send invites to everyone on our client list."

"Sounds like a lot of extra work." He brushed a hand over her hair. "You sound happy."

"I am happy." She stilled, absorbing the encouragement in his caress. "My team will help. The fact I'm holding it despite Grandpa's death might bring a few more people than usual out of the woodwork." That was her goal, to shift interest from her to Niall, to seek paying work for him, so he'd clear his debt faster. "Will you come?"

"When are you planning to hold it?"

"In a few weeks. Late afternoon, early evening. I'll get it catered, finger food and drinks." *And I'm not asking you to do any of the work.*

"I'm not—" he began, and she sensed a refusal, when his presence was essential.

"Please say you'll come. I'd love your support."

"Of course." His reluctance created an itch between her shoulder blades. Telling him her plans might hex them. Promising something she couldn't deliver would be even worse. He took the tea she handed him and went back to the restoration work she'd steamrollered him into.

Propping her computer on the table under the window, she sipped her tea. A cliché, but he was poetry in motion. Competent, focused, his body bent, stretched, squatted, reached as his muscles responded to the demands of his task. With his attention absorbed, she rechecked his website, confirming her concern—no new pieces for sale. The site was unchanged since the first time she'd looked at it. Niall was too kind for his own good—a fruit bowl for her and a cradle for his brother and sister-in-law. She admired his professional integrity. He'd redirected the florist to a friend when the woman had pushed for a higher number of the frames she wanted at a cheaper price.

But he'd lost income.

Her fear of debt stopped her brain and made her flounder like a beached whale, who knew safety was on the other side of a breakwater but couldn't find its way there alone. Niall wasn't so much afraid of debt as uncomfortable at the stain on his self-respect. Love leavened his actions, a commitment to honesty and excellence in whatever he did. Taking advantage of others wasn't in his DNA.

Why had she taken so long to work that out?

Her hand crept to her throat. She'd stolen his time and his skill. Saying sorry wouldn't cut it. Niall let his actions speak for him.

Like her gran, he showed he cared through acts of service. So could she.

\* \* \*

Dawn was breaking on a crisp autumn Sunday morning. Niall had been in his workshop for an hour. Pushing himself for an extra fifteen minutes or a half hour or an hour had become routine. Alerted by his system of flashing lights, he pushed himself upright, pulled his goggles around his neck and rolled his shoulders. He checked the message from Anna on his phone, drained his tea and returned to dismantling the second Gothic chair for Lucy.

"You can avoid me for just so long, boyo, then you're dead meat." Anna pocketed her phone when he swung the door wide thirty minutes later, and tilted her head to one side, listening. "Paul Simon's 'Wristband.' That's a blast from the past."

"Lovely to see you, Anna. He suited my mood." A six-foot-eight guard baring all comers from Niall's door would have been welcome this morning. "How can I help you?" He braced for her succinct annihilation of his excuses.

"You can answer my texts and emails and tell me why your page for the exhibition isn't live on your website yet?" Anna stabbed a finger into his chest. "It should have been live two weeks ago."

"I'm having second thoughts." He turned his back on her, always a dangerous move.

She grabbed his arm and, because she worked out and was stronger than she looked, she tugged him back to face her. Scanning his face, her expression went from irritated to concerned at what she saw. The woman could read body language across a crowded room, so what hope did he have?

"Tell Anna all about it." She tucked her hand through his arm and half-pulled, half-dragged him to the table under the window. She pushed him into a chair but remained standing. "And I mean *all* about it. This is not a good move."

"I haven't finished enough pieces," he said the words aloud for the first time, although his head was near to bursting with the brutal reality.

"Stop everything else and make more." Anna excelled at identifying solutions.

"I'm still under contract with Leopold's." For another two weeks, until the last job was finished, but non-negotiable. He'd promised his brother the money, and he'd never broken a contract in his life.

"That's a self-imposed penance, and why the Quinn brothers have to compete for saint of the week is beyond me." The flamenco tap of her boot heel was a dance of frustration.

"He's carried the load a long time." He played his strongest card. "Don't you think he and Kate deserve a cushion now the babe's coming."

"Not gonna catch me on that one. I can be as sooky as the next person about babies, but this isn't about Leopold's contract." She paced off the line of finished frames resting against the side wall. "You were juggling the frames and the pieces for the exhibition very nicely six weeks ago." She came to the end of the line and stopped in front of a set of two mahogany Gothic revival side chairs. "More restoration for Lucy."

"Perhaps." He shrugged.

"No perhaps about it. They're antiques, they're broken, and they're sitting in the middle of your workshop on a *Sunday*." She invested the word with all the loathing of a vegetarian for a piece of rare steak. "There's not even a scent of a Quinn piece in the place."

"I owe her granda a lot." He gripped the back of his neck and rotated his head, although the ache was in his heart more than his muscle memory. Cam had put both Niall and Lucy in an impossible position with his will.

"She didn't strike me as a selfish cow." Anna tipped up one chair and examined the fracture down the straight back leg. "She said she liked your work."

"She's not. She does. Cam left complications for Lucy too." Niall would defend her as long as he had breath. His quibbles were with the old man's machinations.

"Just a guess here, my carpenter friend. We all had to keep shtum about the exhibition last week because you haven't told her about it."

"Correct."

"Single-word answers don't cut it with me." She wandered back toward him, her arms crossed—Athena on the warpath. "You must be confusing me with my sweet, somewhat distracted sister."

"Never." He loved Anna's loyalty to friends and family, her pushiness when she was worried.

"Another one-word answer," she muttered.

"Couldn't resist." He rose and wrapped his arms around her, resting his cheek on her crown, so she couldn't see his face. "Her granda gave me this workspace, gave me the opportunity to create the pieces for the exhibition. She needs some help to get through this early grieving period."

"I'm guessing you're giving her more than your days."

"Lucy's working on a special opening at McTavish's, but yeah, we're spending some time together." Late meals, snatched lovemaking, falling asleep in each other's arms, and getting up early to do it all again. In the hushed conversations before sleep, mostly he asked about how her plans were progressing, and kept shtum about the collapse of his own.

"You're in love with her," she said, half-question, half-statement, and her words made his heart race with impossible longings.

"I can wait a bit longer for my exhibition."

She pushed back in his arms until she could meet his gaze, gripping his upper arms and shaking him. "Lucy won't forgive you for not telling her what her little requests for restoration are costing you."

"They're costing me feck all. I didn't have a big market before I planned the exhibition. That hasn't changed."

"You had a dream. And everyone who loves you has a share in that dream—Liam, Kate, your mum, me, even the babe. It will kill"—she searched his face and praise the saints; she kicked him metaphorically in the balls—"it is killing you to let this go. If you care for her, don't do this."

"I care," he said.

Lucy had lost the first stable home she'd ever had. Cam's generosity to him had helped tip her into debt. Niall wasn't blind about his choices. A successful exhibition might attract serious monied buyers and prove he was a worthy mentor for the McTavish foundation.

"She needs to feel in control of her granda's business." Lucy was adrift. She'd asked him to help. Whatever the cost, he wouldn't let her down. "It's for a short time. I can give her a short time."

"How long before you have to make the decision to

cancel the exhibition?" Anna was back to brisk efficiency.

"A few weeks." It was sheer stupidity not to do it now.

# CHAPTER ELEVEN

Ten o'clock on Wednesday night and Lucy had sought refuge in flannel pyjamas, thick green and pink-striped woollen socks, and her gran's quilted dressing gown. She glanced in the hall mirror before she opened the door and saw what she already knew. She was pale and a bit haggard around the mouth. Period pain did that to a lot of women. It was nothing to be embarrassed about, but neither did she feel like a temptress. She and Niall had only been lovers for ten days.

"Hi." She forced a smile.

"Is something wrong?" His eyes were dark grey tonight, deep pools of patience. His scent settled her nauseous stomach.

"Come in." She pulled the door wider and stepped back. She was new to real intimacy with a lover and unsure of herself. "We can talk in the kitchen. Bottom of the hall on the right."

"I know where the kitchen is, Lucy." His jaw jutted forward in reproach. "I don't spend all my visits in your bed."

"Sorry. I know you don't." She offered an apology when she hadn't intended to offend. "You make tea and toast and serve me breakfast in bed."

"Do you want tea and toast now?"

"I want to sit down." She brushed past him to enter the kitchen first, taking a seat. "Do you want a drink? Tea, beer, Grandpa's whiskey?"

"I don't want the politeness you serve your customers."

"I should have called." She held her hair off her forehead, searching for the right words.

He remained standing near the door. "If you don't want company tonight, just say so." He paused and seemed to come to some decision. "We're having an affair, for feck's sake. You can call a halt at any time. Just say the word."

"I'm having a hard time with the arrival of my period." She glowered at him, because after sharing sex that got better with each encounter, she'd expected more perceptiveness from him. Perceptiveness and silence. *How dumb is that?*

"I considered the possibility, along with various disasters at the shop. I decided you'd tell me if you were feeling unwell." He pushed himself off the door jamb and strolled closer.

"I'm feeling miserable and uncomfortable and unattractive." And she remembered her mum's fear of her value to any man if she wasn't flat on her back and able to perform.

"I'm sorry for the first two"—he sank into the seat opposite her—"but from where I'm sitting, you're the same beautiful woman I saw yesterday. Do you always have a hard time?" The lullaby in his lilt was causing cramping muscles to loosen their death grip.

"Enough for painkillers. Enough to turn me into a werewolf," she said. Doug had always been uncomfortable around "women's business." Because he only had brothers, he said. Niall was one of two boys, completely discrediting Doug's excuse.

"That's bad." He reached for her hand and linked his fingers with hers. "Do hot water bottles on your tummy help? My mum liked heat. I've known a few other lasses who like the comfort as well as the warmth, but it's an old-fashioned remedy."

"Did your mum talk about having periods?" What a curious conversation to be having? She'd been too young to have the conversation with her mum. Her gran had been matter-of-fact but inclined to talk about it out of Grandpa's earshot.

"As part of her birds and bees' instruction." He grinned. "She's a demon for romances, so we got the proper way to woo a woman, along with the mechanics of reproduction and sex. Dad chipped in anything he thought she left out."

"Mum called it 'the curse.' She hated when she got a period, and she cursed. That's where I picked up some of my best swear words. I realised later she had irregular periods because of her drugs." Lucy was just now realising there were other ways to talk about periods with men.

"Mum spoiled me for formal sex education. But I'd be keen to hear some of your curses." He was drawing circles on her knuckles with his thumb, and the ripples spread in an ever-widening circle through her body.

"I stopped swearing for Gran. She was *such* a lady." Lucy had been flummoxed by the contrast with her mum, then discovered mother-love and grandmother-love were different but lovely. "I only half-listened to my teacher. What she was describing sounded like nothing I'd seen at home."

"I can share a bed without making love to you." He studied her as if she was a maze and he wanted to unlock the puzzle. Not to conquer but because he liked puzzles. "I like being with you, talking to you, holding you—if that helps in any way."

"Come upstairs." She stood, her hand still in his.

He spooned along her back, his body heat burning off the last edges of her pain. His hand rested gently on her belly. She fell asleep with him caressing her womb and woke to the dream of carrying a child.

\* \* \*

Niall arrived at McTavish's Antiques Centre toward the end of the Sunday afternoon event, his mind still on the cedar table he'd started this morning. He'd been cutting timber to the requisite sizes and mulling Anna's latest text message—*Well!?!?*—when his alarm reminded him of his promise to Lucy.

He'd lectured himself on the drive over, repeating words drummed into him as a toddler. "*If you can't be gracious, don't bother to speak or to come.*"

He'd be gracious if it killed him.

McTavish's had been turned into a bower of flowers for the spring sale. Pink and purple, yellow and white tulips stood in perfect upright vases. Ranunculus in the same colours spilled from cheerful pots, and statuesque branches of wine magnolias kept sentinel in dark corners. Huge crystal wide-necked vases took pride of place on nineteenth-century cedar tables, their aromatic lilies in shades from cream through to crimson. They provided the sweet notes riffing to the base note of beeswaxed floors.

Clever Lucy had designed a space to saturate the senses. Gleaming glassware and highly polished mirrors reflected the premium pieces from multiple angles. The soaring strings of Vivaldi from a string quartet in the corner accompanied the fizzing effervescence of popping champagne corks. The crowd moved easily through the large space, exuding the cultivated indifference of people used to doing business in any city in the world.

"You're here." Lucy appeared out of nowhere wearing a simple black dress, shot through with green. Her hair was loose, two combs scooping it off her face, letting her rich tresses fall to her shoulders in waves. Her gran's pearls were twisted around her throat to make a choker. Her usual low-heeled pumps were replaced by stilettos. Elegant, and he wanted her with an intensity that frightened him. She wrapped her hand around his arm, smiling with quiet contentment.

"Looks like it's going well." Kidnapping was a capital offence, so he gestured to a cluster of pieces adorned with red dots, rather than steer her toward the privacy of her office. At a conservative estimate, he'd say half her inventory was sold. The place was awash with energy and serious money.

"Better than I hoped." She pressed closer. The haunted woman who'd appeared on his doorstep bare months ago had been replaced by a vibrant, sophisticated chatelaine of a top antiques house. She twinkled at him. "I had a quiet chat with Grandpa before the start."

"What'd he say?"

"He said, '*Whisht, girl, what are you waiting for?*'" The air around her was electric, her success generating a glow bright enough to lift even his mood. "Come with me. There's someone I want you to meet." A waiter hovered with a tray of drinks. "Look at me." She fanned her face with her free hand. "Not even giving you a chance to get a drink."

"You're happy." He snagged a beer.

"Very." She quickened her steps. "I'm hoping you will be too." She wove through clusters of people, responding to greetings, unaware of the interest she stirred. She might not want to be the centre of attention, but she was luminous. "Peter Bradley, meet Niall Quinn."

"You're the secret weapon Lucy's been telling me about." The grey-at-the-temples, handsome, blue-eyed, Armani-besuited, mid-forties man thrust out his hand.

"Secret weapon?" Niall returned the handshake. Bradley's grip was firm, not the tussle of wills he'd expect from a rival.

"I'll leave you two to chat." Lucy released his arm, patted his butt, and was gone.

Niall sipped his beer, noticing Peter watched Lucy's disappearing form.

"Cameron was proud of her, but he would have been

prouder still that she pulled this off so close to his death." Peter's gaze swivelled back to catch Niall's. "Don't you agree?"

"Any granda would be proud of his granddaughter." Niall made his brogue a little thicker.

"But I'm talking about Cameron and his granddaughter in particular." Peter's look grew speculative. "Lucy said you knew him well and are responsible for the exceptional restoration of an eighteenth-century Serpentine Fireplace Mantel I bought earlier this year."

"It was a piece that rewarded effort." Niall's shoulders slumped as he absorbed the body blow. He'd felt like shite before tonight's shindig, and Lucy had introduced him to a wealthy antiques collector as a furniture restorer.

"I have a few more that would reward your effort," Peter murmured.

"I'm not free to take on new work at the moment." Niall stared into his beer, no longer thirsty. He should have said "I'm working on an exhibition."

"Lucy was *positive* you had time for one or two pieces." The man's insistence raised the hairs on the back of Niall's neck. "In fact, I got the impression she was canvassing for work on your behalf."

Niall glanced across the room. Lucy appeared engrossed in conversation, then turned her head as if aware of his stare. Her tentative smile proved Peter's claim. She'd sold his time and his skills without asking him.

"One." He turned back to Peter. *Was this what it felt like to be a kept man?* Cam wouldn't have expected him to be at Lucy's beck and call, but the old man must have known Niall would never walk away from an obligation.

*"It might take longer than you hope before you get the recognition you deserve."*

And it might never happen.

*Did you factor that in, Cam, when you decided to order people to suit your bidding?*

He returned his beer to a passing waiter.

*Is that what Lucy wants? Me doing her bidding?*

Like Cam, she hadn't warned him about plans involving him—a gut punch.

*Steady, boyo, you haven't told her about your exhibition.*

"Here." Peter slid an embossed card from his wallet, turned it over, and wrote an address on it. "I can be free any evening this week."

"A banker." Niall hoped he kept the hellishness out of his voice.

"For my sins. A family tradition I was expected to follow. Pity my father didn't own McTavish's." Peter's smile was a mix of banker calculation and hopeless romantic.

"Tomorrow night. About seven." Niall didn't want to like the man. "One piece."

"Ah! But I get to pick the piece."

"Don't tell me you've got a warehouse full?" Niall joked, because the thought Lucy had wanted to tie him up in restoration work indefinitely was too bleak to contemplate.

"Enough to provide a steady wage to the right person for months. My word carries weight. I could be a useful referee in your role in the McTavish Foundation." Peter waved to someone across the room. "Until tomorrow night."

Lucy had manoeuvred to set him up with a steady wage and a banker, spruiking Niall's *restoration* skills. *Praise the saints and all the little fishes.*

Turning his back on the room, he pretended the Norman Lindsay etching of a female nude had his full attention, when he couldn't see a thing. Lucy loved antiques. She'd made no secret of her preference from their first meeting. He should have pushed back when she'd asked him to restore pieces for her. Told her his plans for the next few months were set and might even benefit the foundation.

Instead, he'd let his empathy for Cam's death dictate his actions. When he'd lost his da, he became truly helpless. He'd wanted to help Lucy, and if restoring a few pieces of furniture distracted her for even a few minutes a day from

Cam's loss, then he'd been happy to give her an escape. He hadn't needed to talk about his own work.

Now, he was trapped in wanting to give her more.

Anna's perfume gave him a second's warning. An arm came around his waist, a head rested on his shoulder. "My darlin' boyo. Why the glum face?"

"Anna." He draped his arm across her shoulder. "What are you doing here?"

She turned into his arms, her penetrating look skewering him. "Rescuing you. If that's what you want?"

"I love you, Anna Turner." He made himself smile. "But you're about a decade too late."

"You're cancelling the exhibition, aren't you?" She gripped the lapels of his only decent jacket, disappointment clear in her downturned mouth, her frustration a fraction of his own.

"Postponing, due to circumstances beyond my control." He mocked himself. When she opened her mouth to argue, he pressed two fingers to her lips. "Not here. Not tonight. And I still don't know how you found your way here."

"Lucy invited Hunter. Neither of us is sure why." She rested her hand against his cheek, and he accepted her sisterly comfort. "Hunter's intrigued, so here we are."

"Maybe we should look for them." He turned her to face the room. Lucy's interest in the successful property developer was another unwelcome guest at the feast.

"They're consenting adults," she responded with a tart snap.

"I'm not worried about Lucy and Hunter." *Or not much.* Hunter represented the world Lucy rightly inhabited, and she'd been slumming it with Niall. He scanned the room and couldn't see either. "I always forget you refuse to be jealous."

"If I spent my time worrying about what Hunter was doing when I wasn't with him, and vice versa, it wouldn't say much about trust." Her reply was a rapier sharp reminder he was keeping secrets from Lucy.

"The show is wrapping up. I don't have the stomach for any more introductions," he growled.

"Do you remember why you agreed to appear in my billboard campaign?" she asked with deceptive sweetness.

"You asked me."

"I did. And the other reason?" She steered him toward a large sideboard. They were just another couple admiring the merchandise. Except there was purpose in Anna's abrupt change of topic. Experience had taught him to surrender to the inevitable when she started an interrogation.

"Liam had lost himself in work, trying to pay off Da's debts. He didn't tell me about them, wouldn't talk to me at all. I thought he'd lost himself, full stop. Was afraid money was all that mattered to him." Niall had been helpless to bridge the rift. "I wanted to do something to shock him into noticing me."

"He was unhappy. You're unhappy now and just as stubborn as he was. By the way, we're heading for that delicate little hall table near the redhead." Anna would skewer him if he stepped away from her side. "It's okay to accept help."

"I accept help," he muttered, uncomfortable with her assessment.

"Tell that to someone who doesn't know you as well as I do. You and Liam both tend to manage disasters by yourself. You get it from your father, I suspect."

"You never met him." He glared at the unknown redhead. She startled and scurried away.

"I didn't have to meet him to know he was a white knight sort of fellow. Fighting valiantly for just causes, coming to the rescue of a damsel in distress. Us damsels are more inclined to rescue ourselves these days." She stopped and turned to him. "We want to share, not be sheltered. You wanted to share Liam's load. And *you* were not a happy camper being left out." She was brutally loving. "Now, you need to go after that redhead and play nice. Tell her I stabbed you with a pin or something."

The situations weren't the same. Cam, not Lucy, had created the debt. He dredged up a smile. "Introduce myself, you mean?"

"You don't need a stomach for introductions. You need a backbone and a little charm. Practise for when you do finally get your exhibition." She sauntered away.

"On my current trajectory, it'll be posthumous." He was talking to himself.

Irritation was an itch between his shoulder blades. Even the elegance of Lucy's bedroom mocked him tonight. Having sex in a queen bed on high thread-count sheets, nestled in a goose feather eiderdown would heighten anyone's pleasure. For weeks, he'd slid over her, she'd slipped under him, hairy bare skin had brushed silky bare skin while rolling across luxurious bedlinen, each texture a delicious torment. All he could offer was a double bed, cotton percale and a hand-me-down quilt. Their bedding spelt out the contrast in their lifestyles. Lucy's cash flow problems were temporary; McTavish assets would always buy more than basic comfort.

"Why did you ask Peter to offer me work?"

"Because you cancelled the frames you were making for the florist." She turned her back, lifting her hair off her neck. "Can you undo my zipper, please?"

Her scent was sweeter at the nape, more vanilla than rose. He leaned into her smell and couldn't resist brushing his lips across the exposed skin to taste her. With her scent enveloping him, and his mouth on her body, he wished life was as simple as her answer. He guided the zipper down her spine before anchoring his hands at her waist. "Can you check with me next time?"

She spun to face him, her eyes concerned. "Did I do the wrong thing?"

*Yes*, he wanted to shout, but the word wouldn't come.

"Just check. Please."

"He asked me about our restorer. Not for the first time. And you want to repay your brother as quickly as possible." Her words of explanation tumbled over each other, an apology when she wasn't sure how she'd sinned.

"Yeah, I do." He'd loosened his tie on the drive home from her gala, now he discarded it. "But I've got that covered."

"You could have said no." She pulled the dress off her shoulders and stepped out of it. Her pretty bra and pants had sprigs of green leaves embroidered on them. She looked as vulnerable as she had when she'd first shown up on his doorstep, and like then, he couldn't fault her conclusions.

"Bradley implied no wasn't an option." Niall unbuttoned his shirt, his heart hammering in his chest when she slipped off her stilettos, then set her foot on a stool and bent to unclip the suspenders she was wearing.

"That was naughty of him." She glanced up, one silk stocking halfway down her calf, and his mouth watered. "I said I'd introduce you."

"And that I had time free." *Praise the saints.* He must be mad to be belabouring the point when she smelled like heaven, looked like every fantasy he'd ever had, and was within reach. Tonight he'd take the time they hadn't had in the last fortnight to draw out their pleasure.

"I might have." Her brow wrinkled in thought. "Although, I'm more likely to have said you were finishing a contract and might consider the right offer."

"He mentioned being in a position to promote the foundation." *And I'm worse than a dog with a bone.*

She chuckled. "He's hoping our mentee gets hooked on antiques in year one and abandons all other dreams."

"I'm meeting Bradley tomorrow night." He'd misunderstood and over-reacted, and he was an ungrateful bastard when she'd thought she was doing him a good turn. She hadn't pledged his time—the banker had finessed him.

She shook out her second stocking and laid it over a

chair. "Would you like to help me get rid of the rest of these clothes?"

"If you help me first."

"Did I thank you for coming tonight?" She unbuckled his belt, sliding her hand inside his trousers to cup his balls.

"I think you're about to." He tilted her chin to kiss her. Her soft lips moved against his, her mouth opened in welcome, and the angst of the evening faded. He couldn't parse all the elements in her kisses: sweetness, hunger, caring. She was strong, but her vulnerability called to him. She made him feel as if together they were whole. "This is lovely. You're lovely."


Much later, she curled around him, her cheek resting against Niall's heart. By inches, by cup of tea, sandwich, shared meal, shared conversation, exchanged smile, she'd become the keeper of his heart.

"Your deal with Peter has nothing to do with me." Her leg rested across his thighs. "You decide your rate, and Peter pays you."

"Uh-huh." He stroked her back, liking the clean lines of her, the straight spine, the still too prominent shoulder blades, and he'd worry about juggling Peter with her bookcases tomorrow.

"Hold off on my bookcases," she said sleepily. "They can wait."

*No, they can't.* He'd given his word and wasn't about to add a new debt to his growing list. Fourteen Mondays he'd promised her, six left.

"And in the spirit of checking first"—she yawned and tucked herself under his shoulder—"I do have some other contacts if, and only if, you decide you want more work."

She thought his biggest problem was the debt to his brother and had seen a way to help him pay it back sooner. His fault for not sharing all the interlocking pieces of his financial plan, including the exhibition. Initially, he hadn't told her about it, because he didn't expect to fall for her, to become so caught up in helping her, being with her, that it threatened his goals.

Then he hadn't told her, because she'd feel guilty for taking him away from his work. And while Cam had backed him into a corner with the bequest, she was innocent. He wouldn't tell her now, because she'd blame herself for him cancelling it. She wasn't responsible for his decisions. He was a grown man. A "consenting adult," as Anna would have it.

Tonight, he'd consented his way right out of his exhibition.

# CHAPTER TWELVE

"Hi." Lucy pulled her front door wide, welcoming Hunter with a smile. "I love a guest who's punctual. To be honest, I love anyone who's punctual."

"Something we have in common." He joined her in the wide, tiled hallway, and visibly inhaled. "The roses remind me of my aunt's."

"These are from my gran's gardens." Lucy fingered a yellow petal and bent forward to catch the delicate fragrance. "Roses in the hall was a tradition for her."

"My aunt's hall isn't as elegant as this one." His survey was interested, his intent friendly. She knew in her entrails his assessment wasn't always so well-disposed. "Her sideboard and mirror don't store hundreds of years of perfumed memories, but the welcome's the same."

"Thanks for coming to the house."

"Hopetoun Cottage?" He made the name a question.

"My grandparents' tribute to their Scottish forebears." Lucy gestured down the hall. "Straight ahead, the last door on the right." She rubbed clammy hands down the sides of her straight skirt. If she didn't fight her fear, it would swallow her. "I hope you don't mind a meeting in the kitchen."

He paused beside her at the kitchen door. The large, airy room had been renovated in her early teens, making the space surprisingly modern in a house filled with antiques. She and Gran had chosen the appliances together and walked the layout they wanted before bringing in an architect. Huge wide-ledged windows filled with pots of parsley, basil, and thyme overlooked the garden. Fridge, stove, sink and benchtops were within easy reach of one another. The only concessions to the family business were a country sideboard, a large table, and six chairs. Lately she'd been thinking a different kind of table—a long golden-hued, hand-crafted table—might be a better fit for the life she wanted to create.

For all the years she'd lived in this house, the kitchen had been the centre of family gatherings, intimate chats and boisterous lunches. What did Hunter see?

*What deductions is he making about me? About my invitation— my second invitation—the gala and now, a few days later, this more private request?*

"You spend a lot of time here," he concluded.

"Not as much as I used to." She shrugged, then answered the speculation in his gaze. "I've been skipping meals, getting takeaway, eating at Niall's. When Grandpa first died, I wandered for miles, rather than come home. I've developed a love-hate relationship with the place. Whisht, that's the first time I've admitted how complicated my feelings about my home have become. Please, sit down. Did you train with the Spanish Inquisition in a previous life?"

"Success in business is about sixty percent reading people and the rest managing money." He shucked his overcoat, draping it over the back of a chair before taking a seat. "But you'd know that, having been raised by Cameron McTavish."

"Grandpa was interested in people." Her grandpa's trick had been to match a stranger with the perfect vase or table or chair or lamp for them.

"Whereas I'm not." He wasn't offended.

"You're alert to attack," she replied. Hunter Thompson's wariness was matched by a ruthless determination to protect his own—a modern-day warrior.

"I was a builder's labourer before I was anything else. Dangerous places—building sites."

"And now you turn anything you touch into gold." Lucy's move was audacious, but procrastinating with a busy man wouldn't win his advice. "Tea?"

"I'd prefer coffee. Black. Or water if you don't have coffee."

"I can do coffee. Grandpa developed a taste for it in the last few years." She turned on a commercial-sized coffee machine and rested her hips against the bench while waiting for it to heat. "We also entertained a lot at home, until recently."

"Why did you ask me here, Lucy?" His hands rested on the table, palms down. Long-fingered, tanned, neatly manicured, his hands had almost as many nicks and scars as Niall's, although none of Hunter's were recent. The hands of a capable, controlled man.

Turning back to fiddle with the machine, she sorted words, trying to find a reasonable explanation. "I said I had a business proposition." *Which wasn't strictly true.*

"My business interests don't include antiques."

"You didn't need to come here to tell me that." She'd at least piqued his interest. She set a cup under the nozzle, listened for the kerchunk to signal the fresh beans had been ground, and watched the trickle of black gold drip into the cup. "Sugar?" She set it in front of him.

"Please."

She passed him a sugar bowl before turning to make tea. The rhythmic tinkle of the metal spoon against his ceramic cup communicated patience, a hard-won skill for a man in a hurry. Or maybe he wasn't the man depicted in the business press? She slid onto the chair opposite and raised her gaze to meet his. "Actually, I want your advice."

"Why me?" He leaned back, at ease with himself and her,

but he'd recognise a lie.

"I have an accountant and a lawyer I trust, but this is more personal." She'd sounded out both indirectly and done some of her own research, when she'd woken from her grief coma and seen how illogical her actions were. Like any self-respecting sleeping beauty, Niall's kisses had woken her.

"And I'm connected to family?" He made the deduction, saving her the embarrassment of confessing. "Except, I'm not."

"Anna took you to meet her family. That's rare, and I'm betting you know how rare. She trusts you and trusts you around people she cares for." There was a rock-solid decency about the Turner and Quinn twins. She attributed the same characteristics to Hunter by dint of his connection.

"Interesting conclusion." His eyebrows rose, and she wasn't sure if he was flattered or annoyed at the dent in his inscrutable persona. "Niall took you to meet his family. Does that make you trustworthy?"

"I'm trustworthy." But she was shaking her head. "Kate invited me. A kindness because of Grandpa."

"We can agree to disagree on that point." He sipped his coffee, while she held her breath waiting for his next move. "Is that why you invited me to the gala?"

"I invited you so you could get a sense of the business, its products and clients."

"You'd planned a second meeting before we had our first." One eyebrow disappeared into the hank of hair sweeping across his forehead. "I'm impressed.

"You have no interest in antiques. Your reputation is mixed. Ruthless according to some, fair according to others." Lucy ticked points off her fingers. "And then there's Anna." Continuing on the same path wasn't an option, because Lucy's actions were harming Niall.

"Anna's got nothing to do with my business."

"You're dating her. I'm judging you by the company she keeps."

A wolfish grin streaked across his face, his predator instincts diverted by the surprise attack. "Did you inherit your approach from your grandpa as well?"

"Might have." Maybe falling for Niall and not knowing how he felt about her had heightened her awareness of others in the same situation. Hunter would protect the people Anna loved.

"Congratulations on choosing your grandpa's business model." He toasted her with his remaining coffee.

"Did you ever meet him?" She soaked up new stories about Cameron McTavish.

"I did some research before accepting your invitation." He steepled his fingers in front of his mouth, his inscrutable gaze assessing her. "What sort of advice are you after?"

"When I was a little girl, we were dirt poor." She took a quick sip of tea, the hit of caffeine reinforcing her decision to use him as a circuit breaker. "Occasionally, my mum would disappear us overnight"—Lucy flashed her teeth—"that's how she described it when we took off because she hadn't paid the rent. There were other bills, visits from debt collectors, times when we couldn't buy food. The upshot is I entered my teens paranoid about debt."

*I've said it aloud and the world hasn't ended.*

"Any debt."

"Makes sense." He wasn't judging her, which made her next admission easier.

"For the last five years I've managed McTavish's books. We take items on consignment, but we also buy outright, backing our judgment that we'll sell what we've bought and won't default on the overdraft. Since Grandpa's death, my brain's gone haywire. I've become obsessed with building huge cash buffers in case even the smallest bill can't be paid." She stared at the unmarked folder sitting at the end of the table. Evils had flown out of Pandora's box before she'd slammed it shut. Only hope had remained.

"Sounds like you've identified your problem."

"I have." Last week she'd asked Clem for her

professional assessment.

"*Is it possible that Grandpa's death catapulted me back to childhood? Made me helpless again?*"

Money was the security blanket she'd craved as a child, and debt had been the out-of-control monster stalking her dreams.

"Then you're more than halfway towards a solution." He drained his coffee and set it aside. "You don't need me."

"My banker, my accountant, even my lawyer told me to make my assets work harder; that cash flow wasn't the monumental bogeyman I was turning it into." She pushed her empty cup around the table, huffed out a breath and tossed him a half-smile. "Pity I didn't lock myself in a room for a month before making any decisions."

She prayed Niall would forgive her blundering demand to restore additional pieces. She'd stolen his time. Her grand idea of extra restoration work for Peter was another kind of theft, because she was arrogantly making Niall's choices for him. She stifled a groan. His father's debts were real, whereas she'd worked out hers were childhood nightmares that should have lost their power to dictate her actions.

"I'm not your financial adviser, but I'm prepared to consider hypotheticals." From Hunter, that was capitulation.

"I can do hypotheticals." Lifting her chair, she carried it around to his side of the table, bringing the folder with her. "Let's say someone has taken out a loan for a few hundred thousand dollars for two years with repayments of roughly fifteen thousand a month."

To his credit, he didn't blink. "What'd you spend the money on?"

"Most of it is sitting in the business bank account." *I'm an idiot.* Or an orphan paralysed by loss. "Twelve months operating costs, staff salaries and benefits, quarterly utilities, an allocation for buying new product, marketing—"

His hand covered hers on the table. "You don't need me to tell you anything."

"I need someone"—she paused—"knowledgeable, and not in a relationship with me, to remind me of what I spent years learning. I could have taken a smaller loan, brought the spring gala forward, and the normal cash flow would have serviced that loan."

"What are you going to do about it?" He leaned back in his chair.

"Renegotiate the loan." *And beg Niall's forgiveness.*

\* \* \*

Niall had waited until the last possible moment to ring the influential gallery owner. *Hoping for a miracle?* He pocketed his phone and buried his head in his hands, the woman's final words ringing in his ears.

*"Don't expect another chance in this city."*

She was pissed off, and with reason. She'd have to shuffle other exhibitions, change timelines, and it would cost her. More in time and effort than actual money. He'd given her enough notice to cancel the bulk of her promotional activity and agreed to pay any existing out-of-pocket expenses.

"You're a fool." Her anger-laden description lay curdling in his belly. "Wasting the best chance you're likely to get."

Decisions had consequences. *Well, feck, I know that.* He raised his head, elbows on his knees, and scanned his workroom.

He called Lucy, infusing his voice with regret and good humour. "Something's come up. I can't make it tonight." He was no kind of company tonight.

"Of course." Her ready acceptance sparked a different kind of unease. But his mind was a blank. Words dried in his mouth.

The wind-tossed path meandering along the headland above Watsons Bay suited his mood. Stars were pinpricks in a dark-sky-quilt above an even darker sea. No moon, but the lamps lighting his path danced shadows all around him, and white tops coated the waves. His head was packed with shadows tonight.

He'd thought he had plenty of time to make his mark.

Nest eggs were for old men.

In his early twenties, he'd never bothered about making money, because he was too intent on learning his craft. He'd accepted food and board on more than one occasion to work alongside someone with a new skill to offer. He'd given pieces to fellow artisans, who'd admired them but lacked the funds to pay even for his labour.

After meeting his ex-fiancée, Sinead, in Dublin, he'd started to put money aside. Not enough, so when he'd let a friend have a piece at cost, Sinead had gone ballistic. His art had held him in a mad lover's chokehold, she'd claimed, her contempt wild and mean. He was earning peanuts when she had a right to a little luxury. He'd walked away from everything he'd built in Ireland, a fire-sale of belongings. In a desperate act of "you can't hurt me," he'd flown his tools back to Australia first-class freight.

And found a different failure confronting him at home. If he'd had any kind of forethought, he'd have had a bit put by—for Sinead, to pay Liam, to be able to say "thanks, but no thanks" to Cam.

A pub loomed out of the darkness. Music spilled through the door. The smell of fried potatoes mixed with the salt spray, a quintessential Australian scent, beckoned. Through the picture windows, he could see the happy crowd, chatting or dancing or sneaking kisses in corners. Turning his back on the wind, he retraced his path to his vehicle.

If he'd been any kind of provider, he'd be able to access the money to bankroll Lucy until she'd regained her confidence. Folding forward onto his arms across the steering wheel, he shifted through possibilities. One skill he'd mastered was starting with nothing. He could do it again.

This time he had more than nothing. Liam's debt was

almost paid. He could help select the first scholarship winner for Cam's foundation, finish the work he'd agreed to do for Peter and Lucy. He'd surrender the workshop at the end of his original contract with Cam, and Lucy could sell it. He'd explain the situation, ask for the year to sell what he had in storage, to make more, to actively promote his work, to make himself a viable mentor.

Ask Lucy to give him—them—time.

\* \* \*

Lucy tucked her phone back in her pocket. Niall had sounded … "off" in the call, despondent. Hearing the uncharacteristic defeat in his voice scraped at her conscience. She needed her girlfriends, and Kelly was finally back in town.

Thirty minutes later, Lucy walked into a bistro she hadn't been in for months and was directed to a table tucked in a corner. "Thanks." Two women rose at her approach. She hugged one first then the other.

"I've been back in town ten days." Kelly Manners dropped back onto her chair. "We were waiting for you to call."

"Although the clock was ticking down on that." Clementine Gonzales believed in tough love. "One week more was our limit, and that was only because you like to brood your way to a solution."

"Thank you for the feedback." Lucy gave their usual reply when Clem had skewered one of them with her insight, and settled into the cosy-as-Ugg-boots-on-a-winter's-night comfort of a girls' night out.

"I'm sorry I missed the sale night." Kelly held up her hands. "Arabella fell off a ladder I told her she should never have been climbing. I couldn't leave her."

"Is she okay now?" Lucy asked. Arabella Manners was family to Kelly; she'd provided a home for the sixteen-year-old runaway. At eighteen, Kelly had taken Arabella's surname.

"She has titanium for a spine, she tells me." Kelly sighed.

"I'd believe that." Clementine snorted, filling a third flute with their favourite prosecco.

"She dodged a bullet." Kelly shook her head. "Was backing away fast from a dirty big spider, so only fell three steps. On to concrete."

"Only." Lucy winced at the memory of her gran's fall. Arabella Manners was younger and fitter than her gran had been, but accidents were called accidents for a reason. Niall had helped her see that.

"I called the shop the next day"—Kelly continued—"but you were out. Looks like it was a huge success."

"It was," Clementine added. "Jamie and I were early enough for me to pick up a stunning Maud Bowden art deco vase for his mother's birthday."

"You didn't stay long." Lucy didn't mean to sound accusatory. "I wanted to introduce you to Niall—Niall Quinn."

"The man who's been locking you in a workshop on your one free day a week?" Clem was asking a question.

"He knew Grandpa. He talks about Grandpa. In some ways, he's a bit like Grandpa." That realisation surprised her. "I needed the link."

"What ways?"

"He's patient, a bit eccentric." Lucy thought of his mismatched crockery, his insistence on changing seating positions all the time. "Generous, gifted, modest, protective." She hadn't realised she'd collected so many words to describe him.

"Wow! You left out the important one. Hot?" Kelly fanned her face.

"On a scale of one to ten," Clem added.

"Eleven and rising." Lucy grinned.

"Now you're being mean—you know I'm not seeing anyone," Kelly teased.

"That's because you're a workaholic," Lucy pushed

back.

"We've all been guilty of that." Clem stopped smiling.

Someone turned up the background music, the only downside they'd discovered for this bistro. Cyndi Lauper's girl-power anthem 'Girls Just Wanna Have Fun" boomed through the speakers.

"Hey, they're playing our song." Kelly's head swivelled toward the bar. The owner's wife's hand was still on the volume button. "Remember when we made that pact."

"It was after you went to that horrible town with the creepy cop." Lucy had returned to the care home at the same time, after the boy had tried to molest her at the foster home.

"We're not talking about that tonight." Kelly had been sixteen when she'd fled that particular disaster. "Besides, that's ultimately how I met Arabella."

"And Arabella is wonderful."

"It was before Gran and Grandpa found me," Lucy said. "And now they're gone."

"I was the lucky ring-in from the third bed in the room. And Arabella and your gran made sure we hooked up again." Clementine stared into her drink. "No children. That was our pact. Because how would we know what to do, how would we be able to mother a child? A lot's happened since then."

"You mean you've met a wonderful man." Lucy toasted Clem but remembered her own hesitance about entering Kate's nursery.

"Jamie wants to have children."

Kelly set her drink on the table. "That's huge."

"I've asked for time to think." Clementine traced a finger through the condensation on the side of her glass.

"You'd make a wonderful mother, Clem." Lucy touched her hand.

"Jamie says that, but how do you know? What's different about now and then? What if I stuff it up?"

"Jamie won't let you stuff it up," Kelly said matter-of-factly.

"I really love him." Clem sounded exhausted. "Have you told Niall about your childhood demons?"

"I planned to do it tonight, but he had to cancel," Lucy admitted.

Tonight, she'd planned to share all her secrets. To tell him the rest of her story, about the muddled lessons she'd learned from her mum's death, her irrational fear of debt, her conversation with Hunter, and the size of her ridiculous loan. She'd spent her life trying to avoid mistakes and come scarily close with Niall. She'd also planned to apologise for taking advantage of him.

"Sorry, that sounds like you two are the consolation prize."

"I wouldn't have said no to 'hot,'" said Kelly, when all three of them knew Kelly's dog, Boo, vetted all her male companions.

"Are you scared?

"A little." Lucy dribbled the last of the sparkling wine into their glasses.

"Right back at you, sister." Clem grimaced.

"Next bottle's on me." Kelly spoke into the sombre lull following Clem's remark. "My excuse for not seeing you lately is a series of visits to interstate libraries. I've been asked to act in a more senior position, and it might become permanent. I'm about to become an important person in my little world. That gives me the power to banish fear."

"Remember when we …"

Lucy let herself think about Niall for a second, then threw herself into retellings of their childhood disasters and victories. Kelly and Clementine knew many, not all, of her secrets.

A few hours later, Clementine tucked Lucy into a cab and gave the driver Lucy's address. At the first corner, Lucy leaned forward and said, "Wrong address," and recited Niall's instead.

Her friends made her believe she could choose the

future she wanted. She giggled. Niall was gorgeous, all sexy beast and best friend. She'd become accustomed to his smell, to his presence, to him reaching for her in the night, to the simple intimacy of a cuddle and talking about her day and what was ahead. She wanted that tonight.

Tomorrow, when she was sober, she'd tell him the rest of her story.

She paid the cab and watched it drive away before wending—weaving—her way to Niall's gate.

The sensor light on his veranda flashed on. She swung her head to face it. Bright enough so she raised a hand to protect her eyes.

"Hi, Lucy."

"I had dinner with my girlfriends." She hiccupped. "I told them you were sexy and smart, although I used more words." She'd explain everything in the morning. Now, she wanted him to hold her in his arms.

\* \* \*

"Looks like some party." Niall scanned the street. "How'd you get here?"

"Cab." She stumbled up the few steps. "Whoops."

He extended a hand. The scent of her addled what few brains he had left. He disengaged himself. "I should take you home."

"Wanna stay." Her smile was naughty.

Earlier tonight, when he'd called to say he had something on, guilt had stung like a bite from a sand fly. It would have been wrong to hold on to her, when his skin was tight and his limbs heavy with a frustration he couldn't shift. His life had been upended. He had the bare bones of a plan to move forward, but he needed time alone to shape it.

Lucy was solid and good. She wasn't to blame for his mistakes, but for a fleeting second, he wished she hadn't come. The loss of the exhibition was still too raw.

He hadn't had time to parse the loss. He held tight to the joy of creation, of seeing people respond to his work, but making a living from his craft seemed to be drifting further and further from his reach.

Quinns pay their way. He didn't want to be a feckin' mendicant, smooching off McTavish goodwill. Without an independent income, he'd never be Lucy's equal.

Before dawn, Niall woke to find her mouth on his cock and her hand cupping his balls.

"Lucy"—he placed his hand on her shoulder—"wait." But he wasn't sure she heard.

She was everywhere at once, desperate in her need to mate. She straddled him, rocking backward and forward. No gentle touch, just a madness to possess. The physical rush shot through him. His body was responding. Even as she tugged on a condom, he was pumping into her.

"Slow down," he repeated his plea. Tension circled higher and higher. His body teetered on the edge, ready to explode. She tended him, touching the places he'd taught her brought him pleasure. She used every secret he'd given her in tender, endless loving to trigger a sharp, blinding orgasm.

"Has anyone ever told you you could make a living as a lover," she purred and stretched, like a cat warmed by the sun, and the word "fuck buddy" came unbidden to his mind.

"No one important." *Until you.* Niall lay on his back, covering his eyes with his forearm.

She'd told him she was comfortable with her body and sex. Lucy was uninhibited, attentive to his needs, but also taking her own pleasure from him. He wanted that. *Praise the saints*, he wanted her to feel in control, but her throwaway line cut deep, exposing insecurities he'd thought he'd left behind.

Stupid when he'd welcomed similar attentions from her

at other times.

Last night, he decided to talk to Lucy about ways and means so he could stay in her life. This morning he faced reality. Once she'd got past her temporary cash flow problems, she'd still have McTavish's money and a lifestyle alien to him. She'd work out soon enough he was a burden.

*I'm a Class A eejit to think we might have anything lasting together?*

If Cam hadn't thrown them together, they'd never have met; their social circles didn't overlap in any area.

Each day in her workshop, in her home, with her paying his way loaded him with more obligations, more debt. He'd already decided to leave the workshop. She'd be able to sell it immediately and have the financial security she needed to find her balance.

If he refused to be the foundation's mentor, she could choose someone else, someone with a name, with their own studio.

Hell, he could give her a list of names.

They'd never promised forever. She'd never promised forever, while he'd given more of himself each time he touched her, until now he couldn't conceive of a world without her.

Except they lived in different worlds.

"I need to get to work." Niall rolled out of the bed.

"Me too." She propped herself on her elbows, tousled, impossibly beautiful, and—if he was honest—out of his reach. Falling for her was the biggest mistake of his life. She gave a half-smile. "I'll come and say goodbye before I leave."

Niall let himself into the workshop. Frames were propped along one wall, waiting to be picked up. His last commission, because that's the sum he and Liam had agreed. He hadn't told Lucy he'd made his last frames either. Peter's bruiser of a sideboard occupied prime position on the right-hand side of the workshop. He ignored it as well, moving to the kitchenette to make tea.

He opened the fridge. Lucy always cooked more than necessary, leaving him leftovers. She filled the fruit bowl before it was empty, topped up basics in his fridge like he was some bloody beggar. Niall figured this was what a fish felt like after it had been gutted. She'd increased her contributions since they'd started sleeping together, and her charity reinforced his sense of failure. The gallery owner whispered in his ears, "*No reputable gallery owner will touch you.*" Desperation kicked him in the balls.

Without conscious intent, he found himself standing in his storeroom.

He studied his hands, flexing and contracting them until his knuckles burned white. They'd let him down. His hands hadn't worked quickly or cleverly enough to keep up with his dreams. He slammed one fist into his other palm before pushing to his feet. Feck, he was a bad-tempered bastard. And it was a bit bloody late to discover that he'd sabotaged his relationship with Lucy.

To meet as equals, he needed Lucy to witness his success.

By cancelling the exhibition, he'd lost that chance.

"I can't do this anymore!" he roared. He needed the world to stop—needed time out to think. He texted Liam: *I'm refusing the bequest.*

Twenty minutes later, he heard pounding. When he opened the workshop door, he realised Lucy was gone. No goodbye. Probably for the best, given his mood.

"For the love of Mary and Joseph, what the hell are you doing?" Liam pulled him tightly against his chest.

"I can't see any other way." Niall rested his head on his brother's shoulder.

"What can I do?" Liam asked.

"Make it happen fast." Niall walked back to sit at the side table.

His brother swallowed a mouthful of tea. "This is stone, motherless cold. Don't worry. I'll make more. Tell me what you need me to do."

# CHAPTER THIRTEEN

The click of the front door closing reverberated through the small house and into Lucy's body. She groaned and buried her head under Niall's pillow, seeking his scent. Decency and honour melded in the scent and the man, and she'd jumped him like he'd been a stud for hire. She'd been tipsy last night, a last hurrah for demons slayed. Or Clementine's demons slayed. In the middle of second serves of gelato, Clem had blurted out she was going to accept Jamie's proposal.

This morning Lucy had woken still shaken by Clem's decision to become a wife and mother. Her world had turned upside down, and her mum's story had stuck in her throat. Mindless sex had been an escape, and *another mistake*. She'd known before Niall rolled out of bed. He'd withdrawn emotionally. She shivered.

"A goose walked over my grave." Lucy tried to dismiss the sense of foreboding, but it followed her on her search for a towel. "If you explain, he'll understand."

Opening a drawer, she found flyers for a Quinn exhibition and her foreboding became real, sucking the air from her lungs and dropping her to her knees.

An hour later, Lucy spread the promotional material

she'd stolen from Niall's bedroom drawer on her office desk. The tooled, green leather of the antique desktop framed the photographs and blurb promoting a Quinn exhibition. With unsteady hands, she pinned the top of a sample website page with her grandparents' photograph. She used her laptop to pin the bottom. Then she brought up Niall's internet site. No change since the last time she'd looked, but the date and the promise on the sample page was for a Quinn exhibition a week from now in a top Sydney gallery.

Nausea swirled in her stomach. Her body started to tremble as she did more searches of the internet, of social media, of any account she could find where the exhibition might be listed. When she wanted to gag, she covered her mouth with her hand.

*He'd cancelled it.*

Pictures scrolled through her mind. She'd sat at his Huon pine table the first time she'd met him, then it disappeared from the kitchen. Kate insisting on seeing the table, then whispering to Niall. Lucy hadn't heard the words, but she'd picked up distress, which had made no sense then. A storeroom part-stocked with Quinn creations, none of which were listed on his website. He never talked about the occasional items in the middle of his workshop shrouded in sheets. He'd been preparing for this exhibition when Lucy had burst into his home accusing him of fraud and theft and cheating her grandpa.

"What have I done?" she whispered, gripping opposite elbows to control the shaking.

When her phone rang, she checked caller ID and identified Henry Dawson. She froze, fear keeping her silent.

"Lucy, are you there?"

"I'm"—she moistened her mouth—"Lucy McTavish here."

"Why didn't you tell me you were going to refuse the

bequest?" Lucy asked when Niall opened his workshop door a few hours later.

"Henry rang you." His stance changed, bracing for attack, which was fine by her.

"Did you swear him to secrecy?" Lucy strode past him. "Of course he rang me." Unease propelled her toward the side table where they'd shared so many meals and confidences. She halted, disgusted by the lie those memories represented, and spun back to face him. "You didn't give him a plausible reason. Did you plan to explain your duplicity to me? Or just slink away without a word?"

"I never said I'd accept the mentorship." His mouth set in stubborn lines. "Quinns pay their way."

She dragged a hand through her hair and tugged hard. "What the fuck is that supposed to mean?"

"You don't swear." He looked stricken, and he damn well should, while Aretha sang low in the background, *"Chain, chain, chain. Chain of fools."*

"I try not to swear for Gran, but your bastardry inspires me." Lucy wanted him to know he'd hurt her in ways she couldn't yet begin to count.

"I've refused the bequest. That's between me and Cam. Nothing to do with you." He was throwing a cover over his decision like he'd thrown covers to hide his furniture.

"Like hell it's got nothing to do with me. Why now?" The memory of jumping him as if any male would do was dangerous flotsam in her jumbled emotions.

"Cam didn't know he was robbing you by setting me up in the foundation. He'd never have put your financial security at risk." He held his hands wide in a plea for understanding or forgiveness, and she snapped.

"My financial security isn't at risk." Knowing she'd beaten her debt phobia pumped fresh fire into her blood, despite the aching fear she was too late. "I don't have a cash flow problem. I went into a funk after losing Grandpa. I became my ten-year-old self, terrified where my next meal was coming from."

"Right now, you've still got the loan." Niall sounded remote.

He wasn't hearing what Lucy needed him to understand.

"I planned to explain last night. Tell you about that frightened little girl. But I had too much to drink, and this morning …You know what happened this morning." She walked closer and poked her finger into his chest. "Because you went straight from our bed to your brother, Liam, to sever our business connection."

"That's not why." He threw his head back, the muscles in his throat tight cords of tension.

"But refusing the bequest means you don't have to have anything to do with me?" Had the sex repulsed him?

He lowered his head. "I'm trying to separate us from Cam's bequest and money." His gaze was steady while she tried to untangle his reasoning.

"What's us?" She poked him harder in the chest.

Aretha bellowed, "*I'm just a link in your chain.*"

"I'm not sure." Niall rubbed a hand where she'd stabbed him in the heart.

"'Not sure?'" She stamped a foot, the jarring from her court shoe slamming into concrete a different pain. "I'll help you. You don't want to screw me anymore."

"Please don't use that word." He grimaced and stretched a hand toward her.

"Why not? Do you have a better one?" She crossed her arms, rejecting his overture, the adrenalin draining from her system when she spotted the empty spaces behind him. "Where are the new artworks?" She'd been so caught up with the gala she hadn't seen the slides for the new batch.

"I finished the contract." He stared at the empty space with her.

"You've paid Liam." She clutched her stomach, the news a punch to her gut. He was clearing *all* his debts. "Quinns may pay their way, but that doesn't make you honourable." Aretha sang while Lucy's heart stalled. "Why didn't you tell me about the exhibition?"

\* \* \*

Niall closed his eyes. She looked more fragile and lost than the day he'd met her. "How did you find out?"

"I went looking for a towel this morning and found Anna's sample webpage printouts filed under face washers." She retraced her steps to stand beside the table under the window.

His limbs ached with the weight of his decision.

"At first it wasn't relevant. We were strangers. Your passion is antiques. Mine is crafting the new." Niall studied his hands, then pushed them into his pockets. "Then I agreed to help you restore a few pieces."

"Because you owed Grandpa?"

"I didn't want my success to be at the price of your peace of mind."

She'd needed him, whether she'd known it or not.

"You owed Grandpa, and you pitied me. That's insulting." She was visibly donning body armour, her shoulders straightening, her spine stiffening, because without meaning to, he'd painted her as a victim.

"I've just spent a year making bloody frames to pay my brother back. I didn't want another debt I'd spend years regretting." His justifications sounded pathetic spoken aloud. "But my feelings for you were—are—complicated."

"You're not making me feel any better."

"Your dream is to keep McTavish's running, and you worked out the best way to do that. My dream was my business. What right did I have to insist my dream was more important than yours? You needed some financial breathing space. I thought I could juggle all the balls at once. If I'd told you about the exhibition, you'd have felt guilty for asking me to work."

"Or I might have seen the importance of the exhibition to Grandpa's foundation," she said solemnly. "You didn't give me a chance."

"What do you mean?" He was weary of fighting his critics, himself and now her.

"The chance to decide if my dream was more important than yours. If I could achieve mine differently. If your dream was a better way of honouring my grandparents."

She'd been consumed by despair when she'd met him. Not the most rational starting point to make clear decisions. Niall knew because he'd been there.

"My brother put his dream on hold to pay back my father's debts. I never knew the truth, until we talked last year."

"And not talking to your brother gives you the right to make all the decisions in our relationship?" She shook her head at his highhandedness.

"I told you my da died suddenly. Shortly before he died, Da was swindled by an Irish woman. Da asked me to check out someone when I got to Ireland. I made a few calls, got a few 'not available at the moment' brush-offs, and didn't push hard enough. After all, I was doing something important. I was a big man. I'd won a prized mentorship. People were keen to meet and be with me." He'd swaggered all over the place, keen to buy strangers a beer, stuffed to the gills with ill-fitting pride.

"If I'd pushed harder, sooner, I might have found out she was a swindler." He stared at Lucy, breathing hard, his heart and mind still ruptured. "My da might have kept his money and his life."

"Does Liam know you blame yourself for your father's death?" Her face had softened, and her pity was as unwelcome to him as his was to her.

"I've told him about what Da wanted me to do."

"What did he say?"

"That he and a private detective spent months trying to track the woman and the funds down. They drew blanks again and again when they thought they had a lead." Niall had interviewed the private detective and found no gaps in their research.

"But if *you'd* persisted in those few days you had before his death, you'd have solved everything. That's remarkably arrogant. It's worse than arrogant not to tell me about the exhibition when it has material bearing on the success of the foundation. And it's monumentally stupid to think Grandpa would class me as disposable property in his will."

"You think I'm a patronising idiot. Face facts. You can rent or sell this property as you originally planned. You'll have the funds to establish Cam's foundation, and I can stop second-guessing myself about what the hell crazy plan he had in his head." Niall cursed himself for his incoherence.

"You've got no idea what you've done," she accused. "Whereas I have to live with the knowledge that every decision I've made from the day I met you has led to you having no workshop, no home, and no exhibition." Each criticism landed like a whip tip on the tenderest of his extremities.

"I didn't expect to fall for you." *Not the time for this confession, Quinn.*

"You're claiming you've fallen for me?" She scoffed, and he deserved her disbelief.

"Restoring furniture took time out of my schedule." Niall took a half-step toward her, and she stepped back. "Wanting to be with you was the bigger issue. I didn't want you to feel responsible for me not doing my own work."

"Arrogant and blind. Not a pretty combination from where I'm standing."

"Maybe not." He'd spent hours trying to balance all the equations and failed. "But my self-respect is important to me. I'm not a good provider." In defence, he voiced the bitterness building since he'd added up all the contributions she, not Cam, made to his budget. Poison she didn't deserve spilled out of his mouth, because self-respect had to count for something. "Not the right kind of man for the heir to the McTavish estate, who, when the dust settles, is stupidly rich. I can't be a pet poodle, bankrolled by your money."

"Screw you, Niall." She threw a hand in the air, like a

toreador signalling the coup-de-grace was imminent. "Now you're being offensive. You object to me cooking you a few meals, paying for a few groceries. Your family has shown me hospitality.

"You keep adding to my debts." Like a punch-drunk fighter, he listened to himself blame her.

Her head jerked back, as if hit by an uppercut to the jaw. "You don't owe me anything." Her voice cracked. "If anything, I owe you. That's what I wanted to tell you last night. I finally figured it out."

"Figured what out?"

"My demand for you to restore furniture was miserable, bloody, unreasonable, and unfair. You should have called me on it." She whirled in a circle, her distress like a whirling dervish's skirt, keeping him at a distance. "I was incapable of seeing the bigger picture—the connection between your work and the mentorship. You should have told me. Instead, you've rejected Grandpa's bequest."

"I don't need charity." His hands formed fists.

"Grandpa wasn't offering charity—"

"I'd be taking money under false pretences. I'm not a suitable mentor."

"The exhibition would have given you publicity and showcased your work. Grandpa knew that. I bet he also knew how stiff-necked you are and how you dread being beholden to anyone. He was offering you a chance to repay a debt that's largely in your head by mentoring people in his foundation.

"I haven't offered charity either. Friends help each other. But you won't accept help from me. You throw it back in my face, with the most obscene insult you can think of— charity! *I* haven't shown you an inch of charity." She turned on her heel and paced across the floor. "I demanded you restore furniture when you'd already squared your account with Grandpa. I offered your skills to rich collectors who could wait for their restoration. You turned me into a thief. *A thief.*" She stopped, her gaze stricken. "I didn't focus on the right things," she groaned.

"What things?" he asked, afraid of the defeat dragging at her body and echoing in her voice. She was revealing something important, and he couldn't read the cues.

"It doesn't matter." She waved him away.

"*What* things?" he almost shouted.

"You're a brilliant craftsman. I kept wondering why you didn't do more with it. Why you'd settle for restoring furniture, even though it's a desperately hard time to crack the market. I accepted your excuses despite them being inconsistent with the man I was getting to know." She shivered, tears filling her eyes. "Because I didn't push, didn't ask the right questions, didn't open the right door, I've left you to die."

"That's melodramatic crap," he protested, although her insight, that cancelling the exhibition was a kind of death felled him. Watching tears he'd caused spill down her cheeks, he took a step forward, but she held up a hand to stop him.

"It's not melodrama." She scrubbed the tears from her cheeks. "It's a tragedy."

"I care about you, Lucy."

"Not enough to tell me what's important to you. Not enough to trust me with your dreams. Not enough to tell me you're dying inside, because that's what the last few weeks have been about. You've been locking me out bit by bit." She lashed him with the truth.

"I'm thirty-four and can't make enough money to support myself much less anyone else."

"You need to take a hard look at yourself. You've been making a living for yourself and profit to share with your brother. You have numerous options to make a living for yourself, but you claim the only real one is Furniture by Quinn. Maybe you're just afraid, Niall. That you haven't got what it takes to be a master craftsman." She cut through to the underbelly of his insecurity. "That if you come out into the harsh light of day, you'll be shown to be wanting."

"Without Cam's advice and money, I wouldn't have considered an exhibition." Creatives breathed doubt every minute of every day, although he'd started stockpiling pieces before he met Cam.

"Keep telling yourself that bullshit. At the risk of repeating myself"—she sounded annihilated—"you've cancelled the exhibition. You've refused the chance to do your own work and mentor others. You're moving out."

He nodded. "I'll leave at the end of the initial agreement period."

"So, you've decided that in a few weeks you'll give up your home and your workshop." She skewered him with her contempt. "Worst of all, you've shown disrespect to my grandpa."

"You're wrong. I respect him. More than I can say."

"Look around you." Her gaze travelled around the room. "You're squandering his belief in you. Why? Sainthood or martyrdom?"

"I don't have the pieces for an exhibition," he roared, his hands forming fists.

"Your brother and his wife have a cradle and a table, maybe more ..." She stopped with her back to him, her spine rigid, and her courage highlighted his cowardice. "You've made other sales. You could assemble an exhibition by borrowing back some of your best pieces instead of wallowing in manufactured guilt about Cam and me." She grabbed her bag and headed for the door.

"Don't leave," Niall called, searching for a better way to explain himself. He'd made the wrong choices, not her.

"You're the one who's leaving," she said.

The door banged shut.

* * *

Lucy clung to her righteous rage for three blocks because he *had* left her. He'd bolted from her bed and torpedoed their business and personal relationship. Her hands gripped the steering wheel until her knuckles bled white. *Damn the setting sun.* Bouncing off her rear mirror, it was an obscene reminder the planet continued to turn on its axis, when her world had come to a stumbling halt. She tried to swallow the sobs building in her body. Chest heaving, she pulled into the side of the road, her blurred vision making it impossible to identify hazards.

*"Don't leave."*

Meaningless words when his actions and the dramatic changes in his workspace screamed "*I'm moving on.*"

No new frames only told half the tale. Niall was working on Peter's half-finished piece on a Saturday, not using the Mondays she'd handed back to him. The other half of the story leaked through his small resentments. He objected to her filling his fruit bowl, cooking him the occasional meal, whereas he'd offered her cake and conversation and a space to grieve too many times to number. He'd locked her out, even if he hadn't admitted it to himself.

"You lied by omission," she whispered to the shadows sharing her car. "You didn't tell me about the exhibition."

Fear beat a relentless tattoo in her blood because she'd hurt him. She loved him, and if the major gallery he'd been booked with spread the word he was unreliable, no other major gallery would take a chance on him for years. Realising the harm she'd caused, she screamed every cuss she'd learnt as a child, filling the car with curses.

*Damn me to hell because I lied too.*

Lucy hadn't told him about her demons; she was irrationally terrified of having no money, she still blamed herself for not being able to save her mother and gran. Even when she'd had the chance to tell him this morning, she'd frozen. Last night, her girlfriends had issued a new challenge—a week to exorcise her childhood devils. But Clementine and Kelly didn't know all Lucy's secrets.

And Niall's unhappiness had bubbled too near the surface for Lucy to take the risk, especially when she couldn't put her finger on the cause of his discontent. This morning, she'd promised herself there was time, without realising time had been up days, if not weeks, ago. She dashed a hand across her cheek to swipe away fresh tears. The McTavish wealth repelled him as well.

Automatic doors and sensor lighting guided her safely into her garage. The bright lights stung her eyes, hurrying her from the car and into the quietness of the garden, where the scent of Gran's beloved gardenias hung in the air. Lucy sank onto the stone bench set amongst them, letting their soft perfume comfort her as it had when she'd first arrived here.

She'd sabotaged whatever she and Niall might have had. At their first meeting, she'd accused him of theft and fraud as a distraction from missing Grandpa. He'd served her sandwiches and tea in mismatched crockery and absorbed every blow she'd delivered. Her grief-charged rage had set the tone for their relationship. Niall had been a stranger, yet he'd provided a bulwark at her back when she'd worried about money, and when they'd met the over-perfumed Tomas Bechet.

He'd allowed her to hide in his workshop Monday after Monday and pretend she was helping.

An honourable man, who saw her as an obligation, while she'd been falling in love for the first time in her life.

He'd pitied the grieving granddaughter and resented the antiques heiress.

"I don't want to be seen as less or more but equal." She sighed to the night breeze. Lifetimes together aren't built on power games or secrets.

She pushed herself to her feet, her limbs dragging on the walk to the door. Her house smelled of Niall, and that was pure imagination. His woody fragrance might linger in her room because he'd left a few of his clothes and toiletries there, but nowhere else. She baulked at her bedroom door, unwilling to sleep alone in the bed they'd shared. Arriving in this house as a world-weary ten-year-old, she'd claimed she was too old to climb into Gran and Grandpa's bed.

Gran had poohpoohed her objections after Lucy's first nightmare. Night after night, Gran had spooned against Lucy's back when she couldn't sleep, ready with a made-up story about one of the shop's treasures. Her soft-voiced stories were part history lesson, part travelogue and pure comfort.

"I miss you, Gran." *And the safety of discovering I was still lovable.*

Why did Niall's desertion have to be darker and heavier than other losses?

Aching in every cell of her body, she crawled between the sheets of Grandpa and Gran's bed. Her grandparents had owned the big four-poster all their married life and by example had shown her the best of love. She curled into a tight ball.

When she woke, her body was stiff. Glancing around the room, she was momentarily disoriented, before the memory of her conversation with Niall tumbled back.

"You've shown disrespect to my grandpa," she should have added, "And me. You've disrespected me."

Anger had always worked for her, a crutch to propel her through the worst moments of her life. In the past, a lot of her anger had been self-directed. When her mum had died, she was child enough to accept the blame. Anger deserted her now. Black misery was her new companion, and it made her clear-sighted.

"I wasn't to blame for Mum's death." She rolled her shoulders, shedding doubts that had dogged most of her life. "I made mistakes with Niall, but I won't take all the blame for his unhappiness. I deserve to be trusted.

"I deserve the right to help.

"I deserve to be loved."

Lifting her head in the shower, she let warm water cascade over her hair, her face and down her body. She turned around, nudging the temperature up a notch. Hot needles of spray massaged her back, and a plan plopped fully formed into her mind.

A black suit, a white shirt and the reflection in her mirror showed a pale-faced businesswoman, who'd probably spend her life alone. Adding Niall's green scarf was an act of defiance. In the kitchen, she made tea and started making calls.

"I'll be late at McTavish's. If you need me urgently, I can be reached through Henry Dawson's office."

*I have options, if I choose to use them.*

*I can change my mind.*

*I can—I do—refuse to be powerless.*

Lucy loved Niall, but love didn't mean a damn thing without mutual trust. She'd dared to dream Niall was beginning to love her. She'd been wrong. "*I'm sorry for your loss*" had metastasized to an obligation, which for him had drifted from the friendly to the lustful to the how-the-hell-did-I get-myself-into-this-mess?

She'd probably never get another chance to tell Niall her secret. That she was terrified of making mistakes that led to physical harm for the people she loved. She'd been so busy guarding against one kind of mistake, she'd tumbled over a different precipice. She'd worried about his physical well-being, even his financial well-being, whereas self-confidence was his soft underbelly.

*Pity it took you so long to work that out.*

"Stop your dreamin'." She shivered as the loneliness of the empty house pressed against her. Her new plan might not work, but fair play demanded she try. Grandpa had written a story about his wishes and Niall's future. She needed to finish that story.

An hour later, Lucy sat in her lawyer's office.

"What you're proposing isn't legal." Henry was probably regretting giving up his weekend for her.

"It's ethical"—she'd driven her staid, pillar-of-the-community lawyer to uncharacteristic snappiness—"and the only way I can think of to ensure Niall benefits from Grandpa's bequest."

"It's his right to refuse." He lifted a hand, and she waited for him to snatch at his hair in frustration, but he lowered his beautifully manicured paw and pressed his palm flat on his desk.

"Whisht! He's only refusing because I messed it up." Lucy's heart sank. She couldn't fail at the first hurdle. "Tell me honestly. If you'd notified him, and I'd stayed out of it and away from him, do you think he'd be refusing the bequest now?"

"Maybe. He's a proud man."

"Pride and stubbornness are second cousins." She huffed out a breath.

"What's going on, Lucy?" Henry was back to being calm and calculating, having dissected her outlandish request into its various parts.

"He'd scheduled an exhibition. Given his skill, it's likely it would have cemented his name and reputation and been a launchpad for his mentoring role in the foundation."

She'd stolen every moment of time she could get with Niall, stolen time from his work.

"I was floundering, missing Grandpa so much I wasn't seeing straight. We both know I didn't really need money from Niall. Imagining debt everywhere I looked was sheer panic on my part. But he gave up days to my restoration projects, and minutes and hours and half days when I dropped in unannounced to talk about Grandpa. He cancelled his exhibition."

"You blame yourself?" He steepled his hands on his desk.

"The bulk of the evidence points that way." *Although I've decided to apportion blame equally.* "He's convinced he's not a suitable mentor."

"You do know anyone in Australia can ask to see a copy of a deceased's will?"

"Isn't there some other kind of legal agreement that might work? A codicil?" She sighed. "I'm trying to buy some time here, make him rethink his decision."

"A cooling-off period?" Henry's eyes twinkled. "What

are you planning to do in the meantime?"

"I'm still working on it." Niall had said "*don't leave*." He'd left a door slightly ajar. She'd be a fool not to look inside.

# CHAPTER FOURTEEN

Niall waited on his porch for his brother, the image of Lucy from the first Sunday she'd visited him crystal clear in his mind. Exhausted, grieving, and even then, he'd been shaken by her courage. He was bigger than her, stronger than her, and she'd been prepared to confront him on behalf of her grandpa. He admired the hell out of the way she wouldn't turn tail when she was afraid.

She hadn't known why Bechet scared her, still she'd dealt with him professionally and regularly.

Her grandpa had told her stories to distract her while he was dying, and she'd played Cam's game to comfort him.

She'd told Niall about the whispers following her gran's death. Told him her lover had accused her of being deliberately out of the room when she was babysitting her gran. The bastard's betrayal would have hit harder than a back-hander and felled any other woman. She'd retained her dignity and goodness. Because after Niall and she had found their rhythm, everything she'd done for him had been driven by kindness.

She'd eased his guilt about his da's death using logic, compassion and a smack of rage to acquit him of neglect.

She thought he'd kept the exhibition secret because he

didn't trust her. Why hadn't he seen he'd fixed the game to make her blame herself?

"Waiting for me?" Liam called from the gate.

"Thinking," he replied. "Come on in."

Sitting opposite each other in the kitchen, Liam hauled a bottle of Jameson's from his briefcase and set it on the table. "You'll want a drink for what I have to say."

"I'm guessing the sun's over the yardarm somewhere in the Irish-speaking world"—Niall leaned back on the chair legs to collect two Vegemite jars and set them on the table—"but you're making me nervous."

"You deserve to be nervous. I met Lucy's lawyer this afternoon." Liam splashed whiskey into both jars.

"Maybe I need water." Niall pushed his chair back this time and crossed to the sink.

"Only if you plan to swim."

"Was Lucy there?" Niall set a jug of water on the table but swallowed a mouthful of raw spirit. He was hungry for a sight of her after twenty-four hours.

"We were the only witnesses."

"That sounds ominous." Niall stared into his jar, the lingering taste of Jameson's nutty tones no balm for his building panic. He'd made Lucy cry.

"Fascinating is closer to the truth. I emailed Mr. Dawson the letter refusing the bequest. He acknowledged receipt. Today he asked for a meeting." His brother let the words hang in the air. Working on a Sunday. Not good.

"Tell me." Niall had met Henry, a master of the non-committal expression.

"He told me there's a codicil to Cam's will." Liam poured water into his jar, swirled it, then looked up. "If you reject the bequest as it stands, you're to receive fifty thousand dollars cash."

"Praise the saints. She doesn't have that sort of money on hand." Niall slammed his jar on the table. "Do you believe him?"

"Stop abusing the fine glassware," Liam muttered. "And

I don't like my chances if I accuse Henry Dawson, a lawyer with a sterling reputation, of lying about a will. But, no, I don't believe him. What did you do for Lucy to rub your nose in her wealth?"

"I said she was stupidly rich," he confessed with the penitence of a devout Catholic. "That I couldn't be a pet poodle."

"You're some kind of dumb ass. What brought that tirade on?"

"She stocked my fridge."

"What *was* she thinking?" His brother's sarcasm made Niall wince. "I might have to go down to McTavish's and abuse her myself."

"Don't mock me. It might sound like a small thing, but it was the last in a long line—" He stopped, appalled by what he was saying.

"Of kind actions." His brother finished for him. "You tend to show your feelings through actions rather than words. Sometimes you need to say the words."

"She said I turned her into a thief." Whereas for a man who insisted his self-respect was inviolable, he'd made her question the honesty of every moment they'd shared, and triggered an old pain.

Liam whistled.

"Can I refuse this bequest too?"

"I asked if there were other codicils? He suggested there might be a series of escalating offers, each more valuable than the last. Then he smiled, part white-pointer shark and part guppy."

"That can't be legal." Niall raised his jar to his mouth then set it down untouched. "Can it?"

"I've not come across something like this before." His brother drummed his fingers on the table. "I did say there were no witnesses."

"Why is she doing this?" Niall rose to pace his small kitchen, struggling to reconcile the Lucy who was careful with money to the profligacy of this potentially endlessly rising offer.

"You've given notice that you're leaving in a few weeks, leaving you without a home or a workshop. You've cancelled the exhibition and rejected secure employment with the foundation. You've beggared yourself and made her feel responsible." Liam took a small sip of his drink.

"I didn't want her to think I was hanging on to the foundation because of the money. Without the exhibition, I'm not mentor material." Niall returned to the table, picked up the drink, stared once more at its contents, and set it down.

"Do you blame Lucy for losing the exhibition?" Liam asked.

"She asked if I was aiming for sainthood or martyrdom." Niall scrubbed his face. "Anna says we get that from Da."

"If you said Lucy was stupidly rich and you couldn't be her pet poodle, then I'm not surprised." His brother toasted him, then downed another mouthful of fine whiskey. "You've made her wealth the issue, and she was supposed to hear 'I love you'?"

"She's terrified of debt, of not being in control, yet she risked ruining herself to have twenty-four-seven, hospital-in-the-home care when Cam got ill." Niall was missing something.

"Offering you fifty K puts a lot of money in play now."

"I've got it all wrong." Niall slammed his fist into his other palm.

"You're alone with that, boyo, because I'm always right."

"We'd need years to list all your wrong decisions, but I'm happy to make a start." Niall allowed himself to be momentarily distracted.

Liam splashed more water into Niall's whiskey. "Okay, I've made the odd mistake."

"I didn't follow up for Da, because I was basking in the glory of the mentorship." Niall scratched at the old scar. Liam, meanwhile, had been paying their father's debts to let Niall finish his mentorship and build a career in Ireland.

Liam's sacrifice hadn't been Niall's first seed of self-doubt, but guilt had landed in fertile ground.

"For the love of Mary and Joseph, we dealt with that. We did. There's something you're not telling me about Ireland." His brother visibly scrolled through his prodigious memory. "You were coming home with a woman and then you weren't. We weren't talking enough then for me to ask why."

"Sinead changed her mind."

"Why?" His brother had honed his cross-examination skills since childhood. He practised silence as torture.

"She said I only cared about the craft and the glory, never mind food on the table. She was right. I wasn't about to give up my dream for anyone, even the woman I planned to marry," Niall said. Her words were the poison he'd tried and failed to dislodge from his mind, feeding his doubt about his grand plan for his future.

"What else?" his brother demanded.

"What do you mean, 'what else'? Isn't that enough?" He swallowed, his mouth suddenly dry.

"You've never mentioned her, so you can't have been too desperately in love with her. I'm guessing there was a sting in the tail."

"She called me a 'fuck buddy,' said I'd make a better living selling sex instead of furniture." Confiding in his brother lessened the horror somehow.

"And Lucy's paying you for sex." Liam's expression was flat.

"She's wealthy. I'm living rent free in a property she owns," he let fly. It sounded crazy saying it aloud. But Niall had been weary in body and soul when he'd arrived back in Australia, and seeking to find his balance ever since. "And that's insulting to both of us. But what the hell does it look like?"

"You tell me." His brother's steady gaze locked onto his.

"She hates debt, but doesn't care about money." *And I'm a feckin' eejit.* "Family. That's what counts, and she keeps losing it."

"And that insight gets us precisely where in unravelling this puzzle?" His brother was watching Niall fumble his way to some truth Liam had already worked out. "Sinead was wrong. You've spent the past year making frames, which require little of your genius to produce, to pay me back. In the past few months you've added restoring pieces for Lucy and for her fancy client. You take work to pay the bills. You've also made the cradle and alphabet toys for me, Anna's got a new mirror, and I bet you've got a design for Lucy on the go. You more than pay your way. I'm proud of you, and I admire you."

"I love you." Niall knocked back the rest of his whiskey.

"Good thing I watered yours. Did you hear what you just said?"

Liam balanced on the tipped-back chair while Niall joined the dots. For the people he loved, Niall always found time. Ipso facto, he hadn't loved Sinead.

"What about Lucy?"

"I love her too."

"Have you told her?"

"She's too angry to listen to me."

"Do something so she's not angry." Liam made it sound easy.

"The only thing that might make her listen is if I organise another exhibition." Short of grovelling, an exhibition was the only idea Niall had.

"Should be child's play if you put your mind to it." Liam drained his jar. "I'll tell Lucy's most unorthodox lawyer we're considering his very generous offer. We need a fortnight."

"Will he accept?" Niall asked. Without Lucy, two weeks stretched to eternity. Two weeks was the timetable from hell to organise an exhibition.

"I feel sure I can convince him a matter of such significance needs a little time to contemplate." His brother pushed to his feet, a man ready to move mountains on

Niall's behalf.

"Lucy's seriously pissed off. She might not talk to me again even with an exhibition." Niall met his brother's gaze, seeking reassurance.

"When you're down to one option, it makes sense to go with it."

Two weeks later Niall leaned against a wall in a grand, whitewashed warehouse space. The spartan cavern showcased his work better than the gallery he'd originally signed with, and the vestibule display provided a slice of what visitors could expect. He figured he'd chatted and glad-handed everyone in the room, because he owed himself and his family the courtesy of making this show a success. From the smile on Kate's face when she placed red dots on various pieces, people were buying as well as looking.

With his family's help, he'd managed to assemble about thirty pieces, including frames and Lucy's washstand in the vestibule. Part of his apology to her. Part of making peace with who he was and what he might become, if Lucy listened to him.

Only there was no Lucy, and he hadn't prepared for her no-show.

Pushing off the wall, he fixed a smile on his face and prepared to re-enter the fray. In three weeks, he'd leave Cam's workshop. He had an unsigned contract for a smaller space further out of town and was so exhausted he'd almost forgotten his name.

"She's not coming." Niall tugged at the silk tie Anna had brought with her tonight and insisted he wear.

"She's not here *yet*," Anna replied.

"She hates being late. Did she tell you she was coming?" he demanded, because he needed hope to sustain him for the next hour.

"Not in so many words." Anna grabbed the lapels of his

jacket and manoeuvred him around to face her. "This is the last time I'm fixing this tie. Now stand still and look at me as if you're interested in what I have to say and simply ecstatic at how the show's going."

Niall looked at her. She and Kate had sweated blood to get this show together in the tight timeframe. "I can't thank you enough." He kissed her forehead.

"Yes, you can. I won't get tired of hearing how grateful you are for, oh, I'd say a decade or more." Anna patted his tie. "Did you send Lucy an invitation?"

"I sent two, one to her at McTavish's and one to the house."

"Leave the man alone." Hunter arrived at Anna's shoulder. "We know she got the one at McTavish's because I recognise half this crew from her spring gala sale. Her customers have eclectic tastes, or else she strong-armed them."

Kate waddled up and took Niall's right arm.

"I feel surrounded," he murmured.

"If you still plan on saying a few words, you should say them soon, whether Lucy's here or not." Kate was staring at the entrance. "Your mum's keeping watch and will let us know as soon as Lucy arrives."

"How did you convince Mum to leave Newcastle?"

"You're kidding. She wouldn't miss her brilliant son's exhibition for quids, plus she was due a visit to talk babies with me." Kate patted her large baby bump.

Crazy to feel excitement and a gnawing emptiness at the same time, but Niall's last two weeks had been spent on a seesaw tipping from exhilaration at finally achieving a goal he'd worked for to despair at Lucy's absence. In a strange way having the fake codicil hanging over his head formed some connection, as did finishing her washstand. He'd buried himself in work, creating smaller pieces and designing more.

Sleep eluded him. When he closed his eyes, he saw Lucy standing on the other side of the room. Each time he took a step toward her, she stepped back, and the distance between them became endless. He woke in a sweat.

The idea to display drawings of new designs came to him in a rare, hopeful dream. Lucy had been standing at his shoulder in the workshop, looking at drawings for Leopold's picture frames, and he'd heard her voice in his ear: "*Whatever you do, it's the same basic principle. People buy based on the design. If they see a finished product, they buy more.*"

Hard as it was to accept, Leopold's had provided him with options. They'd told him to come back if he was interested in a new contract, offered a deal based on three or six monthly deliveries, rather than every few weeks. He could enjoy designing frames if the job was a one-off, not a necessity to pay down debt.

"The natives are getting restless, despite our fine selection of beer and peanuts." Anna interrupted his thoughts. "Showtime."

"Don't listen to her," Hunter said. "I added fine wine and canapes to the spread. The punters are stuffing themselves and can wait until you're ready. If there's no speech, so be it. To be honest, the works speak for themselves, carpenter. I'm very impressed."

More praise, and still this hollow in his stomach.

Would Lucy let him in if he turned up on her doorstep? Begging held growing appeal.

\* \* \*

The warehouse hosting Niall's exhibition sat on the other side of the quiet suburban street. Still, Lucy hesitated, her stomach switching to some vicious internal spin cycle, making it hard to stay upright. She reached instinctively for her pearls. Her thumb and forefinger moved from gem to gem as she recited the lessons her gran had taught her. Honesty was essential for love to survive. Forgiveness came a close second. She hadn't been honest any more than Niall had, and she wasn't sure he'd forgive her.

*But he'd listen.*

Because he was an honourable man—stubbornly honourable some days. She exhaled to the count of six and settled.

She pushed through the entrance doors to a large vestibule, and gasped. Her washstand was spot-lit on a raised dais, meticulously restored using the Breccia Oniciata pink marble Grandpa had stored for decades and her gran's beloved jug and basin set. Her gaze flew to the flyer advertising the exhibition taped above it. The print copy was about three metres by four, showcasing the Huon pine table, with Lucy's bowl filled with lemon and ruby grapefruit toward one end. The caption *Quinn, by design* was artfully scribbled across the other end of the table in the poster.

"The contrast does rather take one's breath," said a white-haired woman sitting at a simple, elegant Queensland walnut table near the entrance. Lucy would swear the table was a Quinn original and the woman his mother—she had the same grey eyes.

"I thought the exhibition was of Niall's furniture." Lucy absorbed the multiple images. On the left-hand side wall were a half-dozen frames of different sizes, each holding a copy or a fragment of the poster. On the opposite wall were six framed mirrors, reflecting the posters, and the washstand. The message seemed to be *I'm all of this.*

If there was a clue to whether he'd accept Cam's bequest or call her bluff in this display, she couldn't interpret it.

"Niall's *work*," the woman explained.

"I'm guessing this is a family affair?" A redundant question when Lucy knew the Quinn and Turner twins fiercely defended their own. Kate had called at McTavish's to collect the fruit bowl, absolving or depriving Lucy of a chance to drop it off. She could have insisted on delivering it and on seeing Niall. But the two weeks Liam had requested to consider her cash offer flashed as loudly as any *No Trespassers* sign. "The poster looks like an Anna design."

"You know my daughter-in-law's sister?" Niall's

mother's expression held the same mix of shrewd speculation and kindness as her son's. Lucy had known Anna was family, but the warmth in Mrs. Quinn's voice confirmed it.

"I've met her." The loss of Lucy's family was a permanent ache. "Was it her idea to change his business name? I like Quinn, by design."

"Niall's idea." The woman glanced at something on her phone. "I'm his mother, Mary. Just for our records, are you already on our invitation list, or were you lured by Anna's clever advertising?"

"An invitation." Relief had blinded her to the content of the flyer, although it had contained a fragment of the poster. More importantly, the personal invitation gave Lucy a legitimate reason to see him, to see his exhibition, and to apologise for her messy temper tantrum. If the opportunity to ask what he planned to do about Cam's bequest came up, she'd take that too, because the two-week deadline expired tomorrow. Niall's mother was waiting for her to introduce herself. "I'm Lucy McTavish."

"Cam's granddaughter," Mary said matter-of-factly.

"You knew Grandpa?"

"I met him once, but he believed in my boy, so I was inclined to like him. I can take you through if you like." She checked the front door. "I doubt many more will come. The show's closing soon."

"Please don't. I'm sure you're busy. I'm happy just to wander around," Lucy gushed. The older woman held up a hand, and Lucy shut her mouth, before she developed verbal diarrhoea. The Quinn and Turner families had believed in Niall for years, whereas she'd almost cost him this chance. "I'm sorry I'm late." Lucy didn't want company for her first conversation with Niall since their fight.

"Whisht, lassie. No need to apologise. You're here now," Mary said, revealing more shared qualities with her son. "Some of your friends visited earlier. At least, I assume they were friends because they listed you as the source of their information about the show."

"I forwarded the invitation to a few people." She'd created McTavish history by promoting an exhibition other than their own, but hadn't hesitated before forwarding the invitation to her entire client list with a strong personal recommendation. "I guess I follow the music and chatter."

The music was a subtle riff underscoring the hum of cheerful voices. Mary waved her through the door. The single large room with bare rafters, double-height windows, white-washed walls and polished cement floors didn't pretend to be a professional gallery, but someone with a clever eye had turned it into a cathedral of art. Probably Anna, but Niall would have known the empty spaces would draw the visitor's gaze to the elegant simplicity of his designs.

Niall was responsible for Icehouse's national anthem *Great Southern Land* playing in the background. Australian pop royalty backed by a full orchestra and choir suited the blend of awe-inspiring old and new creations spread out before her. Niall's skill was formidable, but his artistry stole her breath.

Despite the grandeur of the space, the Huon table attracted all eyes. Lucy recognised pieces from the storeroom, plus Liam and Kate's table and cradle. An exquisite mirror decorated with a frieze of gumnuts was new to her. She smiled involuntarily. She'd bet Gran's pearls he'd designed it for a child. A girl.

"Hello, Lucy." The wrong voice spoke near her ear.

"Hello, Hunter." She liked the man, but he wasn't Niall. "Have you been delegated to see me out?"

"We both know you have an invitation." He slipped an arm around her waist, as if he feared she'd disappear. "Unless you're planning on doing something to get yourself thrown out?"

"I needed to see his success." She surveyed the animated crowd, noting the sold dots on every item. Some really were for sale. "It *is* a success, isn't it?"

"Financially, it's a success. Creatively, it's a success. But there are other measures."

"Now you're talking in riddles." She freed herself. "Niall deserves the creative and financial success."

"Money and fame aren't enough to nourish the soul." Hunter was notoriously private, making his low-voiced reflection echo like a confession.

"Without buyers, he can't make furniture." She'd thought Niall had doubted he'd find buyers for his designs. Hunter upended her assumptions. Niall's father's debts hadn't brought him home. They'd been his welcome. What had brought him home? "If you haven't been delegated to throw me out, and we're agreed I'm not here to make a fuss, why are you shadowing me?"

His dimple appeared with his grin, making her see why Anna was attracted. "Moral support. And any other support you want."

"That's kind. But Niall and I have unfinished business, so I'll have to speak to him at some point."

"And you think there's safety in a crowd?" He *tsked*. "You poor, deluded woman."

"Is he here?" She hungered for a glimpse of him. She'd taken a happy snap of him in his workshop one day. Lucy had known she was lovesick when she'd started carrying a print copy in the sleeve of her phone, checking it more often than incoming calls.

"Ladies and gentlemen." Niall stepped onto a small stool, so he stood above the crowd.

She couldn't tear her gaze from him. The workshop photo missed his power—a facsimile of a good-looking man. Energy and a sense of purpose bounced off him.

*Please accept Grandpa's bequest. You don't have to deal with me if you don't want to.*

"Thank you all for coming tonight. It's a pleasure to see familiar faces." Niall's gaze rested on her. "And faces I hope will become familiar as years pass. Quinn, by design is my work, but the result of the faith and support of many people.

Two people not here deserve special mention. My father, Mick Quinn, who planted the passion for wood in me, and Cameron McTavish, who's been a more generous patron than I deserve. My extended family have been relentless in helping put this show on." A woman nearby cheered. "Liùsaidh McTavish has been an inspiration. To all of you, my thanks."

The world stopped. The music died. Lucy could hear her heart pounding. Niall had called her Liùsaidh before his closest family. *An inspiration.* Mary had been generous with her welcome, but she was the greeter at the feast. It was Mary's job to charm visitors regardless of her son's opinion of them. Niall's tongue had lingered over the vowels in Liùsaidh. Lucy adored the simple caring at the core of him.

"Earth to Lucy." Hunter nudged her, and she stared at him. "Sounds like he's ready to speak to you."

"You're right. This isn't the place." Hope was a resilient emotion, ready to overtake good sense because the man you loved called you an inspiration. "I should find somewhere without an audience."

"Give me half an hour, and I'll clear the place." He sauntered toward Anna.

Lucy and Niall had each let slip small moments when they might have told each other the truth, a zero-sum game where the final outcome was a refusal by each of them to make a commitment.

*"I'm thirty-four and can't make enough to support myself much less anyone else."*

She was thirty on her next birthday and still had occasional nightmares where she stood accused in a court of law for her mum's murder. *"There's no statute of limitations on murdering your mother,"* some ghoul recited.

She exhaled, exorcising the fears and uncertainties that she'd tripped over too many times. Never murder, rather an error in judgment forgivable in a ten-year-old.

# CHAPTER FIFTEEN

Niall had thanked Liùsaidh, not Lucy, while the people who mattered most in his world were watching. With her arrival, a weight had lifted from his chest. Niall hadn't planned to say her full name, a name he whispered when they made love, turning the word into a benediction. But he liked the sound of it in his head. Liked even more the way her mouth curved into the smile she reserved for him. It had taken her walking out of his life for the hammer to drop hard enough for him to realise he'd been falling in love with her since the day he'd first seen her.

He just hadn't been prepared to admit it.

Didn't think he had the right to burden her with promises other women had told him were worthless.

Standing in the centre of the warehouse, she was working her gran's pearls with the speed of spinning reels at an Irish ceili. Probably worrying about her welcome, when he counted her presence tonight as his crowning achievement. As the minutes had become a half hour, then an hour, then two, he'd begun work on a Plan B, involving kidnapping and locking her in this exhibition space until they fought themselves to a standstill. Fighting with her was better than losing her. He took a step in her direction.

"Niall, a moment." The Michael Portillo look-alike, whom Anna had identified as a major art critic, stood at his elbow. The lemon jumper slung across his shoulders was a direct steal from the train-travel aficionado's wardrobe.

"Good of you to come." Niall spotted Anna signalling him from across the room, her hand gesture threatening murder if he didn't play nice with Mr. Crimson-slacks-and-purple-dress-shirt. He tracked Lucy moving in the direction of the makeshift bar positioned under a window.

"I nearly didn't." His blunt words caught Niall's attention. "I don't usually report on furniture, but your marketing manager was very persuasive."

*Marketing manager?* "You mean Anna." He flicked a glance toward his sister-in-law, who waggled her fingers at him.

"She hounded me"—the critic smiled, destroying the English upper-class gravitas he'd been channelling since his arrival—"in the nicest possible way. She supplied a full bio, plus photos of your major pieces. Your work's even better than she promised. My review will be uploaded tonight, the digital version's available after midnight. How about a shot to go with my text?" He held up his phone.

"Where do you want me?" Niall glanced around, a photo a small price for freedom.

"Where you are works. It's an elegant sideboard, and the bowl of old-fashioned yellow roses accentuates it nicely." He snapped a few shots. "Is Anna here?" he asked a little too innocently. "I'd like to put a face to the name for future reference."

"She's responsible for the roses." Niall grinned. "Over my right shoulder. One o'clock. Black dress with a necklace of coloured beads." The dress was demure, but Anna was luminescent tonight.

The man's eyes widened. "*She's* your marketing manager?"

"She's outstanding at her job." Niall kept his expression bland. Anna looked delicious, although his personal vice was a sedate antiques specialist wearing her gran's pearls, sipping white wine, in one of her standard black business suits, and moving with elegant grace through the dwindling crowd. He needed to catch her before she disappeared. "If you've finished with me, there are some other people I need to catch up with."

*Please be finished with me.*

The critic smiled and headed in Anna's direction.

Lucy stood with her back to the room, in front of the gumnut mirror. Niall absorbed her scent as he drew closer, pausing to breathe in her presence before reaching her. He'd felt invincible in her bed. Who knew invincibility was having the woman you loved tucked against you during the night, her hand in yours? He missed the sensation.

"Thank you for coming," he repeated the words she'd used at her gala.

"You came to my show," she replied, colour flaring in her cheeks as if the memory was uncomfortable. "And I delivered you immediately into Peter's determined clutches."

"A useful introduction," he contradicted her. "He came earlier tonight, brought some buyers with him." Niall mentally measured the ground he needed to make up since their last conversation.

He'd waved his self-doubt like a magic wand over Lucy's head and turned her from a generous, warm-hearted companion into a polite stranger. Politeness was her default shield.

"I had an army of helpers." He continued. "Mum handled personal invitations. Anna handled social media, plus design and, by some magic known only to her, guaranteed the appearance of one of the top arts reporters in Sydney. Liam stitched up insurance and security. Kate phoned my old clients and asked to borrow back items for the show. But you know that." I'm babbling he thought, unable to help himself.

"I was with a client when she called, so didn't have time

to ask her much. It's a great venue."

In the background, William Barton's didgeridoo drifted on an orchestral wave, a lyrical repertoire of barks, yelps, squawks and bird and bush sounds.

"Anna suggested I approach Hunter." He'd missed talking over the venue, the arrangement of the pieces, even the music selection with Lucy. Although Barton was in tonight's playlist because Lucy loved the power and passion of the sounds coming from a length of termite-hollowed wood.

"Because he has empty warehouses?" she asked.

"He has properties, friends with properties and access to more through business connections. He conjured this space at less than gallery rates." Niall allowed some of his bewilderment to surface. The guy had been helpful, and refrained from scoring points or calling him an idiot or even mentioning Lucy's name, when Anna must have outlined his stupidity. Niall had wanted to howl at the moon.

"Are you afraid you'll owe him?" Her head tilted to one side, her gaze considering.

"I paid the amount requested. I said thank you. He was plausible about a gap in occupancy. We're doing each other a favour." Niall wasn't 100 percent convinced, and he was also accruing personal debts with a nonchalance that a few weeks earlier would have shocked his cautious soul. "How have you been?" She looked alive, vibrant, as if his absence had allowed her to bloom.

"Busy," she said, and he'd lost the right to push for details. "You look tired."

*I'm tired of being tired. I want more in my life than my craft. I want you in my life, on any terms you care to grant.*

"But you must think it's worth it"—she made a show of sniffing the air—"I smell success. Congratulations." Then she waved her wine in the direction of the room. "How many times have you sold the table?"

"Three, the two new orders will have different timber. I doubt I can get another piece of Huon pine of the same quality," he said. She'd demanded he take a hard look at himself. The reflection in his mirror hadn't been pretty. "Your bowl's another reason for my success. Half a dozen orders for something similar—a riff on a theme. I appreciate you letting me borrow it after I was such a fool."

She sipped her wine, studying him over the rim of her glass. "I don't believe I called you a fool."

"Not to my face." He winced. "Can you stay? I mean, can I buy you a drink after the show's over?"

"I'd like that. We need to tie up a few loose ends." She looked over his shoulder. "Kate's signalling to you."

"I should be circulating." He was afraid if he turned his back she'd vanish. "*A few loose ends*" sounded like a short conversation, scuttling the hope he'd let run wild with her arrival.

"Circulate, Niall. I said I'd stay for a drink."

\* \* \*

Lucy tracked him with her gaze, while storing up his special brand of sandalwood and citrus scent. Torture to be so close and still have a yawning chasm between them.

She'd expected the show to be a success. How could anyone not recognise his skill? But believing it and seeing it were different beasts, and gave her more insight into his misgivings. He'd laboured for years, won prizes, taken on debts not of his own making, and—he was an artist. Doubt would be a constant, a splinter lodged in an impossible-to-reach spot.

The chatter grew quieter, the waiters packed up and disappeared while Lucy moved from piece to piece, surrendering to the compulsion to touch his creations. She wasn't quite sure of the house rules, so was careful not to let her hand linger. Niall's work drew her like a child in a sweet shop offering free access to her favourite jelly snake. Her finger, trailing across each surface, was a poor substitute for touching him.

Hunter tapped her on the shoulder. "We're off."

"Thanks for the moral support."

"Anna confessed she told Niall weeks ago he was wrong not to tell you about the exhibition."

"I guess without his stubborn streak he might not have achieved so much." Although having the support of the straight-shooting Anna gave Lucy a girl-power boost of confidence. "To be honest, he looks slightly bemused, a man who's overwhelmed by the reception of his brilliance."

"Don't go all soft and gooey on him. If you're interested in him, make him work to win you." Hunter finished before joining Anna at the door. He was replaced by a heavily pregnant Kate.

"I'm glad you were able to make it." Kate rested one hand on her baby bump.

"Thanks for asking me," Lucy replied.

"Niall sent your invitations. Wished on the blarney stone or some such nonsense before he pressed send. Liam and I are taking their mum home. Whatever you said to Niall, it made him see sense."

"What does sense look like on Niall Quinn?" Her free hand crept to her gran's pearls. If he still planned to reject Grandpa's bequest after tonight's success, his principles had destroyed his good sense.

"This." Kate gestured around her. "I gather you told him to stop being such an idiot and just organise an exhibition."

"Whisht. I never called him an idiot."

"You might not have said the word, but you got the message across." Kate lowered her voice. "He'd started to doubt himself and think we were saying his work was wonderful because we love him. He needed a nudge. You gave it to him."

"He'd hate us talking about him." And while he might appreciate her prodding him, that didn't change the past and the secrets they'd kept from each other, and might continue to keep from each other. Niall had them pegged as opposites—attracted—but not soulmates.

\* \* \*

Niall closed the front doors on the final straggler and turned to rest his back against it.

"Don't we leave by the same exit?" She joined him in the vestibule.

"There's a back exit, but I had another idea." *I might only get one chance at this apology.*

"I agreed to a drink." She sounded wary, but willing, and the hopeless romantic in Niall chalked that up as a positive.

"My idea includes a drink." He took her arm and steered her into the larger space. Snagging two chairs from a set of four nearby, he set them on opposite sides of the Huon table. "Please have a seat. I'll be right back."

Niall returned with a bottle of champagne and two flutes to find her stroking the curved back of her chair. Her delight in his furniture was satisfyingly honest. He needed her honesty—and her warmth—in his life.

She turned toward him. "They match," she said, then gasped as he came closer. "French, handblown bowls and cut facets. Late nineteenth century. Where on earth did you get them?"

"An auction," he said, although her reaction justified his lengthy search to find the rare glasses. "You seem to like matching sets."

"I like you, Niall. Despite everything that's happened, I like you."

*Liking* wasn't what he'd hoped for when he'd bought the glasses for her. "Please sit." He eased out the cork, and the champagne burbled into the glasses.

"To Quinn, by design." She toasted him. "It seems to be a larger enterprise than you originally envisaged."

"Someone I respect told me not to be so thin-skinned—"

"I didn't call you a fool, or an idiot or say you were thin-skinned."

"You said I was afraid." He grimaced. "I've done a bit of thinking in the last two weeks. You were right. I was also stubborn, bloody-minded, and content to drown in self-pity." He'd thought the words would stick in his throat, but maybe the ancient Scots who said confession was good for the soul had a point. "It makes sense to use all my skills. I'd prefer the balance to be more furniture, less restoration and frames. After tonight, I might be able to make that happen."

"Why didn't you believe it could happen before tonight?" Her hand curled around the edge of the table.

Niall imagined her fingers trailing over his chest the way they had over each piece in this room. The simple eroticism of her action had started a slow hum, low in his body. The bond between them held, but she was strong enough not to forgive him.

"Maybe because it never has."

She deserved chapter and verse of what had crawled up his backside and made him shut her out.

"And that's a half-arsed answer," he said.

\* \* \*

Lucy considered him across the width of the table. He'd made the kind of admissions few men in her experience were capable of, certainly not any of the men her mum had kept company with. Strengths could be weaknesses. A tired, determined man whose integrity caught him by the balls could at times be stubborn and bloody-minded.

"I want to apologise for pouncing on you the morning after I turned up uninvited. I treated you like the prize in some swinger's raffle."

He mumbled something barely audible. Had he said "fuck *buddy*"?

"Pardon?"

"Nothing." Colour stained his cheeks. *Was he embarrassed?* "Why did you? Pounce on me like that, I mean?"

"I could tell you were unhappy, but I couldn't work out why." Although being called a fuck buddy would go a hell of a long way toward explaining his disgust at being treated like a one-night stand. "Instead of asking you, I channelled Mum. Sex papers over any cracks in a relationship."

"You know that's not true." He stretched his hand across the table to cover her free one. "Do you want to know why I was unhappy?"

"Yes, but I need to tell you a story first." *And see if you're still in the room at the end of it.*

"Do you want me to come around to your side of the table?" He took her consent seriously.

Lucy turned her hand over and linked fingers with him. "I want to look at you while I tell you." *To see if you're repulsed or pitying.* She released his hand and sat back. "I had to look after myself and Mum when I was a kid. Every night I told her I'd wake her in time to walk me to school. She'd laugh and say 'she'd get up when she was ready.'"

"You were always late. You told me that." He, in turn, leaned back, giving her the space she asked for.

"And I always ignored her. I took her a coffee. She loved coffee—hot, strong, and black." Lucy pictured her mum's sleepy grin. "She'd wrap her hands around the hot cup, inhale deeply as if it was some magic potion and say, *'Perfect, baby.'*"

"I've never seen you drink coffee," he broke the silence.

Lucy focused on Niall again. "It reminds me of the day she died." She sipped the sparkling wine, needing to ease her dry throat. "During the week, I'd dress for school, wake her, and leave. She rarely walked me to school, but she'd always call out *'Love you,'* before I reached the front door." Lucy smiled at the memory. "I looked forward to weekends. Mum liked to window shop, to scout out the neighbourhood, maybe line up a date. She'd be up by ten, so I'd wait to make the coffee. The day she died …" She huffed out air trapped by the tight bands encircling her chest.

"Tell me, Liùsaidh." He was listening with his whole body, and compassion shaded his gaze, not pity or disgust. But she hadn't told him the worst.

"I let my mum die." Her chin wobbled.

"You didn't." He gripped her hand so tightly she winced. "Sorry."

"No. I didn't," she whispered, his absolute conviction the missing piece of the puzzle. "But for a long time, I believed I did."

"You've carried this weight since you were a kid?" He eased his hold, shaking his head in disbelief. "You were barely ten years old."

"Yes, and it's taken me a lifetime to work out I'm not responsible." She inhaled his scent, his flavour of patience and goodness, and continued. "She was careless in the company she kept. The night before, a dealer came to visit. I'd seen him once or twice. They disappeared into the bedroom. I saw him the next morning. Leaving. He said she wanted to sleep, *to tell me* to leave her to sleep. I waited and waited. At midday I opened the door. She wouldn't wake up.

"I should have checked sooner." Lucy released his hand and locked her fingers together, her knuckles the bone white of her dead mother's face. "I couldn't wake her up. I called the ambulance. The police came, then social security." Sirens, the sirens had competed with each other to drown out her screams.

"What about feckin' family or friends?" He pushed to his feet.

"No family. You know it took weeks to track down Grandpa and Gran," she said, his anger easing a wound so deep in her heart, the scar tissue had scar tissue. No one had been angry at her mum's death, angry at Lucy's loss. The emotions swirling in her mother's bedroom had been all wrong. "There was a police-appointed counsellor because I was a child. A woman, but I can't remember her at all."

"Some half-trained eejit feeding the doubt in your

mind," he muttered.

"I don't think it was her." *And it no longer matters.*

"You'd lost your mum. You were in shock. And she let you leave without proving your fears were baseless." Protecting the weak was second nature to him. "Someone said something. What did they say?"

"I don't remember who asked what. It all became one joined-up blob." Lucy shook her head, their faces had faded to a blur over the years, until only the questions appeared in block capitals in her dreams. Hounding her.

"Shock untethers you." He'd looked grief in the eye and hadn't forgotten a second of the maelstrom.

"Mum's rule was no later than ten. '*Why didn't I check sooner?*' Someone asked me that." She lifted her head and met his gaze. "The claws from that one question got sharper with the passing of time."

"Keep talking."

"Because talking can defang monsters?" She gave a half laugh, because she'd already used a lifetime of tears on what-ifs. "'*Why did I believe a strange man? Why didn't I check straight away? Wasn't I curious?*'"

"You didn't check sooner, because he"—he held up a finger—"he's the person Tomas reminds you of?"

She nodded.

"Your mum's boyfriend claimed to be passing on her message. Not your fault. She was responsible for you, not the other way around," he repeated arguments she'd only let herself believe since meeting him. "When did she die?"

"They couldn't determine the exact time of death." Another claw from the multi-toed monster haunting her. "Some time in the morning. A range."

"But she could have been dead when her boyfriend left your apartment?" He zeroed in on one of her endless what-ifs.

"Or she could have been alive."

"I want to smash walls."

"Thank you for being angry my mum died. And for

listening."

"I hate that you've lived with this fear." He returned to his chair. "Want to know what I was doing at age ten?"

"Not answering questions from the police?" She swallowed another mouthful, the dance of bubbles in her bloodstream a counterpoint to her tragic tale.

He smiled. "Swinging off a rope into a river. Searching in the undergrowth for bits of rock or wood I might be able to fashion into something. Sweating on getting a new chisel for my birthday. Arm wrestling with my brother. The grown-ups are supposed to be responsible for us."

"The police were careful not to blame me. I remember sitting in a corridor while adults buzzed about me. I knew it was my fault. Why did I change my routine? Every morning I took her coffee. Without fail. Why did I fail on that day?" Her catechism had been different to the fearsome biblical one her Presbyterian gran memorised as a child, but Lucy could recount hers just as fluently.

"When I was a kid"—he reached across the table to tuck her hair behind her *ear*, his fingertip stroking the softer skin there while his thumb brushed her cheek—"I pinched a biscuit from a batch Mum had made up for a neighbour. A mirror in the hall came crashing down. I was positive the two were related. Steal a biscuit and disaster happens. You weren't to blame."

"I wasn't. But for a long time I thought I was."

"Didn't your grandparents exorcise that demon for you?"

"I was in the next room when Gran died. I shouldn't have left her alone."

"Why did you?"

"She was settled in her chair with a photo album. I went to make tea." A routine she and her gran had established.

"But the police came back." His outrage took him the mental step from one death to the other. Her responsibility—cause and effect. "And you had a feckin' useless boyfriend who made a joke about it being natural to anticipate an inheritance, to look away while accidents happened."

"I've been afraid I'll hurt the people I love." Her deepest, darkest shame, and he'd coaxed it from her like he coaxed magic from a block of wood.

*Do you understand I just said I love you?*

"Hence the over-the-top hospital in the home for Cam?" She nodded.

"When were you going to tell me?" His question restored hope.

"That morning, but I chickened out."

"Why not tell me at the workshop?"

"Because I've never told this story before." She sucked in more air. "Because I wondered if treating you like a fuck buddy triggered your disgust enough to cut all ties with me."

"You heard that?" He scrubbed his face.

"I hate myself for that morning. For making you feel less because I got cold feet about telling you about Mum."

"We're all allowed to be scared sometimes," he murmured.

"I hate even more knowing the restoration work I demanded because I went into a funk when Grandpa died forced you to cancel your original exhibition." Her heart stalled. Because he hadn't offered to sit beside her again. Hadn't said one quick screw between lovers was only one beat of a symphony.

"It's not your fault."

"You're right, and I'm over taking responsibility for things that I can't control." Lucy owed Niall for that. Whatever happened between them, she'd always be grateful he'd challenged her to face and defeat her demons.

JENNIFER RAINES

# CHAPTER SIXTEEN

"I'm glad." Niall had worked on a bare bones' explanation for his actions. After all, a man who'd behaved as stupidly as he had still had his pride. Pulling off the exhibition had given his confidence in his craft and his future a sugar hit. Having her within touching distance mattered more. Her searing honesty allowed him to find his own. "You need to know why I was unhappy."

"*I've been afraid I'll hurt the people I love.*" She believed she'd hurt him.

Did that also mean she loved him?

He continued. "This story might take some time."

"I'm guessing you're in charge of locking up here," she said. "So we've got the time."

"Can I pour you another drink?" He shuffled sentences in his head.

"No more bubbles for me on an empty stomach. That's part of why the evening with Clem and Kelly went pear-shaped." Her mouth quirked up at one corner.

"I sent the caterer's leftovers home with Kate and Anna. But I can offer you something to eat." He reached into the chill box at his side and produced two farmhouse sandwiches. "No plates, I'm sorry."

"After the handblown French flutes, I expected Qing dynasty porcelain." She was teasing him, defusing the tension that hovered, and he fell in love all over again.

"They were chipped. Didn't suit the ambience I was creating." He'd start looking for some next week.

"Why are we having this conversation here?"

"The table," Niall admitted. "It's part of our story, and it's being shipped out at the end of the exhibition. I miss it already. Plus, we've got privacy in a neutral venue."

"Hardly neutral," she contradicted him. "Being surrounded by your work gives you the advantage."

"Is that so?" He'd called in every favour his family owed him, and scattered even more IOUs, to gain this advantage.

"You know it's so. Pass me a sandwich."

"I put pickle on yours." He shook out a serviette, then handed a wrapped sandwich across the table. "I cut it in quarters."

"You were feeling pretty confident I'd come," she said.

"Hopeful is a far cry from confident."

"If you're trying to reprise our first meeting, I won't let you ambush me."

"Ambush? How?" Niall had lifted his sandwich to his mouth, but set it down again.

"Reminding me of the good times we had in the hope we can start again where we left off. It's not going to happen. You were unhappy when I arrived that night. I was drunk. We both pretended the elephants in the room were hallucinations. Then, in the morning, we found ourselves in a different country. I've told you about my elephant. Why were you unhappy? Were you sabotaging us or just yourself?"

"I convinced myself not telling you about the exhibition was to protect you. You'd feel guilty knowing I'd cancelled," he said.

"I did." She bit into her sandwich.

"Then stop. I'll show you my order book from tonight." Sharing a simple sandwich with her made finding the words easier for Niall. But no matter how he dressed it up, his answer would hurt her. "The truth is, I was sabotaging us."

She paled and placed what remained of her sandwich on the serviette. "Why?" Her gaze was shuttered; she was mentally summoning her defences, and he couldn't blame her.

"I fell in love with—I thought I fell in love with a girl in Ireland. After Da's death. Unconsciously, I was looking for family and fooled myself into thinking I was in love with her."

She pushed her glass toward him. "I'm ready for another drink."

Niall topped off both glasses. She wasn't drinking any more than she was eating. Glasses were useful props.

"*She* was the person who called you a fuck buddy?" Having Lucy work it out made the next bit easier.

"I asked her to marry me." Niall had wanted to come home and had mistaken what he'd shared with Sinead for family. "She told me not to be an eejit. That I couldn't support myself, much less her and a babe. That I'd make more selling sex than my woodwork." Nausea swirled in Niall's gut, as comprehension chased confusion across Lucy's face.

"She treated you like a body, not the lover of her dreams, and she belittled your work." Lucy's face scrunched in disgust. "She's the reason you think so little of yourself and your skills?"

"She said she loved my carpentry, added her mite when I talked of establishing my own business. Right up to the moment she called me a failure." Niall had been blindsided. And, truth be told, humiliated he'd misread her so badly. "I'd been having my own doubts—most creatives battle doubt on a regular basis—and I wanted to come home. Her plain speaking speeded up my plans."

"Your Irish girlfriend was wrong about your ability," she said. Tears he'd put there, shimmered in her eyes. "I have it on the best authority you're a genius."

"Whose authority?" *I love you.*

"Grandpa. He told his lawyer, his accountant and probably some perfect strangers. It's a pity he forgot to tell me. But I'm starting to understand why he did what he did."

"He loved you. He said you were the sunshine in his life." *And mine.* When the light caught the rich shades in her hair, when she'd danced in steel-capped boots, when she'd given him a sleepy kiss goodbye as he'd slipped from her bed. Niall should have given her the words. "They didn't know you existed. He told me he had regrets, but finding you wasn't one of them."

"What else did he say? Because that's part of this muddle as well. Your ex-girlfriend—what the hell is her name?"

"Sinead. Sinead O'Brien."

"You decided you failed Sinead, you failed your father, you failed your brother. Let's see if I've got this straight. You sabotaged our relationship because you doubted your ability as a carpenter?"

"My ability to make a living from bespoke furniture," he clarified with care. "In my head, the exhibition had become synonymous with being good enough to make a living from my work."

"You're leaving half of it out. Sinead tried to diminish you as a man. And I added fuel to that fire."

"Lovers screw, they make love, and sometimes they go through the motions out of sheer friendliness. They're overcome by lust, and they're swamped by feelings too large to manage. We were lovers in every sense of the word, Lucy. One messy roll between the sheets can't change that." He leaned toward her. "The honest truth is that I turned away from you because I'd decided that the gap between us was too great. I can't provide for you."

"Provide for me?" She stared at him as if he'd sprouted a second head. "What the heck does 'provide' mean?"

"'Providing' was the shared pact among the men in my family. Da always felt he failed because he couldn't save Mum's family farm from development. It nagged at him, and I guess it nagged at me. I've been holding on to the idea I need to pay the bills." He dragged a hand through his hair and clasped the back of his neck. "All the bills."

"Did you hear what you just said? You great, patronising pillock!" She thumped a hand on the table.

"Yeah."

"What did your mother say to your father?"

"They were partners, and that meant taking turns at being the strong, silent type." He'd forgotten his mother had been as outraged as Lucy was.

"But that's not good enough for you." Her scorn was blistering. "How did Grandpa get mixed up in this? Because you decided you failed Cam McTavish as well. What did you promise him?"

"He didn't *ask* for promises. He said you'd need a distraction. That it might take longer than I hoped before I got the recognition I deserved. And he apologised. I didn't know why he apologised until I heard about the bequest." He stopped and grimaced. "Free rent, work as a mentor— he was paying me to look after you."

"And being the fortune-teller he was, he worked out we'd get involved and decided you needed help to provide for me. Have you lost the brain cells you were born with?" She looked magnificent in a rage. "Didn't you consider there's a different way to look at it?"

He'd considered every possibility until he was cross-eyed with fatigue.

"Grandpa knew you. He knew you were a decent, kind man who'd probably be kind to me. Knowing me, he guessed I'd monopolise your time trying to work out your relationship with him. That's why he didn't tell me. He left me a puzzle, an intellectual distraction. Dealing with me would have taken you away from your work, hence, by dying, he'd stuffed up your timeline for the exhibition. Being a decent, honourable bloke himself, he was apologising in advance."

"Cam never told you about me," he repeated, testing her

theory to see if it made sense. "He set us both up?"

"He traded on your kindness and my determination to protect him," she stormed.

"He gave you a puzzle to solve."

"I need to be in control, or enough in control of myself so I don't hurt anyone else. When Grandpa died, it was like slipping off the side of a mountain." Her anger died. "Each time I tried to find a secure foothold, I'd slip further down. I was scrambling mentally, physically and emotionally."

"Can I come around to your side of the table?" Niall wanted to hold her.

"Not until we finish." She held up a hand. "You gave me that foothold. I worked out a few things as well. I couldn't spend as much time with him as I wanted at the end. Asking you to restore furniture gave me a reason to visit you. To talk to you about Grandpa."

"I'm making you cry. You hate crying." He pushed back from his chair. "You were grieving. We all do things we regret when we're grieving. The fault for this entire mess is mine. Quinns pay their way. But they're usually gracious about accepting help. I pushed you away."

"Clementine challenged me to tell you the truth that night." She hiccupped. "Although she doesn't know about Mum. The three of us had a pact. No babies."

"No babies?" Niall hesitated. *Was this another legacy of Lucy's childhood?* "You seemed freaked by Kate and Liam's nursery?"

"Lots of people decide not to have children. Because people are the plague on the planet. Because children should have both a mother and a father, and I'm single ..." She paused—one heartbeat, then another, before she sucked in a breath. "Being an orphan fills up your entire sense of self. It forces you to be alone when you don't want to be alone. I couldn't bear the thought of dying and leaving a child alone, *my* child alone. It's not totally rational, like my fear about debt, but I'm afraid I'll make some terrible mistake and hurt my child."

"All parents are afraid of parenthood." Niall absorbed the slap of her sorrow. He should have guessed her hesitation over a babe had nothing to do with his shortcomings. "Liam and Kate are equal parts terrified and thrilled, especially with the way the world is today."

"Kelly, Clementine, and I got tipsy because time's up. We either take responsibility for our futures, or we blame our crappy childhoods for every mistake we make." She sighed.

"Do they date blokes who are happy to split bills?"

"Forget the bills." She pushed back from the table, tears gone. "You talk to me. You listen to me. You encourage me to do and be more. And you touch me as if I'm the most precious person in your life. You provide everything I need. What do you need, Niall? More importantly, what do you want?" She was fearless.

"You talk to me. You listen to me. You encourage me to do and be more."

"You hurt me by leaving. I want a partner, a lover, an equal, someone who respects me and doesn't see me as McTavish's heir. Don't kid yourself this is about money. I don't need money from you. I need you to love me as I am." She made love so simple.

"I love you, Liùsaidh." His words were a vow. "I should have told you weeks ago."

"Are you sure?"

"I hate that you sound tentative. That I've planted doubt in your mind. I'm sorry for being a great, patronising pillock." He held out his arms and offered his heart. "Can I come around to your side of the table now?"

\* \* \*

Lucy stared at his open arms until his words settled in all the empty spaces in her body.

"I fell in love with you the minute you started stroking my table. I just didn't know it." He stood.

Joy rippled through her, a symphony of colour and light and laughter. "I fell in love with you when you served me tea in a delicate antique cup without a saucer and tricked me into eating a farmhouse sandwich." Lucy stayed where she was.

"I fell deeper when you brought me lunch the next day." He took a step toward the head of the table.

"You gave me your rosewood fruit bowl," she said. The first bridge between her isolation and his friendship.

"In retrospect, I reckon that was a lure"—on his next step, he *swaggered*—"to bring you back. I was wrong not to talk to you about the exhibition. I'm hoping you'll forgive me."

"Not unless you accept the bequest."

He was waiting for her. Tucking his hands into his pockets, he rocked back on his heels. "You want me to accept the bequest?" He feigned disbelief, but he was the one taking the risk, standing alone.

"It's that, or the next offer is one hundred thousand dollars." Lucy gave a take-it-or-leave-it shrug.

"Whisht, lassie, don't be so daft. You don't have that kind of ready cash."

"We can meet halfway." She pushed back from the table and took her first step.

"I'm already here, waiting for you."

His arms closed around her. Pressing her nose against his throat, Lucy inhaled his woody scent. Content to lean against him, the desperation of the last two weeks slipped away. He wrapped her close while her arms found their way around his waist. She took the time to absorb his steadiness, to listen to his heartbeat and to believe in his love.

"I was afraid I'd hurt you too badly for you to forgive me," he whispered against her temple.

"You asked me not to leave. I took a chance you meant that." Lucy slid her hands inside his jacket, letting her fingertips dance over his cotton-covered chest. "The washstand gave me hope you'd decided to fight for us too."

"You didn't say anything about it."

"It's beautiful. You knew I'd never sell it." He'd given Lucy a piece of her history and a piece of himself.

"It's as precious as her pearls to you." He cradled her jaw in his hand. "I'm glad you didn't give up on me."

"It's the best present anyone's ever given me." She smiled, because finishing the wash basin demonstrated more than words ever could that she'd always been in his heart and mind.

"I love you."

"Why don't we give this table a workout?" She loosened his tie, pushing it into his jacket pocket, before flicking open the top button of his shirt. "That's what you were hoping to do, wasn't it?" She smoothed her forefingers along his collarbone, absorbing the warmth of his skin.

"It's a pity to send it off without a christening." His wink was sinful, his hands knowing as they cupped her buttocks to draw her against his body. Widening his stance, he settled himself more firmly between her thighs and gently rocked against her. A foretaste. "I might move the glassware first. Wouldn't want our anniversary glasses to be bounced off the table because one of us is too enthusiastic."

"Anniversary?" She stepped back and draped her jacket over a nearby chair.

"I have a feeling we're going to have many." His eyes narrowed when she started to unbutton her blouse. With more speed than care, he packed the half-eaten sandwiches and glasses into his cool box. "Leave the skirt," he growled, shucking his jacket.

She put her hands under her skirt to push her panties down.

Strolling closer, he unbuttoned his shirt and let it hang open, tempting her to touch with more than her gaze. His fingers took their time on his belt buckle, focusing her attention on his arousal.

"Tease." She tilted her chin and snapped open the front clip on her bra. The soft muslin of her blouse rubbed against her breasts, inciting her.

"Very nice," he drawled, dropping his belt. His grin was pure mischief. "The boots can stay."

Heat flooded her loins. "You *are* in a hurry."

He reached her. Face to face, close enough for her to smell the urgency on his skin. He slid his calloused palms from her waist halfway down her thighs before crushing her straight skirt between his fingers. He dragged it higher, one teasing inch at a time. "Aren't you?"

"What did you have in mind?" Excitement hummed through her.

"I've stopped thinking." He scooped her up and placed her bare backside on the end of the table, before sliding a finger into her damp heat. When she moaned, he sucked her taste from his finger. "Just marking my place."

Her heart raced, and still he waited for her. "Love me, Niall."

His trousers and jocks landed at his feet. Still, he took his time, cupping her face for his kiss. She fell off the end of the world, and he was her only anchor. Waves of hot sweetness hit her, followed by a hunger drenched in tenderness. Dragging his mouth from hers, his gaze was fierce. "I've never loved another before you." He joined them. "You taught me what love is."

She welcomed his possession, and the sensation they were moving as one.

"Liùsaidh," he whispered endearments with each thrust, words she treasured because from him, they were real.

She shattered moments before him, collapsing back on the table. He leaned forward on his hands.

"Now, about that one hundred thousand," she said, sucking in oxygen.

"I'm not negotiating when you've got me at a disadvantage," he panted.

"Take it or leave it." She planted loud kisses down the centre of his chest.

Catching her hands in his, he kissed her knuckles. "I'll

accept Cam's bequest. You keep the money."

"I applaud your good sense." She wrapped her legs around his hips, and he groaned.

"But I'm paying half the costs of running the house." He manoeuvred his hands under her buttocks and squeezed gently. "When the rent-free period of my initial agreement ends, I'll pay full commercial rent. Plus, I want a prenup."

"I haven't heard a marriage proposal." She released her legs and wriggled into a more upright position, her heart giving its own drumroll.

"I was waiting to catch *me* breath." He grinned "Marry me, Liùsaidh?"

"Yes, and I have another confession to make. I started to dream when I sat in Kate's nursery." She stroked his hair back from his brow. "I want you to have your dreams, because then you'll understand I have mine. You'll love our children and let them dream. Yes, I'll marry you. I love you, Niall Quinn."

"Maybe we should stay here all night? Give the table another workout?"

"It'll be in our kitchen in two weeks," she said.

"You bought it?" His look of surprised delight was worth making the purchase through an intermediary.

"It seduced me before you did." She put her hands on his chest. "Come home with me?"

"We're definitely having a prenup. Otherwise, you might be so crazy in love with me, you'll give me a trust fund and present me with matched crockery and crystal glassware."

"Only if you want them." She slid off the table, found her panties, and tucked them in his jacket pocket with his tie. "No prenup, unless it includes a half-share in our babe's cradle, a half-share in the mirror you're planning for me, and a half-share in your life?" She did up enough buttons on her shirt to be decent if they were pulled over by the cops on the way home, and indecent enough to let him know what was in store when they got there.

"Deal." He scooped her off the table and swung her in

a wide circle. "Quinns pay their way."

# AUTHOR'S NOTE

The Huon pine bark to bark table that was featured in this book is real. The woodworker who crafted it, inherited the wood from his father who'd stored that and other precious timbers for decades. I've seen his satisfaction with a finished piece and the delight on the face of the recipient. Artisans fascinate me—woodworkers, silversmiths, glass blowers, cobblers and more— with their ability to conjure practical beauty with their hands and their persistence when so many people grab for the machine made and the new. Being an artisan is a statement of respect for the material and the craft through time. My inclusion of antiques and modern furniture is a nod to the tradition.

I'd like to thank Yezanira Venecia for her thoughtful editing, Melissa Keir, Inkspell Publishing for backing my dreams and the readers who've told me that they love my stories.

# Here's a Sneak Peek at the Third Book in the Choosing Family Series...

## Betrayal

### Chapter One

After accepting the champagne flute of mineral water from the barman, Anna Turner swung to face the marketing conference party crowd. Her penance, as representative of Changing Minds—Marketing Solutions and Services, at this exclusive venue overlooking Sydney Harbour, was to sound out competitors and promote Changing Minds.

"Ditch the scowl, Anna," her friend Beatriz Gomez whispered. "We're here to soothe, not rouse the savage beast."

"I *don't* scowl." Anna beetled her brows. "Remember that exercise at last year's conference with the face-reading experts?"

"They *claimed* a company could increase client signups with the right smile."

"They rated mine as winning."

"Emphasis on the smile, girlfriend." Bea looked her up and down. "And they didn't see you in that dress."

"This old thing?" Anna shrugged, and the décolletage on the flaming-red, figure-hugging short cocktail dress slipped a half-centimetre closer to her navel. The dress was a crude but effective tool for identifying the obvious lechers without saying a word.

"Seeing the stunned disbelief on that company exec's face remains one of the highlights of my short life." Bea didn't waste time on polite fictions, one of the reasons they were close friends. "He couldn't believe you'd chosen that dress to tell him he didn't have a chance in hell of scoring with you."

"The sexist so-and-so deserved it. Claiming his company would cancel their brand marketing contract with Changing Minds because I wouldn't sleep with him. Did he miss several centuries of female emancipation?" Anna infused scorn, disgust and I'll-kill-him-if-I-see-him determination into her voice. Childhood drama classes had to have some benefits.

"There's steam coming out of your ears."

"I'm seriously pissed off." Anna lacked the patience to deal with sleaze tonight.

"I'd never have guessed." And a lot of people never guessed sweet-faced Bea did sarcasm.

"It's worse than when that idiot threatened me." Anna waved her drink in the air, and some sloshed over the rim, just missing her feet—her stilettos continued the blood-red theme. "His boss overruled him. Anyway, that was just money."

"Ah! Money!" Bea sighed. "We don't care about money." Bea had to care about money, regularly helping her immigrant parents pay their bills.

"This is more important than money." Anna curled her lip.

"Your creche." Bea leaned closer and dropped her voice. "Let me get you out of this crush." With a few words and a smile, Bea navigated a path through the crowd away from the packed bar. She made a beeline for the windows overlooking the Sydney Opera House and Harbour Bridge, then tucked the two of them into a corner. "This is quieter. You were meant to sign the lease for the premises today."

"That was before the entire building was subject to a hostile takeover. Some infantile troglodyte in a feud with his equally infantile father." *I worked out too late that competition with some fathers is the first step on the highway to hell.*

"Who won?

"The son. And he cancelled all pending leases. From the few business blogs I checked, if one of them sniffs out a distressed estate, the other tries to beat him to the purchase.

About as logical as teenage boys in a pissing contest."

"I'm sorry, honey." Bea commiserated. "A new owner usually wants to negotiate their own leases. And if the original owner's in trouble, your lease might have gone pear-shaped in a few months anyway."

"That's what Antonio said." She'd been with her boss Antonio Perez, CEO of Changing Minds, long enough that when she'd approached him about the need for better childcare options for company staff, he'd given her the lead on finding a solution.

"What else did Antonio say?" With four younger sisters Beatriz listened to every version of a story before making judgement.

"Sleep on it. We'll regroup in the morning." A perfectly rational assessment. Antonio was better at rolling with the punches than she was. "Normally I love his positivity, but I've promised, Bea." Although Anna's real promise had been made two years ago to three women, one of whom was now dead. Tonight's dress was her roar of frustration at her failure.

"It's unlike you to promise before you have everything stitched up and in triplicate."

"A matter of hours before I signed the lease. Due diligence complete. I was as sure as I could be, and one of my team is holding on by the skin of her teeth. Even with Antonio providing financial help, Nadia's childcare is at one end of town, her crisis accommodation the other, and commuting to the office is an isosceles triangle on steroids. The distances are killing her." Anna was hoping for a miracle before she had to tell the newly single mother the bad news.

"You can't save every woman trapped in an abusive relationship." Bea's pragmatism was as hard won as Anna's determination to make small differences.

"I'm not trying to save every woman. Or even most women. One creche is not a solution to domestic or partner violence, it's an option for a few women under pressure.

Apart from Nadia"—who Anna would lose, if she didn't pull a rabbit out of a hat—"we have two other employees looking for work closer to their childcare. We don't want to lose them."

"What else did Antonio say?"

"The new owner might be financially stretched enough to welcome the offer of a long-term lease on one floor." *Go home now!* Anna's brain screamed.

"He's got a point."

"You're right, and the property's perfect." Anna sighed. "So I'll be charm personified when I try to reopen negotiations, even if the owner has an electronic calculator in place of a heart and a father fetish."

## Coming Soon...

# Be Sure To Catch The First Book In The Choosing Family Series….

## MASQUERADE

*Fool me once…*

Money won't bring LIAM QUINN'S father back, but it'll save his mother's home. A high-paying law partnership is in his sights. To win it, he needs to successfully land a project. Problem is the project requires absolute confidentiality, and he's just discovered his estranged identical twin is appearing life size on a billboard across the city. The second catch is a return to environmental law. His earlier career imploded after his lover was revealed as a mining company spy.

Researcher and soon-to-be-published romance author KATE TURNER needs a disguise. Maybe more than one. Her famous playwright father despises 'trashy' novels. Her ex-boyfriend mocked her 'dirty little secret', then stalked her when she left him. Her identical twin coaxes her into appearing on a billboard to prove she can be notorious and anonymous at the same time. No one connects the billboard model to the dowdy researcher Kate has become, and no one knows about her author pseudonym and second disguise as Ms. Sexy Romance.

Kate and Liam's lives collide when she's hired as Liam's research assistant. Liam's boss laughs off the billboard. Having doubles is the perfect cover for confidential field work.

A masquerade, a road trip, a steamy attraction, the sudden appearance of Liam's old lover, and Ms. Sexy Romance's unexpected arrival in the wrong place at the wrong time, and Liam and Kate discover the steps they took to protect their hearts might break them.

*Award winning author Jennifer Raines' stories combine a love of romance with contemporary conflicts. Her writing is both relevant and heart-warming. Each story is a journey across the world. Jennifer likes to think her readers get occasional hints of the deep passion of a Nora Roberts or the unshakeable loyalty of a Grace Burrowes where love conquers loneliness, distrust and fear.*

**--"A Jennifer Raines romance will make you sigh in the best possible way!"-- Best Selling Author, Grace Burrowes**

EXCERPT

Liam gestured to her report, open in front of him. "Simple summaries of assorted environmental disputes across Australia. That's not a lot to work with."

"Have you read my report, Mr. Quinn?" Kate emphasised his surname, annoyance at the snub for her research trumping her anxiety at exposure. She'd back her research skills against anyone in this room.

"I've scanned it." His shoulder lifted in an offhand shrug.

Arrogant moron. Another man living in an echo chamber, so sure his worldview was right not even a drone buzzing overhead would alert him to imminent attack. Was he hostile because his identical twin Niall had kept the billboard campaign secret from him? Or generally hostile to new ideas? "Then you're being deliberately offensive."

"Not yet," he answered, leaning forward—a panther preparing to spring.

Dismayed to be so attuned to his slightest movement, she stiffened her spine.

Liam had her second-guessing her defence strategy. Until Liam, Kate had trusted that Ms. Dowdy Researcher couldn't be linked to the billboard—the final stress test to confirm no one, especially not her besuited, controlling ex-boyfriend, would recognise Ms. Dowdy as Anna Turner's twin.

# Don't Miss these Award Winning books by Jennifer Raines

## TAYLOR'S LAW

***Tell me a secret and I'll tell you a lie.***

Ella Anderson adores her niece. Despite struggling to make ends meet, accepting her dying sister's request she raise Tessa as her own is a no brainer. Until she receives a summons from a legal goliath on behalf of a wealthy stranger claiming paternity and, potentially, custody of her child.

Jake Taylor has been ripped off one too many times. Yet the letter from a woman claiming his cousin fathered her child feels real. His aunt and uncle are desperate for a grandchild. When the child's aunt shows up in his office in place of the child's mother, he smells fraud.

Secrets and lies bubble to the surface, threatening Ella and Jake's growing attraction. In a minefield of divided loyalties, can Ella trust Jake to make the right decision about custody of Tessa?

*Jennifer's book is great for fans of contemporary romances where attraction blossoms into breath-stealing passion, where mutual respect leads lovers to also being friends, and where humour and tolerance enliven a deep and abiding love.*

*Jennifer likes to think her readers get occasional hints of the deep passion of a Nora Roberts or the unshakeable loyalty of a Grace Burrowes where love conquers loneliness, distrust and fear.*

## EXCERPT

"Who are you?" he demanded.

The tension in his liquid chocolate voice rippled through her. This man couldn't be Tessa's father. The ferocity of her denial rattled her. Every cell refused to accept he'd been her sister's lover. And some remnant of reasoned thought nagged at her. He'd have eaten Chrissy alive.

"Eleanor Anderson." With an effort, she gathered her professional poise. "Chrissy's sister. Ella. You must be Drew." She reached out a hand.

"You know damn well I'm not Drew."

"If you aren't Drew, who are you?" Off-balanced by his instant attack, she tried to steady her jumpy nerves. Withdrawing her hand, she turned to the older man, who was staring at Tessa. "Mr. Taylor, your letter requested Chrissy meet you here about Drew Browning's paternity and …" She stumbled to a halt over the word "custody," then shook her head as a bizarre idea formed. "You can't be Drew?"

"I'm his father, Peter." His presence confused her further but confirmed the identity of the pirate king.

She stretched out a hand for a second time. "Then you must be Mr. Taylor. Good morning."

"Where's Chrissy?" Taylor demanded.

Before she could answer, Tessa's soft voice ricocheted around the room. "Mama's in heaven."

# GRACE UNDER FIRE

*It's deal or no deal when a new threat forces two independent neighbours to face a past tragedy.*

Artisan cheese-maker GRACE ANDERSON lost her closest friend to suicide, then saw her father swindled out of prime dairy land. Abandonment and mistrust cemented her determination to become the fifth generation on the family farm and to do it alone. A deterioration in her mother's health starts the clock. Grace has three months to buy her parents out—a decade sooner than planned—or lose the farm.

Neighbour RYAN WILSON is haunted by the belief he failed to prevent his younger brother Danny's suicide. He's returned to sell his mother's farm. In eight years away, he's built a fortune flipping farm properties and doesn't do attachment—to land or people.

The bank plays hard ball, forcing Grace to consider Ryan's offer to buy part of her land. The sizzling attraction simmering between them is an unwelcome complication. She doesn't want a business partner, he doesn't want to care, but when someone tries to sabotage her purchase, she finds herself turning to Ryan for more than financial help.

Can Ryan convince her accepting help is not failure? Can

Grace escape her legacy of mistrust and teach him how to care again?

*GRACE UNDER FIRE is an award-winning story which brings readers along an emotional journey with the complex characters. Jennifer likes to think her readers get occasional hints of the deep passion of a Nora Roberts or the unshakeable loyalty of a Grace Burrowes where love conquers loneliness, distrust and fear.*

## EXCERPT

Grace had looked to Ryan in the church ten years ago. For help to make sense of the madness? For reassurance? To see if he shared her sense of loss, of waste, of guilt in not being able to prevent Danny's death. Ryan had refused to talk to her after Danny's funeral, abandoning her to suffocating grief.

Ryan had been seventeen then to her fifteen, as tall as now but gangly. He hadn't grown into his build, but the promise of the man had been there. His shaggy hair had been longer. Not long enough to hide his tight, shuttered expression.

The pain of Ryan's rejection had smouldered inside her, only to flare up now. He'd left town straight after her best friend Danny's funeral. Hadn't stayed for the wake or to listen to community condolences. Ryan had spoken to no one. Not even her. Then disappeared. *When his mother needed him.* Grace had struggled to forgive him for that too. She'd taught herself not to need him, not to need anyone other than her family.

"I'm sorry I didn't speak to you." He rose abruptly to his feet, his hands held up in front of him.

She rose with him. Her heart hammered, her hands balled and her legs were planted wide in defiance.

# ABOUT THE AUTHOR

Australian Jennifer Raines writes contemporary romances set mainly, but not exclusively, in Australia – think Malta, Finland, New Zealand or ? A dreamer and an optimist, her stories are a delicious cocktail of passion, mutual respect and loyalty because she still believes in happily-ever-afters.

Jennifer fell in love with romance as a teenager. Starting with historical romance. Everything in the school library and then a personal treasured collection of Georgette Heyer, hard copies, paperbacks and ebooks. Comfort food, she calls them, like Vegemite toast, for those times when she feels low. Her library of comfort food has grown over the years but Georgette Heyer was an early star, under the blankets after lights out using a torch.

Jennifer is a member of Romance Writers of Australia. Three times a finalist in the Emerald competition, including in 2017 (*Common Cause*, renamed *Lela's Choice*), 2018 (*Taylor's Law*) and 2022 (*Quinn, by design* – Choosing Family Book 2). She's a member of Romance Writers of New Zealand, winning the Pacific Hearts competition twice, including in 2019 with *Grace Under Fire*, the sequel to *Taylor's Law*. She's also a member of Romance Writers of America and has been a finalist in chapter competitions in 2019, 2020 and 2021 (*Taylor's Law*). Jennifer won the contemporary romance section in the 2020 Orange Rose Contest for *Planting Hope* and was second overall. Jennifer values competitions for the constructive, honest, not always comfortable feedback they provide.

In 2023 *Taylor's Law* placed second in the Romance Writers of New Zealand Koru Best First Book

Jennifer loves those days when words flow and the joy of writing makes the hard slog worthwhile. She's always made up stories about strangers in the street, in a café or strolling through an airport terminal; finding inspiration in snippets of conversations, news items and the sheer puzzle of human interactions.

Jennifer lives in inner-city Sydney, Australia, with the requisite number of partners (1) and animals (2). Her desk overlooks a park which nourishes her soul when she raises her head from her keyboard. She gets some of her best ideas during long yin yoga poses or walking – anywhere. While Jennifer adores historical romance, she chose to write contemporary because she thought (wrongly) it needed less research while she was holding down a full-time job.

You can find out more about Jennifer and her writing at https://jenniferrainesauthor.com or via https://www.facebook.com/jenniferrainesauthor

Or https://www.instagram.com/romanceauthorjen/

Her book(s) are available through major providers.